Comrades

im Arms

a novel by

Alan Boatman

Harper & Row, Publishers
New York, Evanston, San Francisco, London

The lines on page 148 are from the poem "A Woman Sings a Song for a Soldier Come Home," copyright 1947 by Wallace Stevens. From *Collected Poems*, reprinted by permission of Alfred A. Knopf, Inc.

COMRADES IN ARMS. Copyright © 1974 by Alan Boatman. All rights reserved. Printed in the United States of America. No part of this book may be used or reproduced in any manner whatsoever without written permission except in the case of brief quotations embodied in critical articles and reviews. For information address Harper & Row, Publishers, Inc., 10 East 53rd Street, New York, N.Y. 10022. Published simultaneously in Canada by Fitzhenry & Whiteside Limited, Toronto.

FIRST EDITION

Designed by Janice Stern

Library of Congress Cataloging in Publication Data

Boatman, Alan.
   Comrades in arms.

    I. Title.
PZ4.B6625Co   [PS3552.O25]   813'.5'4   73–4139
ISBN 0–06–010403–1

For Jim Morgan, Roy Nanovic,
John McRedmond

A personal bond, an individual friendship, is found only in animals with highly-developed intra-specific aggression; in fact, this bond is the firmer, the more aggressive the particular animal and species is.

Konrad Lorenz, *On Aggression*

PART 1

Transient Barracks

1

1. Harding was flat on his back in a hospital bed at Da Nang when he got the news. Daniel George Washington Webster, PFC, USMC, had been killed in action while patrolling southwest of the base. Murphy and Green told him about it; they had been present.

It was like a repeat of recent history: the new lieutenant had led the patrol into an ambush, with several men killed and wounded before help arrived. The ambush was set by a small party of VC, what remained of a unit the company had been pursuing for several days and had already met once and largely decimated. Toward the end of the fire fight someone shot PFC Webster in the back with an M-16, emptying the better part of a twenty-round magazine into him, probably firing on automatic. There was of course a good deal of confusion at the time; nobody seemed to know who had done it. It looked as though there would be no investigation.

He would always remember them standing there by the bed, Murphy his usual tough, grim self, not cocky for once—and Green solicitous and quiet, speaking only to ask how Harding was being treated, how he felt—and Harding not asking the question he wanted to ask, settling instead for a variation: "Do you know who got him, Audie?"
—and Murphy shrugging.

"Let's just say somebody got him. Nobody knows or cares who it was."

But Harding cared, and thought he knew.

When his friends left, he lay there watching the dull white ceiling of the ward. He could not move, not even turn over, much less get up to go to the head. He would remember how afraid he had been, and unhappy and lonely, after his friends were gone. He fell asleep, and when he woke up it was night and he was in pain. He wished for a nurse and lay in the darkness, gritting his teeth and remembering Webster's face the last time he had seen it, the ignorant face drained and severe, a haunted look Harding would have thought him incapable of—quite a different look from fear. Why, he wondered still again, why had Webster ever come into the Marine Corps?

He would remember an evening in the rain outside Da Nang, eating C rations and huddling under ponchos. Webster sat a few feet away near the little fire someone had built and protected from the rain by shelter halves, eating ham and lima beans and telling Green and Murphy about the 1967 riot in Detroit. The four of them made up a fire team, with Harding the leader. Webster, a black PFC, was the rifleman. Green, also black, was the automatic rifleman, and Murphy, whose name was Tom but who liked to be called Audie, was Green's assistant automatic rifleman. Murphy and Green were from Texas; they loved the Marine Corps as much as Webster and Harding hated it.

Harding ate his beef stew from the hot can, trying to keep it out of the rain, and listened to Webster tell how he had carried a color television set four blocks and up two flights of stairs on his back.

"Man, I mean. I *wanted* that TV." Webster laughed, a low silly noise, and although he and Green were not close—no one was close to Webster—Green laughed too.

Murphy did not. "It's a good thing the troopers didn't see you. I heard they had regular Army troopers flushing out snipers and looters."

Webster sneered. "That was later. By the time they showed up they wasn't nothing left to take anyhow. But I got all *kinds* of shit."

Murphy, swathed in a green rubber poncho, weighed down with belts and magazines of ammunition, moved over to sit on his pack beside Harding. He spooned beans and franks into his mouth and sipped from a canteen cup full to the brim with coffee. Before Webster had started his boasting, they had been talking about going home.

"Want some of this? I can't drink all this."

Harding held out his cup and Murphy poured it half full. Green was listening patiently as Webster belittled the troops who had been sent into the streets of Detroit.

"Old Webster has to have his audience."

Harding nodded. "I guess he needs to feel his life is affecting something or other. Somebody."

"Yeah. Well, he's not affecting Green any. I don't know why he listens to that shit."

"About thirty seconds ago he had you going too, Audie."

"Bull. I'd rather listen to the rain."

"Hear from your wife this week?"

Murphy sniffed and took another bite. "Yeah. The story now is if I put in for an early out, we can start all over and be good buddies again."

"Sounds fair enough."

"No way. I got almost three years to go. I signed up for them and I'm going to serve them. When she gets that through her head maybe we'll talk it over about new starts." Murphy's wife, after he enlisted, had moved away to live with her aunt in Atlanta.

Webster was droning on. The sound of his voice irritated Harding. It was somehow obscene, faintly depraved. He was talking now about sniping at firemen.

Murphy snorted. "That mother wouldn't have the balls to shoot at a fireman. Hey, you guys want some of this coffee? Willie?"

Green shot him a suspicious grin. "Must be bad if you're givin it away."

"It is," said Harding.

"Hey, corporal." Webster never called Harding by name. "You from Michigan, ain't you?"

Harding considered ignoring him—but one of the damnable things about Webster was that Harding could never ignore him.

"Yeah, Webster, I'm from Michigan."

"Where at in Michigan you from?"

Harding looked at him without answering. He knew Harding was from Detroit, the same as himself. Webster leaned forward and cocked his head. He grinned, his face blank as always, innocent, stupid, black beneath his dripping helmet, his eyes dead-looking, eyelids hanging a shade too low to seem conscious.

"Where at you from?"

"Detroit," said Harding.

"Oh." Webster nodded wisely, grinning as if savoring his victory. "That's right. Hey, corporal, tell Green here. How many of them firemens we shoot? How many?"

"Webster, you've never shot at anything in your life, much less hit it."

"That ain't true. We was keeping them off the buildings the whole first day and night. The whole town like to burn down."

"Somebody was keeping them off. I doubt if you were one of them."

Webster's spoon halted halfway to his mouth. He sat looking at Harding, expressionless. "You think I'm lyin, man?"

"I think you're lying, man. When all that was going on, you were probably in your beddy-bye."

Webster said, almost under his breath, "Fuck you, smart-ass. Smart white-ass corporal. I wish you would of been there, down where I was."

"Oh, I was around," said Harding. "I was around there. And I'm here right now."

"Yeah, I know," said Webster, eating. Green and Murphy exchanged a look. "You here now. That can change."

Harding felt himself growing angry. "A lot can change," he said. "But just remember, PFC, I already know how to shoot. And I'm keeping an eye on you, every minute. For somebody who's never shot a VC since he's been here, you talk mean. I've got a three-man fire team, counting you, but you *talk* mean. You just can't seem to pull the trigger."

"Yeah, I talk mean." Webster sat up a little, flicked Harding a glance and looked at his food. "And you a hard-ass corporal. The lieutenant was a hard-ass, too."

Webster took a bite, ignoring their faces. Their platoon commander, Lieutenant Whitcomb, had been a physical education graduate from the University of Michigan. He had, however, been unfit for leadership or for combat. He had walked the first platoon into an ambush, losing twelve men. The company commander had then put him in charge of Harding's platoon, and there had been grumblings and predictions among the men. A petty tyrant, Whitcomb had not liked Harding, a fellow Michigan graduate and an enlisted man, and Harding had been ashamed of Whitcomb. But the lieutenant had harassed his new platoon once too often, and before he ever had a chance to lead them into a fight, someone rolled a grenade into his tent. Harding had watched the corpsmen work on him, but the lieutenant died quickly and unmourned, except perhaps by Harding, who felt guilty although he was not.

"You wouldn't have the guts to do something like that," he said to Webster, although in fact he suspected that Webster had done it. "You're low enough, but you wouldn't have the guts."

They looked at each other and Webster said, "Maybe I wouldn't and maybe I would. The lieutenant was a hard-ass too."

Murphy laughed, tired of listening. "Shut up your fucking mouth and move out of here; you're a goddamn drag."

Webster glanced quickly at Murphy. "I ain't botherin you none."

"It bothers me just having to see your ugly face. Go on away and hassle somebody else."

Webster curled a lip but said nothing, finishing his ham and lima beans.

"Otherwise," said Murphy, "I'm going to kick your teeth in."

Webster mumbled and looked at Green, but there was no help there. Murphy got up and carefully set his coffee under the shelter half by the fire. He started to take off an ammo belt—but Webster picked up his pack and shambled away, dragging his rifle by the barrel.

"You just have to know how to handle that mother." Murphy retrieved his coffee and sat down again. "You guys waste too much time with him."

"I'm trying to straighten him out a little," said Green.

"The only way to straighten him out is to put a bayonet up his ass."

Green sighed. "I guess."

Harding took a deep breath and let it out. He always felt ashamed after letting himself get angry at Webster, but he was unable to help it. He wondered why.

It was true Webster had never shot anyone. Part of it was that he was a terrible shot, the worst imaginable. He seldom even bothered to fire—to do so was to bring down a shower of tree limbs or kick up clods of dirt ten feet ahead. Harding considered him safer not firing at all. Webster had never been able to qualify with a rifle, even with the M-14, which was easier to aim, much less tricky than the M-16.

Harding thought of him as a coward, but he knew it was not so simple. Webster preferred never to try in any way at all, as if he refused to become accustomed to the Marine Corps. He was a draftee who, like Harding, had chosen the Corps over the Army, but something had caused the two of them to eye each other with distrust at the beginning, and it had grown from that to something much worse.

Sergeant Grant, the squad leader, came by. "We'll be moving out pretty soon."

Murphy tossed his can on a stack of empties, poured out the rest of his coffee and pulled his hands in under the poncho. "I thought we were stopping here tonight."

"Sergeant Dunn wanted to, but he talked to the lieutenant and the lieutenant wants to keep moving. He changed his mind. Dunn is pissed off at him." Dunn was the platoon sergeant.

Green said happily, "Well, a little walk in the rain will be pleasant."

"Why does Lieutenant Melnick want to keep moving?" said Murphy. "Or is that too big a question from a lance corporal?"

"There's a ville up ahead. Some choppers went over this morning and drew fire. The CO wants us to go in around dawn; he's taking the first platoon to flank the ville. Lieutenant Melnick doesn't want to get too far back."

"What ever happened to the third and fourth platoons? Are they still in this company?"

"They got something else going over to the east. We'll do without them a couple days."

"That's very smart."

"No . . ." Green pursed his lips and nodded. "I trust Captain Vincent to know what he's doing. He's here on his third tour, you know that? He was at Hué during Tet."

"It's not him that worries me," said Murphy. "It's these platoon commanders. Guys like Whitcomb—and now we got Melnick. Where's he from, Harding?"

"Dartmouth business school. He's twenty-four years old."

"Christ, *you're* older than that."

"Yes, but he's a trained Marine Corps officer." Harding grinned.

"Yeah, and I'm a trained Marine Corps grunt. I don't like slopping through the mud behind a second lieutenant who wants to be a banker."

"He's a reservist, too."

"Yeah, great. Keep it up. I guess I better clean my rifle; I got mud in it."

"I guess you better," Green told him. "Else I don't want to be in the same fire team with you. You and Webster both is too much even for a professional to cope with."

"Well, you better do it fast," said Grant. "Before we saddle up."

Murphy ducked in under a shelter half near the fire to field strip his rifle. The M-16 would jam more easily than any other rifle Harding had seen. Many marines traded them in for twelve-gauge shotguns that had less range but more impact, and were reliable.

Sergeant Grant stretched and tilted back his head, looking straight up at the rain that fell in his face. "Go ahead, you mother. Rain, you bitch."

"Talking to Mother Nature?"

"I am talking primarily to Asia," said Grant, looking at Harding with water running off his face.

Green laughed. "I got news for you. Asia could care less about the USMC."

"That makes a few hundred thousand of us," said Harding.

Green winked at Grant. "Listen to the amateurs."

Grant looked at him, shook his head and walked away.

2. They moved out later and it got dark and kept raining. After two hours of humping through mud, the column was halted. The sergeants consulted with Lieutenant Melnick, and Grant came back.

"Okay, this is where we crash for the night."

Sentries were posted and the marines settled into the mud. Harding wrapped himself in his poncho and looked for Murphy in the dark, feeling hungry again but without any C rations. Moving along to where he thought Murphy was, he tripped over something, and someone jumped on top of him. Harding rolled and kicked, heard the whining voice and hit him in the stomach, then rolled him over and got a knee into his back. The man made a choked gurgling sound.

"What is this?" Grant had Harding under the arms and hauled him off. "Who is this?" he hissed furiously.

"It's Harding—"

"He jumped me!" cried Webster, stumbling to his feet.

"*Shut up.*" Grant grabbed him and threw him down in the mud. To Harding he said, "What happened?"

"Christ, I tripped over him. All of a sudden I was fighting for my life."

"I thought it was VC." Webster was careful to keep his voice low. "He tried to kill me."

"Shut up." Grant kicked him and Webster made a noise and then kept quiet.

"You want to have the lieutenant down on us?" he said to Harding. "Or worse? We're pretty close to the ville; we don't know how close, but I think we came too far."

"Sorry," said Harding.

"This goddamn rain. Moving troops around at night in the rain and not knowing where you're going is what you'd expect of a businessman. It's exactly the kind of thing Whitcomb would have done. The bastard won't listen to anybody."

He knelt down and said to Webster, "If I ever hear of you laying a hand on an NCO, I'll blow your ass away. You hear me? If he doesn't do it, I'll do it."

"He jumped on me . . ."

"Shut *up*." Grant slapped him with his open hand. "Just keep your fucking mouth *shut*. You either shape up, marine, or you're not going to live much longer. One way or another, I can promise you that."

Harding stood there cursing his big feet and the luck that had put Webster in his fire team, in his squad, in his platoon.

But they had always been together, he thought, lying in the hospital at Da Nang. They had always, in a sense, been together.

They were both from Detroit. They must have entered the Marine Corps at the same time, both drafted, both volunteering. They had come in through Fort Wayne in Detroit, were flown out to the Marine Corps Recruit Depot in San Diego for boot camp, then driven up to Camp Pendleton for infantry training.

Harding remembered Webster in boot camp. If the Marine Corps had not been built up to twice its normal size because of the war, Webster would have flunked out. He was no weaker than most of the recruits, but he was a whiner, a recalcitrant nonproducer. He could not swim or shoot or pay attention, and he would not learn.

Harding and Webster had taken a quick dislike to each other. It was not racial. Harding liked Green, Webster's opposite but equally black. Green and Murphy, Harding's bunkmate, dominated the physical conditioning that made up such a large portion of recruit training. Both were squad leaders, therefore in direct competition, and they became almost as good friends as Harding and Murphy. They were both Texans, four-year enlistees. Green was a black man who had made himself identify with an artificial brotherhood through sheer single-minded ambition. It was easier for Murphy.

Brotherhood, thought Harding. The Marine Corps saw itself as a brotherhood of comrades in arms. It was ingeniously set up—as even a draftee discovered—to instill pride of a peculiar sort, by forcing the individual to identify with the system. Harding had chosen not to resist, once he was in it. Green and Murphy had never had the problem; they were there by choice.

But Webster refused to be motivated—the system was meaningless to him. Harding suspected at times that he disliked Webster primarily not for being a loser, but for his refusal to try, for his indifference to the system from within it, where Harding, who also despised it, forced himself to adapt.

Also, Harding thought now, in the night, Webster and he had reminded each other of too much. When he looked at Webster and knew they had grown up in the same town, he thought of what he missed: downtown Detroit, the Fisher Theater, Woodward Avenue and the Museum of Art, the Lions and Tigers—yes, and the zoo, and the Wayne State campus and Belle Isle Park, WJR radio, the Ford Museum and Greenfield Village and the Ambassador Bridge. Everything that meant home, everything he was away from.

And, of course, the other side of it, parts of the city it made him sick to think about—and the riots—everything he had to think about because Webster was always there, always not cooperating. For everything about Detroit and about America that Harding feared and hated, Webster was there, reminding him of it.

It must have been, he thought now, it surely must have been the same for Webster, in his own dense fumbling way. Harding could only speculate as to what he had reminded Webster of.

3. Lieutenant Melnick refused to try for higher ground, afraid of getting more lost or stumbling into the village. He walked around, followed by his radioman, talking to the marines as they bedded down in the mud. He must have known at that point that they had little faith in him. Harding did not envy the man his job.

Later, as Harding lay rolled in his poncho, the rain slacking and picking up again, he heard Webster and Green arguing. It was impossible to make out what they were saying; Webster went on and on in a whining whisper, and Green would answer with short epithets. Green was the only one with whom Webster had any kind of relationship. Green had some influence with him because he was black and highly respected in the platoon. Murphy, who treated Harding like the older brother he had never had, emulated Green in almost every way. He considered Green—as Green considered himself—a professional. Even Webster, who had no reason to love professionalism, treated Green with deference. Harding thought that if Webster had had it in him to be able to try to accept any sort of discipline and commitment, he might well, like Murphy, have wished to become the cool and efficient Corporal Green.

Webster whined for a while and Harding heard Green say, "Bullshit." Webster said something else and Green said, "For Christ's sake, man, shut up your dumb shit mouth and let me sleep. I *swear* you are the dumbest nigger I ever met."

Webster shut up, and there was only the sound of the rain.

In the early morning the rain stopped. They were moving at dawn, and came on the village after half an hour of slogging through mud. Harding was uneasy: the people were up, standing outside their huts watching as the marines came in. That they had been expected could mean the VC had moved out—or it could mean they had set up an ambush. So much, thought Harding, for the lieutenant from Dartmouth.

They searched the village while Sergeant Dunn and the interpreter rounded up the elders and began to harass them for aiding the VC. The lieutenant watched nervously, reminding Harding of Lieutenant Fuzz in the Beetle Bailey comic strip. He was a tall man with blond hair and an attempt at a mustache, younger-looking than his twenty-four years. He fingered the holster of the .45 worn low on his right hip, as Sergeant Dunn lost his temper and started slapping and kicking one of the old men. The lieutenant kept looking around at the trees, wondering, no doubt, where everyone was: the CO and his first platoon, and the VC. The radio had shorted out.

Dunn worked with evident relish. He hated all Asians indiscriminately, and he horsed the old man around like a drill instructor during the first week of boot camp.

"I don't think we're going to get anywhere with him," the lieutenant ventured.

"Just takes a little time, sir." Dunn struck the old man in the face, knocking him back into the doorway of the hut.

"I think we'd better catch up with the first platoon." The lieutenant was looking around nervously.

"You want us to torch this place, sir?" Dunn pointed his rifle at the remaining old men.

The lieutenant paused to consider, and Harding, watching his face, was making up odds on his decision. At that moment they heard the firing, not far off, a sharp popping of small arms and automatic weapons.

The lieutenant jumped. "Get ready, sergeant. We're moving out."

It did not take them long, Harding remembered. The VC had apparently known about them but had not discovered the first platoon until they walked into it. Harding's platoon pulled around to the left and caught them coming the other way. Sergeant Grant moved his squad directly into their line of retreat, spreading out along a small clearing, picking them off as they came out of the trees.

Harding placed Webster on his left, where there was little action, and he remembered how Webster had held his fire, flattening out on the ground, hugging his rifle. Green was to Harding's right front, firing automatic bursts, and Murphy kept handing him magazines and firing single shots.

Harding, cold and sweating in the night in the hospital at Da Nang, saw it all again. He was down on one knee, pumping rounds into the trees, and he got a stoppage. He slapped the forward assist and nothing happened. He pulled the charging handle to the rear and the round flew out and he released the handle to chamber another round and pulled the trigger, and nothing happened. He hit the bottom of the magazine with the palm of his hand and he was cursing the M-16 and the Colt company, and someone came out of the trees at him. Webster, far to the left, fired a single shot that hit Harding in the back, a few inches below the top of his left shoulder. He twisted and went down, and the VC splashed into the mud and fired at Webster. Webster switched to automatic and churned up mud and water all around the VC and ran out of ammo and Green shot the VC and the VC and Harding rolled around in the mud and the VC died. —And he was conscious then only of blood, an incredible amount of it pumping out of himself all over the ground. He thought *I'm bleeding to death.* Webster was crouching where he had been, looking at him, and then Murphy and Green were there packing pressure bandages into the wound, in front where the round had tumbled and splintered its way out. He looked at his hands and they were covered with blood and so were Murphy's and Green's—and he was losing five pints—*five pints*—it was all he could see, and someone said, "He's passing out," and he thought *I'll bleed to death, I'll go into shock and never come out*—and he could see Webster standing over him looking pale, if that was possible, looking old, looking as if he were bleeding to death, and somebody said *It's okay old buddy, just hang on. Just hang on* and Webster holding his rifle and looking as if he were already dead.

1. The sign, made the same as so many others he had seen, red-painted with bright yellow letters, stuck into the hard-packed fresh-raked grassless dirt that passed for a lawn, was the only example of wit he had seen on the part of the military since he had come into the Marine Corps.

CASUAL COMPANY

said the hand-painted letters, and he grinned and looked at the mountains of Southern California, those low steep rolling hills surrounded by United States military barbed wire and called Camp Pendleton. He had been there before.

But he had not seen Pendleton for almost a year, since he had gone through the infantry school and a staging battalion bound for the war. Now, standing with his green sea bag at his feet, he felt again some sort of flash or déjà vu, as he had coming in on the bus an hour ago. A shifting of time that was at once a telescoping inward and outward, moving away on both ends in his mind from reality. It had been less than a year, seemed ten years, seemed ten days. Or a month. Meaningless.

He hefted his sea bag onto his good shoulder and opened the screen door with his other hand.

"Fresh blood," somebody said.

He stepped inside the door out of the sunlight and blinked into the shadowed length of the barracks. It was Saturday and the place seemed abnormally quiet, everyone gone no doubt to L.A. or San Diego or Tijuana. A phonograph was playing at the far end, but even that was muted, and with his eyes adjusting to the indoors, it was like gazing into a cellblock, or more accurately, with the old-fashioned water pipes overhead, running the length of the squad bay, it made him think of the interior of a submarine, and indeed the two rows of double bunks on either side of the bay were the new Navy-type, gray rather than Marine Corps green. He had lain in one of those for three months, but in a Navy establishment. He had not known the Marine Corps had any.

The barracks was well squared away, the floor recently swept, and had new-looking trash cans with shiny lids, three of them, at intervals of twenty feet. He didn't see anyone until he turned to pick up his sea bag again and someone said, "No, it isn't. Too much hair."

On the rack to his left, or bad, side, the first bunk inside the door, two marines were sitting, their feet propped on a footlocker.

"We get a lot of guys just out of ITR," said one of them, a youngish dark kid in green utility trousers and a T-shirt. The other, shorter, in jeans, with rimless glasses and a barely regulation haircut, looked at him over the top of a Harold Robbins novel.

"Gung-ho," he said. "No hair, calling everybody 'sir.' It's pitiful. On the way to staging and WesPac."

"But not you," said the first, eyeing his civilian clothing as if trying to guess his rank. "Too much hair. You're on the way back."

"You're almost right," he answered. "I'm on my way out."

"Oh, well—"

"Heavy."

"—aren't we all?" said the first with a grin. "Only a matter of time."

"You got a duty NCO?"

A flick of the thumb. "Down there and around the corner. Follow the concert to Lance Corporal Shelby."

"Thanks." He hefted the bag and moved down the squad bay.

A lance corporal was sitting at an old desk set in a niche between the squad bay and the head. Tall and young, he wore the summer tropical uniform of the day and a green duty belt. He was playing chess with himself and listening to Bach on a portable tape player.

"Lance Corporal Shelby?" He put his sea bag down as the other glanced up and turned down the volume. "You the duty?"

"Assistant duty. Just checking in?"

"Right. Corporal Harding."

"Hi. Can I see your papers, corporal?"

Harding dug into his sea bag and handed over his papers. The lance corporal opened a green logbook and made an entry, reading aloud as he wrote: "*1140—Cpl. Harding, R. L. 2575849, reporting in from U.S. Naval Hospital, San Diego.*" He signed the back of Harding's orders and returned them. "They'll want them at the company office Monday when you finish checking in."

Harding nodded. "Got any empty spaces?"

"Oh, yes. Right now you have a wide selection to choose from." Shelby pointed to a door across from the desk. "That's the NCO quarters. It used to be sergeants' quarters, but since the war is, as they say, 'winding down,' there haven't been many sergeants coming through. Just grab anything with an empty mattress. The police sergeant is gone for the weekend. You can catch him Monday and tell him you've moved in."

"Okay. Thanks."

"Wait. I'll lend you some stuff until you can get over to Supply." Shelby opened the top drawer of the desk and took out a set of keys. With one of them, after trying several, he opened a small room and got out a blanket and pillow and some linens.

"Just out of the hospital, huh?" he said as he handed the things to Harding.

"That's right."

"Back from Nam?"

"Yeah." Harding scooped all the things together under one arm and reached for the strap on his sea bag with his left hand. He had forgotten already, and felt a small wrench. The bag did not move. He thought, *Well, I have the rest of my life to learn.* "Hey, would you mind grabbing that for me?"

"Sure." Shelby picked up the canvas bag and followed him into the noncommissioned officers' quarters. "Where were you over there?"

"Around Da Nang for a while. I was up at Phu Bai. Chu Lai a little while."

Shelby put the bag down. "I haven't been over yet. I'm supposed to be a grunt, but they gave me a secondary MOS and sent me to supply school. I got out here this far, but they've just been keeping me here. I raised some hell about it and now I've got a transfer coming —maybe to WesPac. That's why I'm in Casual Company. Just waiting to go."

"Aren't we all," said Harding, echoing the kid by the door. "Well, if you want to get to Nam you'd better hurry before the Corps pulls out. Otherwise you'll end up on Okie."

"No . . ." Shelby shook his head. "The Corps will be there a long time yet. Long enough for me. I won't spend my last year on Okinawa."

"It's safer."

"That isn't the point." After a moment Shelby said tentatively, curious but polite, "You must have been wounded. If you were in the hospital down in Dago."

"Yeah." Harding looked at the bunks in the room. They were all single racks, several made up and the rest, five or six, apparently unoccupied. "What about that one?"

"That's empty. So are the wall lockers, if you've got your padlocks."

"Good enough." He tossed his bedding onto the gray Navy rack with its innerspring mattress, turned and, using his right hand, dragged the sea bag over with one jerk. He looked at Shelby, who stood watching him.

"Well, thanks."

"Yeah, it's okay. I guess I'll go watch the phone. Come out and play me some chess if you don't have anything better to do when you finish here. If you play chess."

"I'll do that." Harding opened the bag and Shelby said, "Welcome to Casual Company." He smiled wryly and went out.

Harding stored his gear in the two wall lockers and attached his combination locks and quickly made up his bunk. Then he sat down on it and looked at the room, rubbing his shoulder where he had wrenched it. He stopped, not liking the feel of it.

The room was spacious enough, sixteen bunks facing out from the walls, eight on each side, with their wall lockers beside them. In the wide center aisle was a sofa with end tables and lamps, and across from that a television set. On one end the door led into the squad bay past the duty desk to the right, or to the head to the left. On the other, far end, a door gave the NCOs a private entrance from the outside. There was a magazine rack on the wall by this door. He could see *Playboy,* some weight-lifting magazines, comic books, *Life.*

On the walls between the curtained windows were several examples of combat art, wash prints depicting Marine Corps operations. The titles he could read were *Search-and-Destroy: Mekong Delta; Helicopter Landing near Chu Lai;* and *Patrolling South of the Z.*

He counted nine other bunks that were made up. On the wall over three of them were photographs. He got up and looked at them. One set showed an aerial view of Da Nang and some pictures of downtown Saigon. Over the next bunk, all the photos were of people: a grinning bunch of Vietnamese kids; a lovely girl, apparently wounded but smiling, her left arm bandaged, carried in the arms of a marine; and a third picture of the same marine in combat gear with flak jacket, helmet and M-16.

Over the other bunk there was only one picture, taken during a body count after a fire fight. The pile of VC looked unreal, yet resembled the children the other man's camera had caught—and in the corner, the utility-clad bodies of four marines, stretched out like men sleeping in the sun. The only living person in the photograph was a marine in a green T-shirt and jungle hat, holding a Chinese AK-47 with its banana-shaped magazine, standing there looking down at the bodies of the dead VC. Someone had written across the bottom of the photograph: *Charter Member, We-Eat-VC-For-Lunch Bunch. Phu Bai 1969.*

Harding started back toward his bunk but hesitated in the aisle and stood looking at the room. He put his hands in his pockets and walked around one of the end tables and sat down on the sofa, facing the TV. He stood up and rubbed his shoulder, took his hand away and slapped it against his thigh. He went over and looked out a window. He could see a street and a building, probably a mess hall, and some trees. A truck full of marines went by, and a sports car driven by an officer.

He looked out all the other windows, taking in the old view, the same on any base. "I'm at Camp Pendleton," he said, trying to make the year disappear; but it would not do that, continued to be with him, and he thought, *I'm back.*

2. The next weekend Harding took a bus to Anaheim and spent Friday night in a hotel bar, drinking bourbon and remembering old songs as he listened to a jazz trio and tried not to think about women. Drunk, he went up to his room and stood under the shower for twenty minutes, and masturbated using Lux as a lubricant, imagining himself in the arms of first one and then another of the girls he had dated at school long ago when he was whole and free and had no nerves. As his seed washed away in the white tile shower he said aloud, "Onanism is death. Is death, old friend," and leaned against the wall with the water cleansing him, and then he stood in front of the mirror and pictured his shoulder restored and well and smooth and white again, and he choked and threw himself wet onto the bed and fell asleep on top of the blankets.

Saturday he slept late, and in the afternoon he went to Disneyland. He had been there once during infantry training; a PFC in uniform, he had wandered in a kind of daze, his hair short, his new green stripes cutting his sleeves like wounds. He had just applied for a change of MOS, for assignment to an infantry outfit and WesPac—West Pacific, the war. Dizzy with freedom from training, and the impact of his decision, he had bought a frozen banana on a stick and paid for it with a ten-dollar bill, not noticing until later that the grinning boy had given him change of a dollar. He had walked down Main Street and gone through the Haunted House, the Pirates of the Caribbean, played pinball and done many other fun things, hardly noticing, a stasis inside, trying to picture himself in the war and finding it impossible, feeling much younger and more naïve than he had any right to be. He promised himself he would come back in a year or so as a near-civilian and compare the impressions, discover by the comparison the extent of his shock and lassitude at the time.

But he had not considered the possibility that he might be in a state of greater shock when he returned—he had perhaps not really expected to return. Now that he was making good his promise, he had forgotten it ever happened and gave no thought to it. Instead, he looked for a woman.

He found her, a girl really, sitting on a park bench eating from a box of CrackerJack. She was small and slim and wore a bright yellow summer dress. She looked cold and was watching the October sky that shook with intermittent sunlight and gray trailing clouds.

Harding sat down beside her and looked where she was looking.

"It isn't going to clear up." She turned and he smiled at her. "I heard it on the radio. There's no use wishing—it will be a cloudy weekend. Maybe even rain tomorrow."

"I know it," she said. Her voice was rather weak, not throaty enough. As she looked at him he saw that her eyes were warm and brown.

"Want some?" She held out the box of CrackerJack.

"At least you were optimistic enough to dress for the sun." He took some and chewed it, peering into the box. "I'm really only interested in the prize." He pulled it out with his finger and gave the box back to her. "What could it be," he said mildly.

"If I were more realistic I'd have worn a sweater. I'm always surprised that southern California can get so cold." She had a Dixie accent.

He tore open the little package. It was a puzzle, four tiny balls in a green maze.

"Oh, boy. The story of my life."

She watched as he tried to get the balls into their slots. "Those are hard to do."

"Yes. I know. I don't have the nerves anymore. Getting old." She laughed and he looked from the puzzle to her. "Are you a regular here?"

A shrug. "I guess I am, more or less. You?"

He shook his head. "Tourist. Sort of."

"Well, you came to the right place."

"I did, huh?" He looked at her steadily, as if it was more than a rhetorical question, one he was really asking her or himself.

She cocked her head. "Well, I *think* so. What do you think?"

"I don't know. Have a drink with me?"

So all right. All right—he thought, and they walked up Main Street, past a troop of characters in bright mouse and elephant and dog costumes trying to befriend a screaming little girl who clung to her mother's skirt and howled with her head thrown back. They went out the main exit and Harding looked for a cab.

"Hey." She took his upper arm. "I've got a car. We can take my car. Okay?" Her small hand felt warm and familiar, yet strange, like something he had known and forgotten, and now remembered again.

"Great."

She led him across the parking lot and they threaded their way among marines in uniform, tourist buses, past several rows of cars to a white Plymouth. She scrabbled in her purse and handed him the keys.

"You drive."

He let the Plymouth out into the Saturday traffic, past the face of Mickey Mouse, past restaurants, motels, thumbing marines and barefoot kids with knapsacks. He made himself relax, feeding his anxiety into the wheel, into the machine that veered through the locomotive madness of California, thinking *Do you really know what you are doing?* Answering *I'm finding out as I go,* not knowing where he was going.

He took her to his hotel and they sat across from each other in a black leather booth in the bar where last night he had been visiting jazz dropout, alone with bourbon and old ballads. Today, quiet piped-in music, red-and-gold chandeliers, dim. They were ahead of the cocktail hour and the place was theirs.

"So." Harding tasted his bourbon and looked at her. "You go to Disneyland and eat CrackerJacks on gray autumn days. That's interesting. What other things do you do?"

"Not an awful lot." She sipped a very fizzy whiskey sour and smiled as if suddenly shy.

"Who are you?" he said. "What's your name?"

"My name? My name is Donna." He waited. "That's my name," she said, nodding. "And you—?"

"All right." He smiled. "You're Donna and I'm Robert. Okay?"

"Robert."

"Okay?"

"Yes. Good."

"Good. Now—Donna—I detect from your voice that you aren't a true Californian."

"Memphis," she confessed.

"Ah."

"Are you—" she said quickly, "are you in the service?"

Harding made a mouth and nodded. "You got me."

"It was just a guess. Mostly the hair."

"Yeah. Well, I'm in the Marine Corps at Camp Pendleton, for a very little while yet. I'll be out soon." He pointed to his shoulder. "Wounded."

"Oh. That's too bad."

"It's all right. Got me out of action before I could be killed. It's a ticket out of the service."

"Well, at least there's that. Does it hurt you at all?"

Harding sipped his bourbon. "Yes. It still hurts me sometimes."

They looked at each other and he said, "What about Memphis? Why are you here instead of there?"

"Oh, I was married. I came out here with my husband. We're divorced now."

"What does he do?"

She shook her head. "I don't really want to talk about him." She smiled an apology.

"Okay. Neither do I. Do you live around here?"

She nodded. "Here in Anaheim, yes."

"Do you work?"

"I'm a secretary."

"Why do you stay here? Why don't you go home?"

"No." She shook her head again. "No."

"All right." Harding finished his drink and signaled the waitress for two more.

Donna sighed. "I'm sorry. I don't seem to be very talky."

"It's all right. I like you anyway."

She put her fingers together in front of her face and looked over them at Harding. "I'd rather skip all that personal stuff for now and just relax and have fun."

"That's fine with me," said Harding. "That's why I'm in Anaheim, all right."

"Where are you from, Robert?"

"Wisconsin originally. America's Dairyland. I grew up in Detroit."

"How long have you been in the Marine Corps?"

"Year and a half. Drafted," he said with a grimace.

"Drafted into the Marine Corps? Wow."

"Well, more or less."

"But you're almost out now."

"Very close," he said. "Very close."

"What are you going to do when you get out?"

"Ha. You would think I'd have a pretty good idea about that, wouldn't you. But I don't. Most likely I'll go back to school. I think I might like it better if I just went on the road for a while. Try to find out about the soul of America. Does that make sense?"

"Traveling does."

"Mm. Yes. Maybe go up north through California and across the mountain states and the plains and cut down through the midwest and go across the south and then up the east coast."

"It sounds like you've got it all planned."

"No. It's just an idea, just one idea. I don't think I know this country."

"Does it matter? You have your own life, don't you?"

"Not so much anymore. It does matter, yes, it does. Let's say it's —necessary—for me to find out some things before I'll have my own life again."

Their drinks came and she gulped her first one, sucking thoughtfully on the cherry while he stirred his bourbon and soda with a plastic swizzle stick. She asked for a cigarette and he gave her one and said, "Have some death," without thinking about it until she reacted. It was a joke among himself and Murphy and Green. He explained and lit one for himself.

She sat back in the booth, apparently sizing him up. The drinks seemed to be relaxing her, and she inhaled deeply and said America was probably the same all over, no matter where you went or whether you came in on a bicycle or a Cadillac. She leaned her elbow on the table and looked at him with a shrug. The lounge was filling up with the cocktail hour group. "It's getting noisy in here."

"Well," said Harding. "I've got a room. Want to go up there?"

She shook her head, looking at the table. "No. No. I want to go back to my apartment. You can take me back there if you want. I can show you my TV. And you can show me your wound. Between us we've got the soul of America." She smiled ruefully. "All right?"

She was a little unsteady on her feet with just the two drinks, and Harding wondered if she had had anything to eat all day besides CrackerJacks. But he decided they could put off food for a couple of hours more, and he slipped his arm around her waist and she leaned against him crossing the parking lot. It was cold out now and the sun was almost down behind the city. He let her in and she slid over and unlocked the door for him as he came around, staying there in the middle of the seat, and he kissed her and moved a hand over her. After a minute she said quietly, "Let's go. Let's go, baby."

3. Donna lived in a boxlike apartment complex built around a pool and almost hidden by palm trees and dark, green, junglelike shrubbery. Harding tucked the Plymouth into its slot beneath the carport and followed her up a flight of stairs, tapping his hand nervously on the wrought-iron railing. The apartment itself was drab: off-white walls, green furniture, a television set and a stereo.

"Nice."

"You want a drink?"

"I want to go to bed with you," he said, grabbing her. "Right now." He kissed her for a while and she finally pulled away.

"Come with me." She took his hand and led him to the bedroom. She allowed him to undress her and he bit his lip and thought, *I don't know you. I'll never see you again. So it doesn't matter what happens or doesn't happen.* He ran his hands over her and felt all right.

"Oh, baby." She started to unbutton his shirt and he pushed away from her and half turned.

"Get into bed. You don't want to see me."

"Yes," she said, "yes, I do."

"Oh, Christ. Hey . . ." He put his hand to his shoulder, feeling the hollow. His passion was ebbing and he tried to hold down his fear. "It isn't pretty. It's pretty bad to look at." But she unbuckled his belt and helped him off with his shirt.

"Don't be silly. I don't care about that. I want to look at you. Don't be shy."

"I'm not. It isn't that. I don't want you to be . . ." He could not find the word. "Upset."

"Don't worry." She sat him on the bed and took his shoes off as he watched her slim body in the half-dark, and she unzipped his trousers and stood him up and helped him take them off. He allowed this, feeling a helplessness choke him, his uncertainty close to panic, and he fought it as she undressed him. She said, "Raise your arms up," and lifted the bottom of his T-shirt, and he took a breath.

"I can't raise my árm above my chest." She didn't answer, but helped him off with the shirt and with only a glance at his shoulder went to her knees and removed his underpants.

They stood a foot apart and looked without touching. He felt her eyes and there was no embarrassment until, the eyes moving up and holding a moment *there,* she then looked into his face and said, "You poor baby,"—and he felt his breath catch and his passion dying, ashamed and angry at himself.

But she moved to him and, reaching out, touched not where he expected but the more sensitive part, her cool fingers moving across the scars and briefly into the hollow, the emptiness he would always have with him, and then to his face, and she kissed him with a desperateness that startled him, and then it was all right again until he came into her and, determined now to do well by her, to thank her in the only way possible, discovered the point was so far off it seemed beyond the reach of either of them. For long minutes he worked for her with no result until she bit his shoulder and cried, "Oh, *hard,*" and he complied, tangling his fingers in her hair and forcing her head back, and it was what she wanted, and it worked.

They rested with a cigarette, and when she said, "You didn't make it," he imitated her hard inhalation of raw unfiltered death and shook his head.

She put the cigarette out and went to work with a persistence that made him gasp, and for minutes he hovered on the edge, with long slow rhythmic strokes, smooth and measured while he fantasized everything he could think of, still so near and far.

She whispered in his ear, "Do you like married women? Some men say they're the best because they know all there is from practice. And they know how to appreciate it. And they love to give themselves to strangers, to see how their husbands measure up. I'll tell you something," she said as he labored on the edge. "I'm married. I'm not divorced at all, it was a lie. While I'm here with you my husband is on Okinawa wishing he could have it. But I'm glad it's you instead of him, because you're better, you're so much better. . . ."

He made it and thought his back would break, thought he would be turned inside out. He lay exhausted with her while she kissed his cheek and stroked his hair and his shoulder. When he had the strength he kissed her and laughed.

"What's so funny?" She moved a leg over him.

"Donna, Jesus Christ."

"So maybe it was a hick cornball thing to do—but tell me, did it work?"

"It worked," he said. "God, it worked."

She reached for the cigarettes. "Besides, it was the truth."

He looked at her in the light from the match. "You really are married? Still married?"

"Why do you think I'm so horny?"

"Divorcees are pretty horny."

"Divorcees get it more often than I do. They don't feel guilty about it. Guilt makes you even hornier."

He laughed. "I'll take your word for it. All right—what about your husband?"

"He's a lifer in the Marine Corps. You figure it. You should know."

"I don't know if there's anything automatically bad about that. I suppose he's been gone a lot."

"He wanted that. We got married right out of high school in Memphis and he got a job in a factory. We were all right until the war came along. He enlisted, did a year in Viet Nam—I stood it all right because it was, you know, the thing to do; it was the war. I didn't know he'd get to like it so much. So much that he shipped for four more. I never planned on being a military wife."

"Any children?"

"No children. We never got around to that. Now he's on Okinawa. In six months he's written to me four times."

"Well."

"And I know all about the sex on Okinawa. He's got all the Japanese cunt he can handle, and he's welcome to it. If he needs that to make him happy . . . But sometimes I get lonely, you know, Robert?" He could see her eyes shining in the glow from her cigarette; she sniffed and he thought she was crying, but when he touched her eyes with his fingers they were dry.

"Yes," he said. After a moment he said, "You know, I had no idea. I mean I don't go around looking for wives."

"I don't go around looking for men, either. Not all the time. But if your conscience bothers you, you can tell it you didn't know. I lied to you, right? So forget it. Besides, you were doing us both a favor."

It rained the next morning, but in the afternoon the sun came out and they went back to Disneyland. They ate lunch and sat on a park bench near the town square, watching the people and waiting for the time his bus would pull up in the parking lot.

"You know," she said casually, looking at the sky, "I'd be happy to drive you down to the base. You could even stay another night. There'd be time in the morning."

"I know." He caressed the hair at her neck, his arm on the back of the park bench. "I think there's a possibility here for something pretty important to get started. We could eventually be seeing each other every weekend. Even some nights through the week."

"It could happen," she admitted. "It could very easily happen."

"And we don't want that."

"We don't?"

He shook his head. "Let's say I'm not prepared right now to take on any emotional responsibilities. I'm in free fall. You have a wonderful body and I appreciated and loved having the use of it more than I can say. But I don't want to give you or anyone more of myself than you had last night."

"It wouldn't have to be more." She laughed. "Just another shot of the same."

"I know how I sound. I'm only trying to be honest."

"No, it's all right." She touched his arm. "I'm not prepared for it either, I guess. But—an occasional lay never hurt anyone. I mean, here I am. No strings."

"That's a hard offer to resist."

"And I mean it. Until you get out or get transferred or find someone else. I'm here if you want me."

He took her hand. "Well, it may not happen. Give me your number. But it may not happen. You understand?"

"I never expect a thing," she said, writing the number out for him.

When the time came he kissed her and wanted to say something, but she already knew. She said, "Bye, Robert," and hurried away from him into the crowd, and he walked up Main Street and out the gate. The bus was sitting off to the right with a line of marines climbing aboard. He felt tired but better than he had felt in a long time, and he got in and watched the drab countryside as the bus headed south.

1. Three sergeants and a corporal were playing cards at a table in the NCO quarters. They were drinking coffee and Cokes from the machines in the head, smoking cigarettes and chomping cigars, and they played a loud and aggressive game, slapping down the cards, arguing over points. The game was hearts and at stake was an evening of free pizza and beer.

Corporal Harding, lying on his bunk six feet away, gave up trying to read "The Encantadas, Or Enchanted Isles" out of Melville's *Piazza Tales.* He had been making slow progress, underlining passages and rereading certain parts, and the addition of four cardplaying NCOs and a stereo that blasted an incredibly raucous group called *Led Zeppelin* was too much for him. He closed the book and shoved it under his pillow, sat up and began putting on his boots. It was Monday night and he wore a clean starched set of utilities; he was the assistant duty NCO for the day. He looked at his watch and noted that it was ten minutes until ten o'clock and lights out. He was off duty until eleven.

After lacing his boots, he wandered out into the squad bay. Sergeant Donovan, a lean, hawk-faced brown-bagger, was sitting at the desk reading a Sergeant Rock comic. Harding sat down on the edge of the desk.

"Anything happening?"

Donovan looked up from the comic book. "Nothing, man. Everybody's over to the movie. They got *The Magnificent Seven* again. Everybody must have seen that flick a dozen times already."

"Well, at least it keeps them out of the barracks. It's quieter here than in our quarters. I ought to move my rack out here."

"You going to relieve me on time? My wife's waiting."

Harding got up. "I'll see you about a quarter till."

"That's good. Good man."

Harding walked down to the end of the squad bay, passing mostly empty racks, and went outside. It was cold out; he could see his breath. Toward the infantry schools at San Onofre and Horno two orange flares burned as they hung in the sky. A cold night for maneuvers, he thought, picturing recruits out on compass marches. He had gone through advance training in October and November, when the Corps was overstrength and crowded. Donna was right: it was incredible how cold southern California could be out in the bush on a late autumn night. They slept in tents that had wooden floors but no stoves for the first two weeks, and they would go to bed fully dressed—long underwear, sweat shirt, utilities—removing only their boots and field jackets. They slept on canvas cots with a blanket and sheet beneath and two blankets on top of them, their field jackets over their heads, and six marines got pneumonia during that month. At night—like now, he thought, looking up—the sky was so clear and cold that the stars were like the bright crystals of rime that formed on the wooden steps, on the canvas tents themselves, gleaming in that hard starlight at men walking the two-hour fire watches. Later they had got portable oil-burning stoves and were ordered to keep them turned off after taps because two tents had caught fire. Nobody obeyed the order; men asleep on their feet during fire watch saw the black oil smoke over the tent city in the small hours of the morning.

Harding decided now, at this late date, that it had been partly fun —partly. But it had been cold, those short nights. Watching the flares fall, he wished he had accepted Shelby's offer to go somewhere and drink. He had opted instead for sleep and reading but had done little of either. Shelby was out there in the night somewhere, pouring suds down his throat and wondering if he would make it to Nam in time. In time for what? Harding wondered.

Marines started coming in from the movie, and he walked back through the barracks to the NCO quarters and watched the card game. The stereo was turned off. Apparently they too had had enough of Led Zeppelin.

The corporal, a New Jersey kid named Venezio, seemed to be cleaning up. Harding asked him how he was doing.

"I'm going to have a hell of a time come Saturday."

"Let me see that goddamn score pad." Sergeant McMullin, a quiet man in wire-rimmed glasses, passed the pad over to Sergeant Barnes, who scrutinized it, moving his lips as he added up the points against him. Barnes was a little overweight. It was he whose wall bore the photograph of the bodies he had helped produce during his tour.

"You can't be this good." He glared from the pad to Venezio and back at the pad.

Venezio winked at Harding. "In a world full of E-5s, a corporal has *gotta* be good."

The other sergeant, a short-timer named Doyle, carefully shuffled the cards. "I'll get these little bastards so mixed up you won't be able to pull any of your tricks."

Doyle dealt the cards. They picked them up and Barnes started growling. When they passed cards, Venezio gave him the queen of spades.

"Jesus *Christ!* You rotten little bastard!"

Venezio chuckled. "Pretty soon I'll be a sergeant too."

Harding went over and collapsed on his bunk, and a short time later the lights went out. The cardplayers gave it up for the night. By a quarter past ten the barracks was quiet except for occasional people coming in from town. Harding lay in the darkness and waited for his duty time. *I want out,* he thought. *I will soon be out.*

He wanted out before he got used to it again. The hospital had been bad enough, God knew, but now he was back in garrison, spit-and-polish, and even Casual Company was petty compared to a combat outfit. He did not want to get used to it again.

For the past week now he had endured the morning formations, standing in ranks with marines who dozed and daydreamed while the company gunnery sergeant read off his endless notices, reminders, duty rosters, come-ons for service-affiliated night schools, and other such useless junk. Harding would look at the hills of Camp Pendleton and feel short, nearly free. It was all such old stuff, checking brass and boots with the squad leader, standing the weekly inspection by the young reservist lieutenant who served as company commander, who would snap Harding's rifle away from him and, while pretending to inspect it, ask how short he was.

"About six months, sir. Unless the doctors come through."

"No word yet," the lieutenant would say, handing back the rifle. Harding would close the bolt, snap the trigger and come to order arms. "You'll be getting the medical, though, I'm sure. Any way you look at it, you're shorter than I am. I'm going over."

Harding would look straight ahead as the lieutenant grinned at him. "Yes, sir."

2. The blower clicked on in the ceiling and its even purr made Harding sleepy. He sat up on the side of the bed, looked at the green face of his watch and decided to relieve Sergeant Donovan. He took his Melville with him.

Donovan was looking alternately at the clock on the wall and an old girlie magazine.

"Go ahead if you want to, sergeant." Harding yawned and put his book in the desk drawer.

"It's a little early," said Donovan hopefully.

"What the hell. The OD's been through, hasn't he?"

"Yeah. And the staff duty was around a little while ago. Should be quiet the rest of the night."

"Go ahead and check me in if you want. I'm going to get some coffee."

"Okay, thanks."

When he came back from the head Donovan had made his last

entry and signed the logbook. He handed Harding the green pistol belt.

"Well, have fun."

"You too. My regards to your wife."

"I'll sure do that. Night."

Harding sat down in the old wooden chair, sipped his coffee and flipped through the logbook. Nothing much had happened this evening.

> 1900: Held sweepdown. Pvt. Alexander refused to help empty GI cans. Threatened to put a charge sheet on him. He complied.
> 2000: Officer of the Day checked barracks. All O.K.
> 2200: Lights out, TV room and pool room secured. Barracks all secure.
> 2300: Barracks all secure. Relieved by A/DNCO.
>
> James N. Donovan, Sgt.

At eleven o'clock Harding checked the barracks and stood for a moment watching the clear sky outside the door at the end of the squad bay.

PFCs Ellis and Harvey, black marines, came in, Ellis carrying a paper bag. He hesitated at the door while Harvey rummaged in a locker.

Harding nodded. "What's happening?"

Ellis grinned. "Our evening just *beginning*. Want some?" He held up the bag. "I don't see no lifers around."

"Just me. What've you got, Ripple?" Harding raised the bag and took a drink from the bottle. It was peppermint schnapps. He handed it back. "Good stuff."

Harvey, in the darkness by his locker, said, "Come help me."

Ellis went, and in a moment they came back with a portable stereo and a stack of records.

"I don't know how you guys can do this at night and work in the daytime."

"It take hard serious practice," said Ellis. "Wanta get the door, please?"

Harding held the door while they carried their things out. "You all take it easy now."

"The only way," said Ellis, and Harvey, carrying the stereo and half the records, grunted.

Harding walked back through the darkened barracks to the duty desk. There were a couple of radios on but they were turned down and he decided to leave them alone. He finished his coffee and wrote in the log:

2300: I assume all duties as A/DNCO.
R. L. Harding, Cpl.

He could still taste the peppermint schnapps even after the coffee. It reminded him of Green and Murphy, who were in North Carolina now, at Camp Lejeune. He remembered them during infantry training, bringing in liquor on the weekends. They would sit on bunks and footlockers after taps, and Harding would sometimes join them.

One Saturday night Murphy got drunk and upset, passing a bottle of schnapps with the Moody Blues playing softly on the stereo, and the Beatles' "Abbey Road." Green was asleep on the floor.

"I did a really bad thing," said Murphy, shaking his head as if unable to believe it himself. "A scary thing, Harding. I want to tell you. . . ."

He and Green had gone to Los Angeles and Murphy had blown all his money on Friday night at a whorehouse. Some of the money he had borrowed from Harding, and he felt guilty about it. He had returned to the hotel with Green and after Green crashed he went back out and walked up and down the Strip and ended up in a bus station. A man in his middle thirties had struck up a conversation, bought him a beer and invited Murphy up to his apartment for a drink. Murphy said okay and went along. He knew what the man was after and he knew what he was after, but he was not sure how to go about it.

The man had a nice apartment and they had driven to it in a Chrysler. On the way the man had talked about himself. He was from

Kansas City, in California on business, selling water coolers. He was single and said he liked it that way. Murphy agreed, and told the man where he was from. He said he was broke and owed money and could not go back to the base without it. The water cooler salesman said not to worry.

"He said he was lonely," Murphy remembered, while the Moody Blues sang and somebody lit a stick of incense, and no doubt a joint, at the other end of the squad bay. The pungent smell drifted to where they sat in the darkness.

Murphy and the man had got to the apartment and the man made drinks for them and talked for a long time. Murphy could not remember much of what he had said. Murphy was wondering why he was there and what he was going to do—but he sort of knew what he was going to do. The man asked Murphy if he liked him and Murphy said yes but he needed twenty bucks to repay his buddy. The man said not to worry and he smoothed Murphy's hair.

"He said I was a beautiful boy," Murphy said, taking a hit on the bottle.

The man had then put his hand on Murphy's shoulder and leaned over and kissed him on the mouth, closing his eyes, his lips surprisingly soft, and Murphy, not certain what he wanted to do, relaxed a moment and then tensed and hit the man a short hard blow into his unguarded stomach. The man made a noise and doubled up on the floor, and Murphy got up and kicked him in the face. When the man cried out and put his hands to his face, Murphy kicked him in the stomach.

"I don't know, I don't know why," said Murphy. "The guy was fucked up, but I could have just walked out. I didn't have to go there in the first place. The guy cried and said, 'I knew this would happen, I knew this would happen.' I got his billfold and there was sixty dollars in it. I took the sixty and left him the billfold and all his credit cards. All the time he was saying he was sorry."

Harding remembered how Murphy shook his head and was almost crying. Murphy said it wasn't because he hated queers. He felt sorry for them but he didn't hate them, and the man had been nice to him.

"I wouldn't ever have done any of it before," he said. "I wouldn't have gone with him and let him think— And I wouldn't have robbed him. I wouldn't have beat him up. But"—he looked at Harding, his eyes bright with schnapps—"it was kind of fun at the time—I mean it was *exciting,* you know? I felt like—a *marine,* and I could take this guy on, like he was the enemy. You know? But that's the first time I ever actually beat up anybody. The first time. This state . . . I hate this goddamn state."

At that time, Murphy had not yet killed anyone.

4

1. A board to recommend promotions to sergeant met on the fifteenth of the month in a small room across from the sergeant major's office, in the building where Harding had been working. Several units were represented, and Harding and Venezio were there from Casual Company. They waited with six others from the battalion, immaculate in their winter greens, fresh haircuts, mirrorlike shoes.

"How do I look?" Venezio patted a careless hair at the back of his head and adjusted the belt on his blouse so the distance between buckle and tip was perfect.

"You look gorgeous." Harding leaned against the wall, wondering why he was there. Venezio was a three-year man with time in grade; he was due for promotion. But not many marines went up for sergeant on two-year enlistments—soon, by regulation, there would be none. Harding had not expected to be there.

"If I look as good as you, I'm in." Venezio put his foot beside Harding's and compared the mirrors. "How do you get such a good shine?"

"I had PFC Harvey do them." Harvey was proud of his ability with a damp cloth and a tin of shoe polish. He did a lot of business for inspections and promotions.

"You too, huh? I gave him a buck to do my shoes for me. How come yours look better than mine?"

"I paid him two bucks."

"That's inflationary."

Sergeant Major McPherson came out of the board room and nodded at the corporals.

"Gentlemen." He was tall, in his early forties, with a pink complexion and pure white hair. Harding had heard that the sergeant major was well liked in the battalion, with a reputation for fairness. The three-stripe, four-rocker chevrons on his sleeves were green on bright red, impressive on the forest-green blouse, with a star in the center of each chevron, and, on the bottom of each sleeve, four green-on-red hash marks representing a minimum of sixteen years.

"We're about ready," he said. "Now here's how it will go. I'll call you one at a time in alphabetical order. When you come in, the members of the board will be sitting at a table to your left. Walk straight in until you are even with the officer in the center—that's Major Pierce, the battalion executive officer. The other members of the board are Captain Kingston and myself." Kingston was the commander of another company.

"Stop and make a left face and report to the major. I will put you at ease. We'll have some questions for you, so answer up and look sharp. Then I'll call you to attention, you will left face and march out. When you come out, you can leave. The results will be forwarded to your section heads in a few days. Is this all clear?" Everyone nodded. "Okay. Good luck, gentlemen. I'll call the first man in just a minute." The sergeant major went into the room and in less than a minute the door opened.

"Corporal Benjamin."

When the door closed again, Harding leaned against the wall and smiled at Venezio, who looked nervous as he got a drink at the water fountain outside the sergeant major's office.

"I don't understand all this bullshit," said Venezio, wiping his mouth. "I never been up in front of a promotion board since I come in the Marine Corps."

"It's garrison duty," somebody said. "They don't bother with this shit in WesPac. They need NCOs too bad to quibble about it over there. But come back to a base stateside and you get this."

"It pisses me off." Venezio leaned over and flicked away a particle of dust from his shoe with his clean white handkerchief. "Goddamn it, I got time in grade. Why should I have to answer a bunch of chicken-shit questions? They didn't ask any questions in Hué."

"It's garrison."

"It's the Marine Corps," said Venezio.

"There it is."

Harding was not nervous. He had decided, or realized, months ago, in the hospital in San Diego, that nothing would intimidate him again for the remainder of his time in the Marine Corps. The worst he could feel now was irritation, frustration at the waiting to get out. It was the only thing he wanted. Instead, he got duties and run-arounds, and promotion boards. The thought of being kept in by such tactics for the rest of his enlistment angered him, and he knew that they could do it. Military inefficiency, intentional or otherwise, had done in many a good man, and in such a way that no one could be held responsible. Harding did not intend to let such a thing happen to him. He was not going to divert himself around Camp Pendleton for another six months while they scratched their bureaucratic heads over his case and robbed him of his benefits by their inactivity, waited him out until he *was* out.

"They're taking a long time with Benjamin."

"He's only been in there five minutes."

"Five minutes is a long time when they're firing questions at you. What can they say to you that takes five goddamn minutes?"

They had put Harding to work in a receiving warehouse, tracking down the origins of unidentified shipments. It was an easy, not unpleasant job; he spent much of his time sitting at a desk in the warehouse office, drinking coffee and talking to the civilians who worked there. It was as good a place as any, better than most, to wait out a military enlistment. If he had been willing to wait it out he would have been satisfied to stay where he was. That was the dangerous thing about it; if he allowed himself to frequent the beach, Los Angeles, San Diego, Tijuana, he would find himself hanging around for another half year, perhaps lose the fine edge to his blade of malice.

He did not think that could happen to him now. Yet he knew too well what compromises are possible in the military and he did not want to find out if it could happen. He wanted out while his bitterness was fresh.

Benjamin came out of the office, heaved a sigh of relief and got some water. He ignored the questions of the other marines until he finished. Then he smiled like a veteran.

"It's no big deal. They take a look at you and ask some questions about where you've been in the Corps and what you think about this and that, whether you think you'd make a good sergeant—just bullshit."

Before he could be more specific, the sergeant major came out.

"You can take off, Benjamin."

"Yes, sir." Benjamin put his cap on and left.

"Corporal Dietz."

Harding was the fourth man called. He walked into the room, conscious of the soundproof silence, stopped and made a left face, looking at the light-green wall three feet over Major Pierce's head.

"Corporal Harding reporting as ordered, sir."

"At ease, corporal," said the sergeant major, taking his seat again.

Harding went to a relaxed parade rest, feet twelve inches apart, hands clasped behind his back. Major Pierce gave him a long look that took in Harding's haircut, his fresh-pressed uniform, his ribbons, his shoes.

"How are you today, Corporal Harding?" he said at last.

"Very well, sir," Harding answered, looking at the major. Major Pierce was a medium-size man in his fifties, balding in front, with short, carefully combed graying hair around the sides of his slightly elongated head. His eyes were deep blue, a little tired looking, small wrinkles in the corners. Harding had seen him here and there but knew nothing about him except that he was not much liked by enlisted men in the battalion. He had the reputation of being a hard-liner. Fortunately the battalion commander, Colonel Tripp, was a more reasonably easygoing man. There was, however, a rumor of Colonel Tripp's impending retirement, and some of the senior NCOs were afraid that Pierce would be promoted to lieutenant colonel and take over the battalion.

Major Pierce flipped through Harding's service record book.

"I see that you are from Wisconsin."

"Yes, sir, born there," said Harding. "Actually I grew up in Detroit."

"You're a college graduate?"

"Yes, sir."

"Where did you go to school, Corporal Harding?"

"Sir, I graduated from the University of Michigan."

"Mm." The major nodded. "Oh, yes, so I see here." He looked up at Harding. "I have a son at Michigan State. Hates the military," he added mildly. "You took a degree?"

"Yes, sir. I have a Bachelor of Arts in history."

"Indeed." The major looked back at the SRB. "Well, I don't suppose you've had much use for that in the Marine Corps."

"Not the slightest," said Harding.

"Tell me, Corporal Harding," the major continued, as if he had not heard the remark, although Harding saw in his eyes as the major glanced up again that he had indeed heard and noted it. "Why didn't you apply for officer training? You obviously have the qualifications."

Harding hesitated a moment. "Sir, there were several reasons. It would have been necessary for me to extend for another year to go to OCS. I was drafted into the service and I wasn't willing to give up more than two years."

"I see. Of course, if you had taken ROTC at school, that problem wouldn't have occurred."

"It wasn't a problem, sir. I was never interested in becoming an officer."

The major looked at him carefully. "Well, that is your prerogative, of course. You no doubt wanted to give the minimum and get out," he said dryly.

"I didn't want to give anything, sir."

The major ignored this, but the captain and the sergeant major moved in their seats. Harding did not look at them.

"How long were you in Viet Nam, Corporal Harding?" Major Pierce was studying the SRB again.

"Almost eight months, sir."

"Where were you?"

"Mostly around Da Nang, sir. Also at Phu Bai and Chu Lai."

"You were—I see here that you were wounded."

Harding did not answer.

"You aren't wearing a Purple Heart ribbon, though," said the major, looking at Harding's ribbons. "If you rate a Purple Heart, why aren't you wearing it?"

"Sir, the Purple Heart was never awarded to me."

"But you were wounded in action. You came here from the naval hospital in San Diego."

"Yes, sir, I did. But it was never awarded."

"Well, that's rather strange, don't you think?" Before Harding could answer he said, "I think I will look into it and see if I can't expedite your ribbon and medal."

Harding said nothing.

The major looked at Captain Kingston. "Do you have any questions, captain?"

"I have one or two." The captain shifted a little and sat up as tall as he could. "Corporal, where were you wounded?"

Harding turned his head to the right to look at Captain Kingston, who was short, heavy-set, energetic in appearance, perhaps forty years old. His hair was worn in the short lifer crew cut, shaved close above both ears.

"In the left shoulder," said Harding.

"No, no; I mean where were you when you were wounded?"

"I was near Da Nang, sir."

"What were your duties at the time?"

"Sir, I was a fire team leader in the first squad of the second platoon."

"But I understand that your Military Occupational Specialty is not 0311 infantryman."

"No, sir. My primary MOS is 3042, but I have a secondary MOS of 0311."

"Was that by choice?"

"Yes, sir."

"That's interesting," said the captain. "You didn't want to go to OCS and be an officer, yet you didn't use your degree to keep a supply job that was assigned to you. You volunteered for combat."

Harding did not answer.

"Is that right?" said the captain.

"Yes, sir."

"How did you happen to do that?"

"I don't think I remember, sir." The captain looked unwilling to accept this and Harding added, "It was right after boot camp. Some of my friends were going over as infantrymen."

"I see. Well, that I can understand." The captain nodded approvingly. "I don't think I have any more questions."

"Sergeant major?" suggested Major Pierce.

"Yes."

Harding turned his head to the left and looked at the sergeant major.

"Corporal Harding, you have an excellent record. You gave up an easy job to go out in the field and you acquitted yourself well as an NCO where it counts most. Do you think you would be a good sergeant?"

Harding did not hesitate. "I doubt it, sir. Average, I suppose."

The sergeant major blinked. "I see. Do you *want* this promotion, Harding?"

"No, sir," said Harding, looking at the brown eyes of the sergeant major. "I don't."

There was a silence as they all looked at him. He kept his attention with the sergeant major. The sergeant major said quietly, "Why not?"

"I'm not interested in any more responsibility, sir. I'm only interested in getting out of the Marine Corps."

"That will do," said Major Pierce. "I don't know what your problem is, Harding, but it's obvious enough you have one. We aren't here to get you out of the Marine Corps, but we can damn well see that your discomfort isn't increased by added responsibilities. That will be all, corporal."

Harding came to attention, made a left face and walked out of the room, closing the door behind him.

Venezio was pacing back and forth in the hallway. "Christ, you were in there long enough. How did it go?"

"Oh, fine," said Harding. "Lovely. No sweat."

"You going to make it?"

Harding smiled and got a drink of water.

The door opened and the sergeant major said, "Stick around, Harding. I want to talk to you. Corporal Nelson."

"What was that all about?" asked Venezio when the door closed.

"Nothing much. The sergeant major wants to learn more about my special problem, that's all."

"You mean your discharge?"

"My discharge." Harding smiled. "My discharge." It sounded so good.

Venezio finally took his turn in front of the board. When he came out he grinned at Harding and got a drink of water.

"Well?"

"I knocked 'em dead. It'll be a cold day in California when they get another sergeant as good as me, and they know it."

"They do?"

"Damn right." Venezio took a deep breath and let it out. He laughed and said, "Jesus, I'm glad that's over." He sighed again. "You want me to wait for you?"

"No," said Harding. "This will probably take a little while. Thanks anyway."

"Okay, man. I'll see you, then, *sergeant.*" He lifted his eyebrows, put on his cap and went out. Harding heard him whistling as he crossed the street.

He waited for another ten minutes and the sergeant major came out of the board room with his briefcase. He glanced at Harding and crossed the hall to his office.

"In here, corporal."

Harding followed him in and stood in front of the desk. The desk was neat, with papers aligned and ballpoint pens evenly spaced on the green blotter. There were a United States flag and a Marine Corps flag standing behind the desk, a coat tree by the rear wall and pretty pastel combat drawings framed on the walls. The carpet was green.

The sergeant major put his briefcase down and fixed Harding with a look while he took off his blouse.

"You had one hell of a nerve coming into a promotion board and acting the way you did. Just who do you think you are?"

"Nobody really," said Harding.

"If you didn't *want* a promotion you could have seen me ahead of time instead of going through your little song and dance in front of the battalion XO. Does it please your sense of theater to do things that way?"

"No, sir. I really didn't think to see you first, sergeant major. Or I would have. I didn't expect to be called up before the board at all, and when I was—I just followed through on it."

"You followed through, all right. Sit down." He hung his blouse on the coat tree and pulled out the chair behind the desk, sitting down to face Harding across the polished surface and the blotter.

"But you didn't *want* to be promoted. All of a sudden you don't *want* any more responsibility. Just what is your problem, corporal?"

"I want out," said Harding.

The sergeant major gave him a cross between a grimace and a smile. "You want out. Well, that's tough. How long have you been in the Marine Corps?"

"Almost eighteen months."

"Eighteen months? And you're up for sergeant E-5 and bitching about it. I've been in the Marine Corps eighteen *years*. I remember when a man could count himself lucky to come out of a three-year enlistment as a PFC. What were you, drafted?"

"Yes, sir."

"Into the Marine Corps?"

Harding hesitated. "No, sir . . ."

"So you had some choice in the matter. You've hacked eighteen months, done a tour and been wounded. All of a sudden you're sour on the Corps. What is it, the wound?"

Harding was silent and looked at the pen and pencil set on its eagle-globe-and-anchor base, next to the nameplate that said: MCPHERSON, J. K. SGT. MAJOR.

"You miffed because they screwed up on the medal?"

Harding looked up. "No. I couldn't care less about—"

"How long were you down there at Dago?"

"Three months."

"So you had a lot of time to lie there and feel sorry for yourself and decide the Marine Corps got you fucked up and so you're through with it. Is that about right?"

"I've done my share." Harding looked at the sergeant major and shook his head quickly because that was not what he meant. "I volunteered to go over and I almost got blown away. I have at least a partial disability. I've been trying for four months to get a discharge and the doctors keep running me around the block. Instead of a discharge I get my Purple Heart expedited, I get a chance for promotion. I don't want any medal. I haven't the slightest interest in being promoted. What I am interested in is having the Marine Corps acknowledge its responsibility to me. I am entitled to a medical discharge and a pension, and that's what I want. That's the only thing I want."

The sergeant major played with the pencils on his desk. "I didn't know you were that bad off physically."

"I can hardly raise my left arm. I'm on light duty. I couldn't run an obstacle course now. I couldn't carry two ammo boxes or an M-60."

"What do the doctors say?"

"That my request is in channels; that I may respond to therapy. *Therapy*..."

The sergeant major picked up a pencil and tapped it in the palm of his hand. "Have you requested mast about this? I'd think you could get some action by taking this to higher authorities."

Harding shook his head. "I haven't done that, sir. It's a little hard to explain why. It's that... I've been what I suppose is called a good marine. I've done the job, more than lived up to the contract. I was badly wounded in action and the regulations seem pretty clear to me. I don't feel I should have to petition the Marine Corps to live up to its responsibilities after I've lived up to mine. I shouldn't have to *ask* them to abide by their own regulations. That's why I haven't gone up the ladder. I'm watching to see how the organization takes care of its own."

"Well." The sergeant major tried with a look to communicate his own certainty, his confidence in the institution. "The Marine Corps takes care of its own, Harding. It does. Sometimes, though, you have to help it along. You have to make it aware of you."

"Well, sir, all things considered, I think the Corps should be aware of me by now. It should be helping me along."

The sergeant major nodded. "Well... yes, you're probably right. By now you should be getting action. I'm going to look into it."

"Thank you, sir."

"It seems to me, though, that you haven't been very reasonable about this, in other ways. Admittedly, if you rate a medical discharge and appropriate benefits, then you have that coming, and you'll get it. But I wouldn't think a little red tape should be enough to put you so down on the Corps that you would refuse a promotion."

"I'm not really down on the Corps," said Harding. He thought a moment and said honestly, "I don't feel anything for the Marine Corps anymore except the need to get out of it with what is left of me. I can't *function* in it anymore. I feel as though my military experience ended when I was shot. That should have been the end of it." He smiled unhappily and added, "If Webster—if the man who got me had been a better shot, I wouldn't have to worry about all this."

"Webster?"

Harding nodded. "Another marine. A man in my own fire team. Shot me in the back. By mistake, I guess."

"You guess?"

"He was killed a few days later." *Murphy,* he thought. "I never got a chance to ask him."

The sergeant major blew softly through his lips and tossed the pencil on his desk. "Maybe I see why you're a little bitter. You gave up a supply MOS to volunteer for infantry and were shot by one of your own men. That probably explains why you haven't gotten the medal, although you're sure to eventually."

"Yes, sir. I don't care about the medal. I care about the discharge."

They sat there looking at each other for a minute. The sergeant major pursed his lips and swiveled back and forth a few inches in his chair.

"You've had some bad luck, Harding," he said at last. "That doesn't excuse your behavior today. But . . . hell, I don't know what else to say to you. I guess you can go. You'll be hearing pretty quick about this request of yours. I'm going to check with sick bay and see what comes out."

"I appreciate it," said Harding.

"Your experience hasn't exactly been typical, you know."

"I hope not, sir."

"It hasn't." The sergeant major sighed. "Okay, that's all. Stay out of the major's way."

"Yes, sir. I'll do that."

2. A few days later, Harding and Shelby, working in the same building, were called to the company office.

"I have a feeling," said Shelby.

"Don't we both."

They stepped out the back door of the building. It was a dark and rainy autumn day, with no sign of the California sun. As they waited under the eave for the rain to slacken, a line of big trucks rumbled by, green canvas-covered half-tons and six-bys, their dim headlights cutting through the fall of water so that it seemed even darker than it was.

"I may never ride one of those again," said Harding.

"You sound nostalgic already."

"I'll probably get there. In a few years." Harding watched Shelby light a cigarette, cupping his lighter flame in the wet breeze. The first gray puff of smoke rolled away and the orange tip glowed and Harding thought of Murphy. *Have some death.* "I guess eventually," he said, "I may feel something about my time in the Corps. But it will be a while. It will really be a while."

"Maybe," said Shelby. "I have a feeling that kind of thing fools you, though. The longer you're out, the more you'll think you remember having enjoyed it. That should start for you right about—next week."

Harding laughed. Oh, but Christ, he thought, it was good to be getting out of it now, without having to adjust to it again. He felt he would not have been able to endure it now. It was something that should not have happened at all, and when it did, it had lasted until that day he had slapped his M-16 and jerked the charging handle, as the round came tearing into him. From that moment it had been over, the adjustment had been made and lost; adaptation had reached its natural limit. He was only sorry he could not see Green and Murphy again.

The rain eased up and Shelby tossed his cigarette away. They jogged through a mild drizzle to the company office, and a lance corporal took them to his desk behind a partition.

"Corporal Harding, Lance Corporal Shelby . . ." He dug into a mass of papers. "I got orders for both of you here someplace."

"I think that will be 'mister,' " said Harding.

"Yeah, here we are." He handed a set of orders to each of them.

"Wait a minute . . ." Shelby sat down on the edge of the desk.

But Harding did not notice Shelby. He was reading his orders—*orders,* not discharge papers. He was instructed to leave the following morning and report in one week to the Commanding Officer, Force

Troops, Fleet Marine Forces Atlantic, Camp Lejeune, North Carolina.

"No." He shook his head. "Hey, there must be some mistake."

"I've heard that one lots of times." The lance corporal grinned. "No, they're straight. Nobody stays in Casual Company forever, you know."

"No, but . . ." Harding looked at the lance corporal. "But I was supposed to have *discharge* papers. A medical discharge. Don't you have any word on that?"

"Nope. Did you put in for a discharge?"

"Did I put—" Harding suddenly felt weak. He leaned against the desk.

Then he was angry. "Hey, I want to see the CO. I want to request mast."

"*You* want to request mast." Shelby looked at him sickly. "They're sending *me* back to North Carolina!"

An hour later they had both seen the reservist lieutenant, Hobbs, their company commander. He was solicitous but unhelpful. Harding's request had indeed been sent into channels. The sergeant major had kept his promise and checked. But Harding was being forwarded to Camp Lejeune as his duty station until his request could be acted upon. It was simply a matter of time, said the lieutenant. But Harding had always known that.

Shelby's case was more complicated. Apparently a mistake had been made. He had been reassigned his primary MOS of 0311 infantryman—but his orders had come in for Camp Lejeune instead of WesPac. The orders had originated at Commandant Marine Corps in Quantico, Virginia, and would take an indefinite length of time to straighten out. Meanwhile, he was to carry out the orders he had received. The lieutenant promised to do everything possible to get Shelby a trip over to where the lieutenant himself was heading in two more weeks. That was the best he could do.

They went to the mess hall, but neither of them was very hungry. They finally gave up, walked back to the barracks to pack their sea bags and sat in the NCO quarters looking at each other.

"You going anywhere tonight?" Harding asked.

"I don't know. I may just sit around and cry. Or get into Venezio's card game. Or maybe go to the flick. There's some science fiction thing on."

"At least it isn't *The Magnificent Seven.*"

"Have you ever had the feeling," said Shelby, "that Fate was trying to tell you something?"

"You'd do well to listen."

"This is going to cost me months, I'd bet on it. I may not even get over now. It's like a sign—do you believe in signs?"

Harding shrugged. "Depends on what they say. Let's get drunk."

"That won't solve anything."

"It will solve being sober."

"Maybe I'm not supposed to go to Nam. But I had it all figured—"

"The Corps will be pulling out anyway. Probably before you finish staging."

"I hope not."

"It's better."

"Maybe. Maybe it is."

They walked over to the door and stood watching the rain.

"Well," said Shelby, "you're going to get a chance to see your friends again."

"Yes. It feels strange not to be getting out. It's like the old days, shuffling around the bases. But it will be good to see Murphy and Green. I didn't think I'd ever see them again."

Sergeants Venezio and McMullin and Barnes and Doyle were setting up their card game. Venezio wore shiny new collar chevrons, three stripes. Harding and Shelby stepped outside under the eave and watched a light rain sprinkle down. The sky was dark and no stars were visible, no moon. A wind picked up in gusts and blew the rain into them.

Shelby had just started a cigarette. "Oh, hell." He tossed it away. Harding thought of the kids in ITR down at San Onofre. He wondered if Echo Company still lived in tents as he had, but doubted it.

That was some time back; now the Corps was scaling down again and facilities that had been overflowing with young men then had plenty of room now. He thought of the kids in BITS, the Basic Infantry Training School, up at Horno, climbing Mount Motherfucker and running along the ridges of Old Smoky. He thought of the marines in staging battalions at Las Pulgas. Where Shelby should have been —Shelby thought—waiting to go over, waiting to go.

"What's Lejeune like?" he asked Shelby.

"It's big. Bigger than Pendleton. Of course, I was only at Montford Point, at the supply school. I never thought I'd be going back there."

"I never thought I'd be going there at all."

"Well . . . maybe it will be interesting." Shelby nodded positively. "We'll see your friends and maybe all of us will be buddies. Then you'll get out and I'll go over. We'll take it as it comes."

Harding answered with a smile, and he felt the rain and looked at the dark mountains, unable to predict, or to entertain a single thought for the future except seeing Murphy and Green again. That was enough to excite him; the vision of all of them finishing out what little time he had left made him take a deep breath of wet air. From the corner of his eye he could see the lights of a column of trucks moving slowly down the street toward him, but he looked not at that but at the mountains that ran the length of California and beyond, some hundreds of miles north to Oregon and yet beyond, and a little way south to Mexico—and beyond. And on the other side, he thought, idly rubbing his shoulder although it did not hurt at this moment—on the other side, stretching east and south and north to the borders and the oceans, was his country. And beyond that, much more than that, he thought, feeling young suddenly again, and excited: the world.

1

1. The young woman finished packing up her car with everything she could squeeze into it for this trip, the last of the weekend. When she was done she made herself a cup of tea and sat down in the window bay to drink it, looking out at the coast of North Carolina, where November waves pounded the shore, scattering sea birds that ran like tiny marionettes, buffeted by the hard cold sea wind. The tide was coming in. The white froth looked like dirty snow all along the beach.

The boy she had seen that morning showed up again as she sat watching the waves. He appeared as little more than a dot rounding a dune up the beach, black against the sand of the high dune. She watched him work his way down toward the cottage, approaching from the New River inlet, walking on the wet part of the sand and stepping back whenever a wave came in. He kept his head turned to the sea and he seemed in no hurry, rather otherwise, as if he was sure something was there if only he could see it.

She watched him, as she had that morning, sipping her tea, wondering why he was on the beach at this time of day, this time of year. On the beach the season had turned early and it was winter, too cold for swimming, too cold really for walking.

He wore a blue flight jacket and jeans and boots, and walked with his hands jammed into the pockets of the jacket. He did not otherwise seem to notice the cold, did not flinch in the wind that tossed the sandpipers along the beach. She knew he had to be cold, because she had nearly frozen loading the car. She felt a little sorry for him, and curious.

While he moved along she was making up her mind to talk to him, and by the time he came abreast of the cottage she had put on her coat and was ready to step outside. When she opened the door, a blast of wind struck her, blowing her long hair across her face and causing her to squint, and as the boy continued without noticing she quickly pulled her coat close around her and tossed her head so the hair was blown back, and hurried out down the wooden steps and across the sand toward where he was moving away from her.

The sea and the sky met in a fine division of blue and gray that seemed very close, and a small white sailboat held itself motionless, seemingly farther out than the horizon, and the boy had stopped and was turned toward all this now and was watching the boat pinned on the backdrop. She called out, "Hi," as she approached, but the wind blew it back in her face and the boy did not move. She came up to him and, suddenly timid, hesitated behind him and finally reached out a tentative hand, but before she could touch him he turned and saw her and jumped.

"Hi," she said again.

"You scared me," he said, his words blowing to her as if picked up by the wind from far away.

"Sorry. You didn't hear me."

He was looking back at the sea. She hesitated and said loudly, as if crying down the shore, "It's cold today!"

She thought he answered something; his mouth formed words, but they were blown away.

"It's a cold day for beachcombing!" she cried.

He smiled briefly and turned and stepped away, looking out again, and she said with a small desperation, "Do you know them?"

He stopped dead and turned. "What? What did you say?"

"I said do you *know* them? On the boat?"

"Boat?" He gave her a slow uncomprehending stare that made her uncomfortable, and looked out to sea again. She thought he said, "Oh," as if he had just seen it, had not even known it was there. He turned back and said, "I wasn't watching that."

She looked at him questioningly and he pointed toward something to the right of the boat, much closer in, and she noticed then a number of dorsal fins just beyond the shallows. She pictured huge fishy bodies lingering there.

"Sharks?"

He shook this off with a single jerk of his head.

"Dolphins. Sharks don't roll like that."

She saw that indeed the creatures were bounding gently up and down, showing their backs, at times flipping their tails. She had often sat on the porch of the cottage and watched them work their slow way up or down the beach, feeding and playing. It was strange she had not noticed these.

"There's not a shark in a long ways from here right now." The boy watched them intently, blinking his eyes as a blast of wind struck, causing her to take a half step backward. "Sharks won't come around a school of dolphins."

"Oh," she said. "They won't?" Her hair blew into her face again and as she tossed her head he looked at her without answering. She gazed back at him. He was young, his face and eyes clear, drawn from the cold, almost pale. A strong mouth, and his hair was short, a little longer in front, blowing away from his forehead. *A marine,* she thought, *from the base.*

"You looked so cold." She shoved her hands into her coat pockets. "That place"—she nodded toward the cottage, sitting back on the hill behind the beach, its front porch balanced as if precariously on stilts —"that's my cottage. Would you like to get warm? Would you like a cup of tea? Or coffee? Hot coffee?"

He looked at her for a moment, dropped his eyes and turned again to the sea. The dolphins seemed not to be moving now; they maneuvered a bit in toward and out from the beach, but were apparently holding up on their journey.

"Okay," he said, turning back. "Thanks."

"What?"

"I said *yes*. Thanks!" He finally smiled, and followed her across the width of beach toward the cottage. She felt her feet sinking into the sand with each step as if the cold were holding them, as if the beach were cooperating with the sea—she had a momentary image of the sea trying to get her—and she glanced back and saw only him. When they reached the wooden steps she hurried up them and threw open the door, and he moved inside quickly enough to tell her that he was indeed cold.

2. "I'll never get warm again." She took off her coat and tugged her sweater down, tossing the coat on a chair and moving over to the heat register, where dry warm air was blowing out. "You must be absolutely frozen. Come on, take off your jacket and come over here and get warm; I won't hurt you. I don't know how you stood it, walking in that wind and spray, up and down the beach. What were you doing out there?"

The boy kept his jacket on, hands in pockets, watching her. He glanced briefly around the room and moved over to look out the window.

"Watching the dolphins. They feed right offshore sometimes. They follow the line of the coast for miles. I've seen a lot of them before."

"Are you from around here?"

"No. Texas. Galveston," he said. "Must be a school of fish out there, the way they're holding up."

"Yes, but why? Why do you want to walk along watching a school of porpoises on a day like this?"

"I like them. Dolphins are really smart animals. The Navy's been training them for years. They're even trying to talk to them—you know, learn their language. It sounds impossible, but—"

"Why don't you take off your jacket." She went over and unzipped his flight jacket for him. "You'll get too warm with the tea, and freeze when you go back out."

He allowed her to help him off with the jacket. "I don't care much for tea. You said something about coffee."

"Oh, coffee. Of course. Go ahead and sit down there." She put his jacket on the chair with her coat and began to heat more water.

He took a last look out the window, which rattled as the wind blew grains of sand against it, and sat down at the table, where he could still see part of the beach. He let his gaze move around the room again and noticed the boxes. "How come you're out here this time of year? I thought all these places were empty in the winter."

"They are. This place will be too in another day or so, when I've finished up."

"Finished up? Moving?"

She nodded, leaning against the stove. "I'm going to miss it. Last year we had a big party here at Christmas. We couldn't have got another person in—or another bottle." She smiled and sighed. "This year we have housing on the base."

"You're married to a marine?"

"Yes. I don't think there will be any parties this year. He just left on a Med cruise. You're a marine, aren't you?"

"Yeah."

"From the base here?"

He nodded. "Camp Lejeune." He was looking out the window again, raising himself to see out.

She rummaged through a box, tearing away newspapers and coming up with an extra cup. She washed it in cold water.

"My husband is a captain." She measured out coffee and he turned back and watched her pour the boiling water into the filtering unit. "I don't see him half the time when he's here, and now he'll be gone for six months."

"Well, I'm only a corporal," said the boy. He watched her pour the coffee. "I've seen you someplace, though."

She stopped and smiled at him. "Well, well. That's very nice, corporal."

"I have, though."

She looked at him, smiling, for a long moment. "Do you ever go into Jacksonville? To the bars along Main Street?"

"Sure. Oh," he said. "You're—aren't you the girl who takes pictures?"

"Very good. I thought they only remembered the dancers. Next time I see you I'll take your picture. On the house."

"Thanks." He grinned. "How about getting Cherry to sit on my lap. You know, the dancer in the Pussycat?"

"I know her. You like her, do you?"

"I sure do."

"All right." She put the cup in front of him and sat down. Thanking her, he sipped the coffee, seeming still a little preoccupied.

"How is it?"

"Good. It's great. Just what I needed."

"I thought you could probably use some." She watched his face, his dark eyes. He seemed to be thinking of something far away from her. She could hear the wind and feel its gusts slapping against the side of the cottage, and she felt cold again, alone.

"You're pretty young to be in the Marine Corps, aren't you?"

He laughed. "I'm old enough for just about anything that comes along. Old enough and big enough."

"Well," she said. "How about that. You look like a kid."

He waited a moment, looking at her, and said, "What kind of a husband have you got, that goes running off to the Med and leaves his wife alone in a beach cottage? What kind of a thing is that for an officer and gentleman to do?"

"Oh," she said, "he loves the Marine Corps. More than anything."

"So do I," said the boy. He started to go distant again and she said, "My name is Madelaine," and looked at him, having hesitated too long, tilting her head to catch his eye as he turned toward the window. "Would you like to tell me your name, corporal?"

"Murphy," he said. "You know, a guy got killed out here last week."

She blinked.

"When that amtrac was swamped." An amtrac was an amphibious tractor, a landing craft. "I knew him."

She let her breath out. "Oh, yes, I heard about it. It was terrible.... Do you drive one of those?"

He shook his head. "No, I'm just a grunt. My buddy too. We were riding on one in a landing exercise." She recalled the sign at the entrance to the base: CAMP LEJEUNE, THE WORLD'S MOST COMPLETE AMPHIBIOUS TRAINING BASE.

"That's terrible," she said.

"Yeah, it was." He was looking at his coffee, and his face had changed. "We were pretty far out and six of us were riding on top. There wasn't any room inside—we shouldn't have been out there at all. And this wave hit us hard and the driver let it turn the amtrac almost broadside before he gunned it. All of us were under water, and when we came up, he was gone. Nobody even saw him go. I was sitting right *beside* him."

"That's horrible," she said. "I'm sorry."

"Yeah. We were together from boot camp, all through training, and we did our time in Nam together. He was an automatic rifleman. He was a professional marine. I mean really the best, the very best. He was one of my two best friends." He was speaking slowly and his eyes had an unfocused look.

He got up and went to the window and she felt a moment of something akin to panic, frustration, a shameful confusion. She followed him and put her arms around him from behind. It was something she had never done before and she was frightened. She pressed herself tight against his back.

"I remember once when we went surfing near San Diego," he said, looking out the window as if she were not there. "We had paddled out pretty far and I was sitting on the board watching him and I saw a shark go right past him. It was big as a horse, just under the surface. He didn't even see it. He got up on his board and went in, and I followed him in and almost fainted on the beach. Because of him. They all thought I'd swallowed some sea water."

He turned around in her arms, but after a moment he broke away to the window, leaving her breathless.

"I have to go. They're moving again."

"Stay here awhile," she said. "Stay with me."

"I can't. I have to keep up with them."

"No, you don't. Please. Please stay."

"Oh, Christ," he said. "Any other time . . . I *can't.*"

He broke away and got his jacket, putting it on quickly. She saw tears in his eyes.

"They never found him. He had on a flak jacket, and a cartridge belt and a helmet. And boots and ammo, and an M-14. I thought maybe at low tide this morning . . . And then the dolphins came. I've heard of dolphins helping swimmers in distress, pushing drowning people to shore. Dolphins are really smart like that, and they like people. So I thought maybe . . ." He zipped up his jacket, shaking his head. "He's probably farther up the beach, anyway. I don't think he could have got down this far. But I can't stand it," he said suddenly, looking at her. "I can't stand the thought of him being out there. I can't go home for Christmas with him out there."

He looked at her for a long moment and slowly shook his head. He went to the door. "Thanks, Madelaine. For the coffee and everything."

"Come back later," she said, and she knew he would not come back, and felt that if he did not she would be as swallowed and lost in the cold depths as his friend. "Please. Come back later. I'll be here. Come back tonight."

"I don't know," he said.

"Will you come back?"

"I don't know. I can't think about it now." He stepped outside and closed the door.

She went to the window and saw him hurry down the beach after the dolphins, blending against the dark sky and the sea. She felt cold and afraid, and put on her coat and sat down on the sofa, holding herself with her arms crossed over her breast. The wind sounded as if it would tear the cottage down.

1. Camp Lejeune was, like Pendleton, a sprawling, self-contained unit, with port facilities at Morehead City, an air base at Cherry Point and a helicopter squadron at the base's New River Air Station. The base was surrounded by forest and swamp. Harding and Shelby, having driven across the continent, were assigned to an infantry unit of Force Troops, an outfit kept in a high state of readiness.

They arrived just in time for a twenty-mile hike. Shelby had been clerking for several months, had been in supply school before that, and neither he nor Harding was in shape for a long march. It angered Harding that they had not been exempted. He was angry to be there at all and he fell out after the first five miles, as Shelby went bravely on. The first sergeant jumped on him, but when he made Harding take off his shirt to prove his claim of injury, he whistled at the wrecked shoulder, wrote out a light-duty chit and sent him back on a truck. Shelby made the entire march, imagining himself on some rescue mission, as he might well find himself in a matter of weeks or months.

They settled in at Lejeune to wait for the changes to come. Harding bought a used Volkswagen. He began haunting sick bay and the naval hospital and was put on permanent light duty while they played with his requests for a discharge.

Too late for Green, he tracked Murphy to a rifle company in the

Second Marine Division, and together with Shelby and a friend of Murphy's named Morrison, went into Jacksonville several nights a week, waiting out the time.

Jacksonville, another sort of swamp, sat five miles from the main gate, on a highway that went to pleasanter towns in both directions. Drinking in a bar called the Hideaway one night, with Shelby and Morrison arguing over the jukebox selections, Harding looked at his young friend—dark-haired Murphy, his face clear and innocent despite everything—and asked him about Green.

Murphy lowered his head and blinked rapidly. His mouth tightened.

"There's not much to tell you. The last time we went out it was to this place, and the Pussycat. We talked about Thanksgiving and Christmas coming up, and leave and all. We talked about that exercise the next day out at Onslow beach."

Harding shook his head. "A landing this time of year."

"Fucking A, that's what I said. All I needed was goddamn pneumonia for Christmas. And he said, 'Oh, it'll be kind of fun. I'm kind of looking forward to it.' No shit, he really was, the crazy bastard. He thought it was fun, riding amtracs. 'Beats walking,' he said, and I said, 'You'll see. It's fucking *winter,* you crazy black-ass.' And he just laughed. And then we went out there the next day. It was nice in the morning, but we screwed around until the weather got rough. And that cretin of a driver fucked it up good. And he was just gone. He was gone."

"It must have been quick anyway. He probably went right down."

"It was so fast nobody even saw him. I thought they'd find him later, but . . . I even went out there a couple of times, just in case he might—you know—wash up on the beach. But no."

Murphy took a drink of his beer and changed the subject. "So how do you like Lejeune?"

"It's kind of a pretty base," Harding admitted.

"But you'd rather be out."

"I'd rather be out."

"They must know how valuable you are." Murphy grinned and looked almost shyly at Harding. "They must be on to you. Man"—he reached out and put a hand on Harding's arm—"I'm really glad you got here. If you have to wait around," he said, sitting back, "this is a damn decent place to do it. The area, I mean, not this lousy town."

Morrison, a tall, mustached draftee from New Orleans, smiled and said, "Hell, it isn't California." Morrison was an ex-LSU student, a part-time head, a grass-and-rock fiend.

"California." Murphy made a face, picked up his beer and chugged half of what remained, setting the mug down with a wet smack. "I hate that fucking state. *This* is our part of the country, man. The South."

"Maybe so," grinned Morrison. "But you're farther from home right now than you'd be at Camp Pendleton."

"Bullshit. Anyplace I got my friends is home, and I'm still in the South and the South is still God's country. Isn't that right, Harding? Harding's an honorary Confederate because he's my best buddy. Isn't that right?"

"Damn right," said Harding, with a look at Shelby.

"Southerners," said Shelby. He snorted. "Pass the hominy."

Harding watched a girl photographer snap a flash shot of some marines in a booth by the door. When their picture was ready they paid her for it.

"Have you been down to see your wife, Audie?" he asked.

Murphy gave him a look. "Ah, damn her. I went down to Atlanta for a quick weekend, swooped down there with a guy. We had a day and a night together."

"Sounds good."

"Yeah, good. She started right off asking when was I going to put in for an early out. She's got that on the brain." He looked around the bar, but Harding pressed on.

"What happened?"

Murphy sighed. "First she worked on me awhile and then her aunt worked on me—like *I* was the one who had left *her* or something—

and then she worked on me some more, came on like she was so glad to see me and we could start over and all. If I just got out early and went back home." He stopped.

"Yes?"

"Well, we sort of spent the rest of the time in bed."

"Good," said Harding. "So it's okay, huh? You going to bring her up here?"

Murphy looked at him. "No, it's not okay. She's been—she's been going out. I mean she's been going out on me." His face took on a look of distaste.

"Well, she hadn't seen you for almost a year. She probably needed to get out a little. Are you going to bring her up here?"

"No," said Murphy. "I think she's been doing more than just getting *out* a little. I think she's been getting a little more than that."

"Did she tell you that?"

"I know her. She took off on me when I came in the Marine Corps and she left Galveston when her old lady died. In a way I almost don't even feel married to her."

"Oh, man—why don't you bring her up here? Things will straighten out. You love her, don't you?"

Murphy looked up quickly. "Yeah," he said. "I love her. But I'm not bringing her up here. She wouldn't come, anyway, to a military base. She hates that stuff. Her brother was killed four years ago, near Saigon. He was an Army man. She wants me to get out and I'm not going to get out for a long time." He thought a moment, and added, "If she's got something like that going, I might just shoot her full of holes. I might shoot both of them."

Morrison said, "Audie, you're crazy, man."

"It wouldn't be much of a solution," said Harding. "The thing to do—"

"Don't tell me any things to do. I mean I don't want to talk about her anymore. I'll figure out what to do."

The photographer had worked her way around to their booth.

"Like me to take your picture? —Well, hello," she said.

Murphy had already seen her. "Hi. Did you get moved?"

"Oh, yes. Everything is pretty much back to normal."

"That's good."

"You didn't find—"

"No," he said.

She nodded. "Well, I never gave you that free picture with . . . Cherry, wasn't it?"

"Yeah," he said, starting to look interested. "It was Cherry. We'll be going over to the Pussycat pretty soon."

"Me too. Well, then, I'll see you all there."

She glanced at Harding and moved away behind him. He turned for another look over the back of the booth.

"Do you know her?"

"Sort of," said Murphy. "I met her once." He watched Harding looking. "Are you interested?"

"I don't know. Maybe I might be."

"Yeah. Yeah. Listen, you might be what she needs right now," said Murphy slowly.

Harding eyed him. "Just how well do you know her?"

"I don't. Really, I just talked to her once. But I think she's pretty lonely. You know?"

"I don't know a thing."

"It might be worth finding out about," said Shelby.

Murphy agreed. "Right." He took a deep breath and smiled broadly. "Well, let's go over to the old Pussycat and sort of see what develops. Cherry'll be coming on."

"It'll just hurt you," Morrison told him.

"That's what you think."

2. Outside, Harding watched the crazy neon of this parasite town. It was cold, and despite the flashing lights' promises, there was no warmth around. The promises were lies. A kid could go to the USO and be handed a free New Testament and charged a quarter for six ounces of Coke. He could buy cheap watery beer in any of a score of bars or dance halls and the waitresses were usually rude and harried poor-town girls he never got to touch, and the dancers were sometimes quite beautiful and sometimes very sad dogs and he still could not touch, and the town was infinitely depressing, a place kids went because they wanted to get off the base and had no cars and it was not worth riding to D.C. and back by bus on a weekend.

Harding watched himself eyed by the pimps on the corner, who were there every night. Most of the brothels were across the tracks in off-limits areas, and a few of the cab drivers were ex-marines and refused to take kids out there. But most of them would, with a warning to be careful and stay in groups.

But every month or so a young marine was found strangled with a coat hanger or stabbed in the ear or with his throat cut. That was why the older hands hated Jacksonville.

Murphy had already told him about one bad time. He and Green and Morrison and another friend had taken the ride one lusty night into the darkness of broken houses and no street lights, across the New River and the tracks, and what happened and almost happened was Murphy's fault, although he never told anyone but Harding.

They had been picked up by one of the pimps on Main Street and driven out in his Cadillac to a falling-down house where a party was on. There were four very pretty black girls, and Murphy, who was not much of a racist when it came to friendship or sex, found that one of them liked him, and they negotiated and had a drink and negotiated some more and made out awhile in a friendly way and decided on twenty-five, a fair price in that town.

Murphy thought of himself as a stud. He had had a lot of girls in the last quarter of his twenty years. He had had prostitutes in California and Tijuana and Okinawa and Viet Nam, and what made him feel like a fool was that this girl took care of him so fast he thought he had been tricked—which, in a manner of speaking, was true.

She was out of her clothes before he had his buckle undone, and she got him down to the necessities and went for him as if she had a bus to catch, and before he quite got relaxed it was all over.

While he lay there wondering what had gone wrong, the girl said, "Come on; buy me a drink."

It's impossible, he thought. *With my experience. I never came that fast before in my whole life.*

"Come on, baby. I need a drink after that. You just too much for me." She made a noise, half in her mouth and half in her nose, and put a hand over her mouth like a little girl. "Come on. I think you need a couple drinks too. You should of had more than one before."

"Yeah," he said, slowly pulling on his shorts. "Well, I'll buy you a drink. I guess it was almost worth that."

"And, uh, just leave the money on the table there."

"Money?" he said, putting on his pants. "Money for that? That wasn't even worth the drink. I'm buying it out of charity."

"Well," she said, "I'm real sorry if it wasn't too good for you. You maybe a little bit fast tonight. We try it again soon."

"Sure," said Murphy.

"That was, uh, twenny-five."

"My ass," said Murphy.

There was a silence in which the thumping beat of the stereo in the living room seemed very loud.

"Just what you mean by that, sonny?" She sat up in the middle of the bed and seemed to harden all over.

"I mean it wasn't worth a goddamn twenty-five *cents,* man. Let's just forget it this time and I'll buy you a drink. Okay?"

"Twenny-five dollars," she said in a voice like breaking glass.

"Up yours," said Murphy

"Hey! Twenny-five *dollars!*"

Murphy winced and started tying a shoe. "Don't get all bitchy with me, honey. I got three buddies out there. Why don't you try one of them? They got money."

She landed on his back while he was leaning over and raked a handful of fingernails across his bare chest. He gasped and fell to the floor with the girl on top of him. She slapped him with both hands and grabbed at his short-clipped hair, trying to pound his face into the floor. He rolled over and squeezed both her breasts until she screamed and then he backhanded her as hard as he could from that position. He expected her to break into tears, but she lay there silently, glaring at him. He got off her.

"Now let's just cut all the shit, okay?"

She got up and ran out of the room.

He had not liked the look in her eyes, and he felt guilty and thought he should have given her the money. But he was still angry at her, at himself, was still humiliated. He had never liked the idea of paying for it anyway, and once in Saigon he had slapped around a little girl for trying to jack up the price on him after a similar performance.

While he was thinking about it, buttoning his shirt, she came back with a butcher knife in her hand. She stopped inside the door as he turned, and their eyes locked—and he had a sudden awareness of how pretty she was, small and slim and black and long-haired there in her bra and underpants and with her butcher knife that he knew she was going to try to kill him with. In the moment that they sized each other up it was hard for him to realize he had just had this girl, or she had had him; it was as if her deadliness now made her a new person he had never touched, and her prettiness and her deadliness almost aroused him again as he watched her step forward, holding the knife like a bayonet, holding it properly, and he stood there fascinated as she came at him. He realized with a shiver that if she did not kill him, he was going to hurt her.

Neither of them said anything. He stepped back and slid off his wide leather belt with its heavy buckle. He wrapped it twice around his hand and got ready for the assault. He did not think she could kill him, and if she failed he was going to take the knife away from her and hit her in her pretty face with his buckle until she cried. Then he was going to grab a handful of her long hair and pull her head back until her mouth came open and he could look at the marks he had put in her face, and he would show her the knife and brush it along the soft curve of her throat to see how terrified she could get. . . .

As he described this later to Harding, his voice showed little emotion, some guilt. He was moderately drunk or, Harding supposed, he would not have confessed it at all. But he was obviously less affected than he had been in California, when he had actually beaten a man. Harding wondered if he would really have done what he was saying. Remembering Murphy as a friend, he doubted it; remembering him in the war, he wondered.

The girl feinted with the knife and two other girls broke into the room and grabbed her. Murphy waited, idly swinging the belt as they struggled. The girls could not get her to drop the knife. They screamed at her and she kept silent, breathing hard with the effort, her eyes on him, and Murphy stepped forward and quickly wrapped the belt around his wrist once more, and put his left hand along the side of the girl's head. She twisted and tried to bite him and then looked him in the eyes as he raised the belt.

"Audie!"

Green stood in the doorway, shirtless, his strong body darkened by the backlight from the other room.

Murphy hesitated and the girl twisted viciously and bit him on the hand. He cried out and started to swing the buckle into her face as the others held her, but Green rushed forward and tore the belt out of his hand.

"What the hell is this!"

"She's crazy," said Murphy. "She was going to kill me."

The girl opened her mouth and began to shriek curses at him hysterically. She still held the knife but had stopped twisting, and stood in the arms of her friends while both Green and Murphy looked at her in amazement.

"What did you *do!*" shouted Green, as Murphy stared at the girl, her curses striking his face from a distance of three feet. She tried to kick him.

"I didn't do anything," he said wonderingly, so that Green believed him. And he believed himself. "I didn't do a thing to her and she was going to— She ran out and got a knife and—"

"Let's get the goddamn out of here before the cops or somebody hears her hollering clear uptown."

Morrison and the other marine were sitting on the living room floor with drinks in their hands.

"What the hell's happening?" Morrison, drunk or stoned, fell over as he tried to get up.

"We movin out," said Green like a platoon sergeant. "Saddle up. Let's get our asses in gear."

"I thought you were both dead. That broad with the knife . . ."

"Just a little misunderstanding," said Green, and his girl brought his shirt and shoes. He kissed her on the cheek. "Listen, we see you all again real soon."

"That crazy bitch was going to kill me," said Murphy as Green tied his shoes.

"Ain't you going to wait for Sam to come back?" Green's girl nuzzled him. "He bring another load and take you all back."

"I think we'll just toddle along." Green hustled the three white boys to the door. "We can get a cab or something. Let's go."

They moved away from the house in the cool black night. Morrison began to sing and Green shut him up and herded them toward the lights of town.

"What the hell happened?" he said to Murphy.

Murphy told them, omitting a certain fact. "I didn't do anything and she wanted twenty-five bucks. Twenty-five bucks. And when I wouldn't give it to her, when I told her I changed my mind, she went crazy and jumped all over me. And I fought her off and she went and got that knife. She was really going to kill me."

"You're lucky," Green told him. "Those girls can be pretty mean."

"Jesus Christ." Murphy stopped and dug frantically through his pockets. "I lost my billfold!"

"Ouch. How much was in it?"

"Twenty-five bucks!"

"Well. I think we better not go back tonight. Tell you the truth, I don't like this neighborhood much after dark. We can get it tomorrow."

"Son of a bitch." Murphy shoved his hands into his pockets and shook his head in the dark. "The goddamn crazy bitch *rolled* me!"

1. For whatever distinction it was, the Pussycat was the best place in Jacksonville. It had the prettiest dancers, the loudest music, played by an on-the-scene D.J. from the radio station, and real beer at the highest price. It was the place to go if a marine did not want to talk or think, if he only wanted to drink fast and stare into the eye-numbing strobe that made a poor sad Carolina small-town blonde look like something out of *Playboy*. He could watch Cherry or Jill or Janie or Rita—all four if he stayed long enough and did not go blind or deaf—climb into the gilded cage, dressed in a uniform of pink or blue or yellow or red satin with sequins, black net stockings with a garter above one knee, and heels that looked hard to dance in. But none of the girls moved their feet much, and nobody was watching their feet. They all doubled as waitresses, and made good money considering the town they were in.

Cherry was the prettiest. She was a big blowzy girl with soft-blown corn-yellow hair and smooth pale skin that wanted to be stroked, or so it seemed to Murphy, who had got a crush on Cherry the first time he saw her. To Harding and Shelby, the Pussycat was a kind of epitome of Jacksonville and all such towns, but Murphy would sit through several hours of pulsing headache lights to watch Cherry dance.

Harding would shake his head when she entered the gilded cage and did her soft, too-slow, unrhythmic, almost shy display. "Audie," he would yell sadly over the noise, "you are a romantic, and are doomed to unhappiness and unrequited love."

Murphy would nod. "I should have 'Born to Lose' tattooed on my ass." He would admit it, sniff once, gulp his beer and think of stealing Cherry away to the Virgin Islands, which he placed somewhere in the Gulf of Mexico, near Louisiana.

Before going out with Harding and Shelby and Morrison that Saturday, Murphy had come into town in the middle of the afternoon, when half the chairs were stacked on the tables, the strobes dead, the ultraviolet off, with a stream of autumn sunlight playing across the bar from a window whose black curtain had been drawn away. He had come in alone after promising to meet the others in the evening, to get started drinking and brood about his wife and wonder what would become of her and of himself.

Sitting at the bar, sipping a beer and talking to an amtrac driver from Alabama, he looked across beyond the cage to the poolroom and saw Cherry standing by the table with a pool cue in her hand. He left the Alabaman in the middle of a sentence about how to bring a trac in when the surf was heavy, and took his beer around the bar to the door of the poolroom.

She did not notice him. She leaned one hip gently against the table, sizing up a bank shot like Paul Newman in *The Hustler,* and although she looked a little ridiculous screwing up her mouth as if something like the Eastern North Carolina Billiard Championship depended on this shot—she was alone in the room—Murphy noticed that, unlike some of the dancers he had seen in daylight, she really was lovely.

As he watched her, she made a little noise with her mouth, leaned forward onto the table and raised up on her toes, her skirt riding two-thirds up the backs of her legs. She fired away and the ball banked off the rim, struck the ball she was aiming at and followed it into the pocket.

"*Darn* it." She stood up and shook the pool cue as if wanting to break it over her knee. "Oh . . . !"

"Now, now," said Murphy. "What kind of sportsmanship is that?"

She turned to look at him with vexation, but he smiled and after a moment she shrugged. "That's easy for you to say. I just blew a quarter."

"What are you doing hanging around here in the afternoon? Don't you have to work tonight?"

"My roommate is using the place today. Her boyfriend is here from Chapel Hill."

"Oh. So you decided to come down early and sharpen your game."

"Right."

"Well, hey." He took a breath. "Are you hungry? You want to walk over to the Fish House with me? I'll buy you a fish dinner."

"Thank you," she said. "But—"

"You don't like fish?"

"Sure, I like fish." She laughed.

"So do I. I mean you have to eat. *I* have to eat, and it's too late to get back to the mess hall in time, and besides, it's Saturday and I'd rather eat in town. And if you're hungry I'd like you to eat with me, and there it is."

"Well," she said, "I'm hungry, all right."

"But if you don't like fish—"

She laughed. "I *like* fish."

They walked over to the Fish House. It was clear and cold outside, the sun almost gone and the tangle of neon coming on like an acid trip. Already busloads of marines were cruising into the evil-looking station across the street, stepping out in their windbreakers half excited and half sad at the prospect of another Saturday night in this town that pretended so much and delivered so little.

Murphy, bucking head on against those odds in his peculiar fashion, kidded Cherry through an ocean perch dinner. Wanting her was enough of a reason to keep him going. He felt that he had to have her.

It had always been that way. He had been a beautiful child and had grown into a handsome athletic young man, and he had never been one who worried about girls—or women, as he thought of them. He was used to having his way and the only mistake he had ever made was to get married. Women were not really vulnerable. Only little girls were vulnerable. His wife had known that and they had used each other for their own ends and it had been all right, a mutual understanding. What made it work was that they were in love—but also that he was stronger. He was a little more used to having his way than she was, and so he had the upper hand. But she was strong too, and the reason he hated her was that she had taken advantage of him when he could not fight back. In real combat there were no rules, but *she* should not have known that. He should never have let her find it out.

Cherry reminded him of his wife. She had the same body and the long blond hair and blue eyes everyone was such a sucker for, although Murphy knew he was not. She began to jabber at him the way they all did and it was almost like the last time he had seen his wife, when they had gone out to Howard Johnson's for dinner and he had watched her coldly while she snowed him with a jumble of words that constantly begged the real question.

He pinched this off and forced himself to listen, to smile and nod, and he got the gist of it. Patricia Tuttle, from Beaufort, North Carolina. Twenty-one, beautiful. Married at seventeen, husband a helicopter crewman at New River; killed in a crash in 1968. Stayed with sister in Swansboro. Sister moved to Kentucky, 1969. Patricia becomes Cherry, queen of Jacksonville dancers, dream mistress to thousands of displaced adolescents, dances in satin and sequins, her life frozen into ten million separate instants, separate conscious hurtings, by the strobe lights at the Pussycat.

"So, like," she said, her smile turning to a grin, "one of us doesn't have to say he was scared to talk about himself. Herself."

"You know"—Murphy leaned a little forward and knew better than to say it even as he said it, because it was the truth—"I really like you."

"Well." And very faintly, like a thin gauze curtain, what she had for defenses came down over her face; it tightened so little only someone like Murphy would have noticed. Probably even she did not notice. He felt that he had to break that fragile curtain.

He paid the bill and they walked outside. After the food smells in the Fish House the cold air hit them like ice cream. The sky had turned a hard dark purple and a quarter moon was out, pale over the hundred neon signs of the bars, pawnshops, stag theaters and restaurants, all burning now, drawing marines as candles draw moths, with cold sweet candy colors, like sugar on fire. It was as if the town could melt and flow like a rainbow under the moon.

"What time do you go on?"

"Around seven-thirty. I'm the last to start. I'll just bring drinks until then."

"Look, this place closes at eleven-thirty. Can I walk you home?"

She shook her head. "I get a ride from the boss, Jill and I. We share an apartment."

"You and the boss?"

She smiled. "You know who I mean."

"Well, then, what about this: why don't you go to the beach with me tomorrow afternoon?"

"The beach? Audie, it's *November.*"

"You wouldn't kid me? I know it's November, but it'll be sunny tomorrow. We can build a fire and have a picnic and walk on the beach. What do you say?"

"Well . . ." She looked at him as if he were a little crazy. "I guess . . . well, okay. It sounds great."

"Yeah," he said. He had thought of it on the spur of the moment. It was what he had done with his wife at the beginning. "Yeah, it'll be good."

She gave him her address and telephone number, and he wrote them down on the back of an advertisement for the Virgin Islands he had torn out of a magazine.

"I'll be back later with my friends to watch you dance. Dance good."

"Okay. Bye."

She went inside and he checked his watch and walked on down the block, looking in the windows of the pawnshops. He felt good. Cherry liked him and they were going to the beach tomorrow, and she was not really at all like his wife, or like any girl he had ever met.

2. The fat man checking IDs at the door of the Pussycat reminded Harding of an actor he had seen who usually played the role of some greasy gangster, although Harding could not remember the man's name. (It was Thomas Gomez.) He looked unhappy in his work: what kind of job, after all, he seemed to be thinking, was this for a grown man?

The place was full of marines, and the four of them, Harding, Shelby, Murphy and Morrison, had to separate and squeeze up to the bar. The strobe was on. Harding blinked as a girl moved like a kinescope image in the cage, like a silent film except that instead of silence there was the other, the pandemonium of rock.

When the song was finished the strobe went off and the girl climbed down and disappeared into the crowd. The room was at once crammed with marines to whom the girls peddled drinks in their skin like erotic dreams from the massed unconscious, yet the mobiles and glowing posters hung on darknesses and mirrors which seemed to fall away forever.

Harding turned and watched the only woman in the place who was not a dancer. It was the photographer who knew Murphy. She carried her Polaroid and moved among the tables, stopping to snap a shot with a pop of blue flash, talking to the boys at the table while their picture developed, then collecting a dollar. Sometimes she would call Rita or Janie or Cherry over, and the girl would sit on a kid's lap and smile for the camera, then be up and gone before the picture was done.

Murphy and Morrison went to play pool and Shelby was lost on the other end of the bar. Harding watched the photographer until she got to one end of the room and she looked over and caught him. He leaned back with an elbow on the bar, sipping his beer, and shifted his attention to Jill in the cage.

The photographer came and set her Polaroid on the counter and the bartender handed her a glass, pouring a beer for her. Harding watched the girl in the cage and the photographer watched too and she was the one he wanted—so he turned away from the cage, looked at himself in the blue-lit mirror behind the bar while he drank, and then looked at the photographer. She was watching him.

"Hi," he said.

"Hi yourself. You're Murphy's friend."

He nodded. "So are you."

She mulled that over and said, "Not really. Did he tell you that?"

"No. He said the same thing but I didn't believe him."

"It's the truth, though. Don't you have any faith in your friends?"

He shrugged without answering, and said, "Are you going to dance?"

"Sure." Her lip curled derisively. "After another winter in this town it will just about be my turn."

"Too bad," he said sadly. "I won't be here that long." He let what he considered a frank and healthy interest show in his face and she looked back at him the same way, or at least frankly.

"Now I'll bet," she said, "you aren't interested in having your picture taken."

"I guess you can spot a cynic when you see one," he said, smiling. "What is it, the mouth?"

"The eyes," she said. "The way you were looking at Jill, there. You're not hungry enough."

"Well, it all depends on the menu," said Harding. "Now Cherry is quite a dish. I could probably go for that."

"Couldn't you just."

"Couldn't I, though."

They stood looking at each other. She was dark-haired, a little older than the dancers. "Well," she said, "grab a chair and I'll immortalize the two of you sitting cozy. Wouldn't you like a picture of that?"

"It would be very nice," said Harding. "But what in the world would I do with it?"

"I don't care what you *do* with it as long as you *buy* it. Send it to your mother."

He laughed. "Is everybody in this town as mercenary as the women?"

She picked up her glass and took a sip and said, "Don't ask me. I'll lie to you." She looked at him as the music started up again, and they held the look, smiling. Marines elbowed past them and around them at the bar and she moved closer. "You can't have Cherry anyway. Your friend Murphy is in love with Cherry."

"My friend Murphy is in love with all beautiful girls," said Harding, looking at her big dark eyes and feeling the warmth from her face as they leaned toward each other to hear. "What's your name?"

"Madelaine. What's your name?"

"Robert," he said over the crash of a drum. "How about taking the rest of the day off?"

She sipped her beer and held up her left hand to show him a ring. He clicked his teeth and shook his head once. "I don't believe it. I think you just wear that to scare away the wolves."

She made a face and set her glass down. "I can do my own scaring away. It's for real."

"All right," he said. "I'll share you. I'm serious."

"I believe you," she said, looking at him quickly and, he thought, with interest. She picked up her camera. "Some of us have to work, though, Robert. Don't think it hasn't been fun."

"But it hasn't yet. Stay and talk to me." He nodded at the camera. "That isn't good for you, walking around with that thing, taking pictures of people."

She hesitated, an amused frown on her face. "Talking to you would be good for me?"

"I'm basically a very nice guy," he said. "Although I do have my ribald side."

She laughed and elbowed a space between two boys ogling the cage, hypnotized by the strobe and the dancer. "See you around, Robert."

"I'll drink myself to death."

"Well, here." She pushed her glass away and handed him the bottle, still a third full. "On me." She winked at him and moved away.

Shelby had grabbed a table. Murphy and Morrison came back and as they settled in, Cherry came to clear away the bottles for them. "Hi, Audie."

"Hey, there. How's business?"

She groaned. "I guess you can see. Want a round here?"

"Yeah. And hey, get Madelaine. She owes me a picture with you, and I want one of me and all my friends."

Cherry went to get the beer and Morrison shook his head. " 'Hi, Audie'?"

"I got a date with her," said Murphy. "She was here when I came in today, so we played some pool and she had supper with me. Tomorrow we're going on a picnic."

"God." Morrison looked at Murphy with a kind of awe. "I don't believe it, you bastard."

Harding said wonderingly, "A picnic? Where the hell are you going to have a picnic?"

"Well, listen," said Murphy, "can you lend me your Volkswagen? We're going to go out to the beach and build a fire and all."

"The beach," said Harding, and shook his head. "In November. Well, for a date with Cherry, how can I refuse? I just hope you don't freeze."

"Man," said Morrison, "I'd freeze my ass with that kind of body any day of the year."

Shelby set his bottle down with a bang and they all looked at him.

"By God," he said. "So would I."

4

1. The sun was warm and there were almost no clouds in the sky as Murphy headed the Volkswagen out highway 17 away from Jacksonville, south toward Wilmington.

Cherry felt good. She had not been anywhere with a boy for over a month, since a sergeant she had liked got drunk one night and tried to take her out of the cage at the Pussycat while she was dancing. The bouncer had got him instead, and then the MPs.

She had never had much luck with men. Her husband had knocked her around when he drank and, she suspected, although she had never let herself think about it since his death, had cheated on her. Jill said Cherry was the worst loser she had ever known, and that was something coming from a two-time divorcee. But it had always seemed to Cherry that she was simply into a run of bad luck—several years of it, in fact—and she knew that luck was fickle, that the only way to beat it was to keep trying.

"This is a neat little car." She patted the seat and watched Murphy, who was imagining he was A. J. Foyt in the Dixie 500. "I ought to get one of these."

"Belongs to Harding." Murphy swerved around an old black man in a 1950 Chevrolet that seemed, from the smoke, to be running on oil alone. "I wouldn't have a dinky car like this myself."

"Harding—which one is he?"

"You met him. Good-looking guy, suede jacket. Shelby was the nervous-looking one who didn't say much. He's from New York. Always has a cigarette."

"I remember. And the other one, with the mustache . . ."

"That was Morrison. He's from New Orleans."

"Have you known them very long?"

"No. Only Harding. Morrison's in my company and Shelby was transferred out here from Pendleton with Harding. Me and Harding and another guy were in Nam together, been together since boot camp. Harding got zapped just before our tours were up."

"You mean shot?"

Murphy nodded. "He spent some time in the hospital; that's why he's just now caught up with me. He's trying to get a medical discharge."

Murphy fell into a silence and she watched the pine woods on both sides as they approached Verona and Murphy slowed down. A sign pointed off to the right toward another little town called Haw. Cherry had never been to Haw. She wondered what Haw was like.

"Have you ever been to Haw?"

Murphy looked at her. "What?"

"That town called Haw. Have you ever been to Haw?"

"No." He grinned, accelerating out of Verona, pulling out to pass a truck that was so rusty it looked as if it had been rained on every day since it was built. "Somehow I always managed to avoid the place."

"Well," said Cherry, "you just did it again."

"I'll have a flat tire or engine trouble around here sometime," he said. "And all the people of Verona will be gone to a camp meeting or a fish fry or a family reunion someplace, and I'll have to go over to Haw. And nobody'll ever see me again."

"They'll hear legends about you, though," she said. "You'll be an old man who lives on the edge of the swamp and plants collards. You'll have four beautiful daughters who are all dead-eyes with a rifle."

"Damn right," said Murphy. " 'Cause I'll teach them myself."

She sat back and watched the ruined woods on her side of the road, yellow and brown but not really dead. It was a pretty day and not cold. She hated cold weather. But today was good.

"What do you think about my job?" she asked Murphy.

Murphy slowed down and turned left on Sneads Ferry Road.

"It probably pays better than mine."

"That's not what I mean." She waited, but he said nothing. "I mean —do you think anything about a girl who has a job like that? It would maybe bother some people a little. I mean would it bother you?"

"If I was a girl?"

"No. Just . . . the way it is."

"Do I act like it bothers me?" He was busy driving fast, rounding the curves in the flat country toward the coast. "Did I buy you a perch dinner and ask you out today?"

"Yes. You did."

"Well, then, don't be a dope." He glanced at her.

She smiled and quickly moved over and kissed him on the cheek. "That's for being a gentleman."

"Well, thanks, I guess. But I'm not making any promises."

"Good. That's smart. I like boys who are smart."

"You see any boys around here?"

"Men," she corrected.

They passed Sneads Ferry, a town composed of seafood restaurants, bait shops, gas stations. There were boats tied up at the dock and people fishing off the bridge that went back toward the base.

Cherry liked the little town. She would like, she thought, to get married again, to a really good boy who would treat her right. And they could live in a place like Sneads Ferry, and when they had children they could take them fishing on weekends, maybe have their own little boat.

While she was daydreaming, the car headed up the steep bridge that arched out over the Intracoastal Waterway toward the beach. Murphy checked the rear-view mirror and stopped at the top of the bridge.

As far as they could see on both sides were the channels of the waterway, like canals chopped through islands of yellow-green sea grass. Ahead of them the beach and its dunes ran from horizon to horizon.

"Isn't it beautiful?"

Murphy nodded. "I always liked the view from up here."

"Look." She pointed ahead to the left where, far up the beach in the distance, a building stood out against the backdrop of the sea. "Is that a lighthouse?"

"Not anymore. It might have been a guide to the New River Inlet once, but it's all deserted now, falling down."

A car approached from the rear and Murphy put the Volkswagen in gear and drove down the long arch, curved around to the right and made a left turn onto the road that paralleled the beach, running along behind the dunes. A sign pointed toward an inlet called Galleon Bay.

He parked on the shoulder halfway between the main road and the deserted house. While he locked the car Cherry was already running up one of the dunes to see the ocean. She stood in her boots and jeans and green field jacket, her long hair blowing, and as he looked up at her she lifted both arms and cried, "Wow!"

Murphy humped up the dune behind her, his boots sinking into the sand. When he got to the top she said, "It's all *ours,*" and gestured at the beach that lay tan and pale in front of them, empty as some primeval shore. He turned his head and looked up and down the beach, and there was not another person, only the sea birds.

Cherry grabbed his arm, cried, "Let's walk!" and jerked him along with her in an awkward run down the side of the dune.

They ran out to where the waves made a dark line of division between the wet and dry sand, and turned north, and all ahead as far as they could see, no other person. The wind was blowing from the south and beat against their backs in little gusts, and the sun was warm. Cherry kept taking deep breaths, picking up shells, scattering the sandpipers, playing at the edge of the surf, which never touched her boots.

"Isn't this fantastic?"

Murphy nodded. "Yeah. It's something."

She threw down a handful of shells and ran up and kissed him, hopping away again before he could react. She picked up a rock and threw it as hard as she could with her left hand; it sailed out twenty feet and plopped into the surf. She kicked a spray of sand at the sea and ran again.

Murphy hunched along behind, his hands deep in the pockets of his jeans, watching the whitecaps the wind blew off the tops of the waves. He could still feel Cherry's warm mouth and he was at odds with himself between a flooding sense of well-being and, deeper in him, the new thing he felt at the edge of the sea, here so close in time and place to where his friend had been lost. He wondered why he had come. He wanted to cry.

Or perhaps run, grab Cherry and throw her into a dune, take her until whatever it was let go of him and he could lie beneath the clear blue sunny Carolina sky and feel only the sky and the sand and the girl's body, and smell the wind and the girl and have nothing else beyond that, nothing inside.

They moved up the beach, Cherry running ahead, Murphy, hands in pockets, watching the sea, moving as he had moved that other time, those several times, his boots leaving a deep, deliberate line of prints, not really looking for anything now, but with the question in his head, behind his eyes, the dumb fright he would admit only as a wondering, a question.

They covered half a mile and Murphy called, "Hey. Let's head back." She had got far ahead of him.

"I want to see the lighthouse!"

"It's another mile or so. Let's go back and build a fire and eat. We can drive over later."

"Promise?" she said, running back to his side.

"All right. But there's not a damn thing worth seeing."

"But promise."

"Okay," he said with a hint of grouchiness. "Yeah, I *promise.*"

She ran up and took his arm and he grabbed her and kissed her with a kind of getting-even hardness that she either did not notice or didn't mind.

"Come on, let's eat." She took his hand and they walked back into the wind and finally his irritation ebbed and he put an arm around her. Just like his wife, he thought. He would go along and let her wrap him around her finger. It didn't seem right. But Christ, he liked her.

2. A little farther down the beach from where they had parked, he found the old telephone pole he and Green and Morrison had used for firewood before the weather turned cold. He did not know where it had come from, but apparently nobody else had bothered with it because it was still intact and about where they had left it. He dug out a pit around the end, got newspapers and kindling out of the trunk of the Volkswagen, with a half-full can of charcoal lighter, packed it all carefully around the end of the pole and got it going.

They sat on blankets on the windward side, protected by a dune, and ate the food Cherry had brought: fried chicken, rolls, radishes and pickles, a bottle of wine and four pieces of devil's food cake. When they finished the cake and the wine, Murphy pulled out a bottle of Rebel Yell and they sat together passing it back and forth. The sky had clouded but the breeze was light now and with the blankets and the fire and the whiskey, they were warm.

"The beach is a good place." Cherry looked all around, and Murphy took a shot of the whiskey and tried not to have it be anything except a beach, a kind of place he had always liked, with no other significance. He had invited her here on a quick impulse because it had always been good for him, had been good for him and his wife too, and it seemed a logical place to start whatever he was starting.

"It's funny," she said. "It seems empty and lonely, and yet right out there, the ocean is full of all kinds of fish and things, and whales and octopuses. It's scary, thinking of all that stuff alive out there right now. It makes me cold." She moved over and hugged his arm. "I'd rather be here."

Murphy tipped up the bottle again, switching hands, taking two hard swallows as she watched him. When he brought it down he said, "Hey, you're a hell of a cook." The whiskey made him shudder.

Cherry sat back on the blanket, her arm still hooked in his. "You're from Texas?"

"Galveston," he said, and for the first time in a while he felt all right about it, did not entertain the thought of his wife, who had left there to be in Atlanta with her stud. For the first time in a while he did not much care.

"I guess you'd rather be back home than here, wouldn't you?"

"I don't know," he said. "Lejeune is all right. North Carolina is all right."

"How did you like California?"

He made a scoffing noise. "This is a lot better than California."

"Really?"

"At least this is the South. California is nowhere. It's like being nowhere."

"That's a funny way to put it."

"Skip it," he said. "Here, have a snort."

"I don't like it much. . . . Hey, you better watch it," she said as he took another drink. She took the bottle and sipped a little. He had really put a dent in it.

California, he thought. Beaches there too. He and Harding and Green had gone to the beach a lot, had done so many things they would never do again now, with himself feeling old and Harding shot up, and Green . . .

"Just be glad you're here with me instead of there," she said. "Or" —she pointed toward the sea—"out there with all the cold fish."

Murphy jerked and said before he could stop himself, "Why don't you knock the hell off that stuff."

Her smile went cold and she blinked at him. "What?" she said faintly.

Now damn it, he thought. He grabbed the bottle and took a long pull—too long; he coughed half a mouthful onto the sand at his feet.

She was swallowing and looking at him as if he had slapped her. "What's the matter? What did I say?"

"Hey," he said. He didn't look at her, he looked at the sand where the whiskey had soaked away around his boots, and he felt the slow wave rolling through his head and thought, *You're drunk, you crazy bastard.*

But he said it anyway. "Hey, did you know my best friend—one of my best friends—got killed out here a couple weeks ago?" He felt his throat choke up.

"Oh . . ." she said, her eyes growing big when he glanced at her to see her take it. "No, I didn't. How would I know *that?* "

"He went off an amtrac and nobody ever saw him again," said Murphy gravely, knowing he was going to cry. "He's still out there, with those cold fishes and octopuses of yours. Did you know that?" He dropped his eyes from hers and felt very hurt, wronged, as if all the unfairness in the world had suddenly come to rest squarely upon his soul.

"Oh, God, I'm sorry. Oh, Audie—"

"So if you don't mind," he said, looking at his boots and lifting the bottle again, "if it wouldn't be too much—too much—" He choked again without even getting the bottle to his mouth, and she took it out of his hand and moved to him. He was sure he had not done it for that, or even intentionally, and she kissed him a long time before he responded, and then he did not really take charge, and they didn't go far. He finally lay beside her on the green wool blanket and she lit him a cigarette.

"Where's the whiskey? Where's the Rebel Yell?"

"I don't think you want any more," she said, smoothing his hair.

"Where's the goddamn Rebel Yell?" He sat up and grabbed the bottle. It had not been full when they started, and now there was only a little left. She let him drink some and then finished most of it herself to keep it from him. She left him the last swallow and when he had taken it he carefully screwed the cap back on the bottle and tossed it over his head into the dunes. He fell back with his head in her lap.

"Do you want to tell me about it, Audie?"

"No." He shook his head and put a hand on his forehead. "Christ, I'm—Ooh." He closed his eyes. "Oh, the son of a bitch is dead. He's just dead. He should've hung on, Cherry."

"I know," she said.

"Oh, fuck him. He should've held *on,* Cherry."

"I know," she said. "I know it."

"I didn't even see him go. You know, I was right *beside* him."

"It's all right. Don't talk about it. It's all right, Audie."

She kissed him and smoothed his hair, and after a minute the cigarette dropped out of his mouth onto the blanket. She picked it up and started to put it back and saw he was asleep. She did not believe he could have fallen asleep so fast even with the whiskey, and she leaned over him and looked at his face to see if he had had a stroke or a heart attack. But he was breathing deeply and she sat up and finished the cigarette, looking out at the surf that the tide brought steadily toward her.

He woke up an hour later. She was tending the fire. She had put the other blanket over him and laid his head on her field jacket, and she needed the fire now for warmth. The sun had reappeared far down the sky and the wind had picked up as the tide came in.

"Oh, boy." He sighed and slowly opened and closed his eyes.

"I think maybe you drank a little too fast," said Cherry. "How do you feel now?"

"Like I been run over by something."

"You're lucky you didn't get sick."

He sat up. His mouth was as dry as if he had been eating sand, and his head spun.

"Well, that's swift. That's really something for me to do on our first date."

"Second," she said. "Remember the perch?"

"Yeah." He nodded slowly, trying to clear his head. "Remember the perch. Like a battle cry. Hey, where's your—" He saw the jacket then and forced himself to get up with it.

"Wow, you're going to freeze. Your roommate will shoot me. Hey, you shouldn't have done that." He helped her put the jacket on.

"You didn't want me to leave your head in the sand, did you?"

"That would have been better than you catching pneumonia." He zipped and snapped the jacket for her. "Man, I really did it good. I did a job of it."

She put her arms around him and held him tight. "Listen, I wouldn't have got out to the beach until spring. Listen, it was *good*. Kiss me."

"No, I gotta get some water first. My mouth tastes like a drainage ditch."

They buried the fire and packed up the car. It was a mile to the old house, then the road went on a little way behind a group of beach cottages and ended at the New River Inlet. The bait shop and grocery was open. Murphy bought Cokes for Cherry and himself and they left the car at the store and walked back to the house.

It was a tall building of cement block, the first floor built on wooden pilings to keep out the tides, and three more floors on top of the first. A large room had been added to the first floor, jutting straight out toward the sea. Murphy was not even sure it was a lighthouse; he did not know what it was, standing like a capital L, with, across the road, a small utility building with spaces to park cars beneath and a single room overhead with three windows facing the taller structure and the sea, this also fallen into disuse.

Cherry clambered across the flattened wire fence. "Come on, let's look inside."

He did not much feel like exploring anything except Cherry, and his head throbbed as he followed her up to the porch and into the first floor. When they got to the top they found an empty room with graffiti on the walls and a view of the beach and the sea.

"Not worth the climb." Murphy leaned against the wall and looked out at the beach. His head was a little better.

"It's wonderful. I could live here."

"Be kind of drafty."

"No, I mean it." She nodded slowly, looking up and down the beach. "I could move right into this place and be happy, I think. Audie, look at it! The sun would come up right over the ocean in the mornings, and we could run on the beach and swim and catch fish for our dinner. And then sit up here at the top, the highest place on the beach, and it'd be like we owned it all, everything we can see."

"Mm," he said. He was looking out toward the north, at the row of cottages scattered out to the inlet. One of them, he could not tell which, was the place where that girl had been, Madelaine, who took pictures in Jacksonville. She had given him a cup of coffee that day which seemed so long ago and was only three weeks. On beyond that, more beach and then the New River Inlet, running into Jacksonville —and across that, the wide military beaches of Camp Lejeune, where the amtracs pounded ashore like sea monsters, like dinosaurs.

"Wouldn't it be great?"

"Yeah, great." He turned from the window with a shudder inside and went for the girl. He pushed her back into a corner and kissed her, moving his hands over her body, and she said, "Listen, I think we better go on back pretty quick."

"No," he said into her hair, running a hand through it, breathing its clean smell. "I don't want to turn you over to your roommate yet."

She laughed quietly. "I got news for you. Jill went to Raleigh with her friend. I don't think they'll be bothering us."

"Oh," said Murphy. "Well, then, maybe we ought to be getting back."

"Yes," she said. "I think so too."

He let go of her and she started away, and as he turned he saw them, not far out, working their way down the beach, bounding slightly, their backs curving out of the waves, the dorsal fins cutting the water, their broad tails slapping. He froze by the window and gripped the steel frame, and a sliver of glass cut his finger but he didn't notice. They were moving slowly to the south, and one of them—or it might have been his imagination—was playing with something, and he could almost see it; in his mind he did see it, saw the powerful body cut toward the beach, nosing its burden in through the surf, nudging it to the shallows and leaving it to crawl out of the foam up the beach to dry sand—except it would not do that, would only lie there, its arms and legs moving with the waves, its head lolling, black in the white surf—

"What's the matter?"

"Nothing," he said, turning away.

"You've cut yourself! What is it?"

He laughed. "Glass in the window frame." They were not turning, there was nothing. They pushed on south without hesitating.

"What were you looking at?"

"Nothing," he said. "Dolphins. Just a herd of dolphins."

"Oh!" she cried. "Let me see!"

1. Friday evening, Harding pulled his Volkswagen into the drive of the little trailer court outside the back gate, where Murphy and Morrison, after trying in vain to enlist Harding's interest, had taken Shelby instead and rented a trailer off base. Harding would have been uncomfortable living with Murphy and Morrison, but Shelby, more flexible, was willing to put up with the rock music and grass in order to avoid barracks life while awaiting his orders.

Harding parked off the pavement in the dirt that passed for a yard, beside Shelby's old Ford and Morrison's Toyota. The evening was cool, with a sea breeze blowing in from the bay at Paradise Point. On the base was a power plant that burned coal, but here there was no trace of the smoke that usually hung over the area.

He got out carrying two six packs, and took a deep breath of the fresh air. He had had the day off and slept most of it after returning from a week-long field problem that had included hiking most of the way to Fort Bragg. They had gone fifty miles in the field and Harding had volunteered to walk much of the way. He was in good shape now except for the shoulder, and he felt good.

He went up the steps and tapped on the door of the trailer. Inside he could hear the pulsing music, and he banged harder on the door, taking a half step back as it opened a few inches on a chain.

"Who dat?" An eye appeared in the crack.

"CID. You're all under arrest."

The eye disappeared and the door slammed, to be opened by Murphy, in jeans and a sweat shirt with U.S. MARINES across the front in red letters.

"Jesus, not *now*. I got too much time left to serve it in the brig. Come on in."

Harding stepped up into the main room of the trailer. "Good evening."

This went unheard, the words lost in the noise.

Morrison sat on the floor beside the stereo, a plastic bag of marijuana and some yellow cigarette papers on a newspaper in front of him. He glanced up and fingered his mustache.

"Hey there, Harding." He was engaged in rolling a joint, and Harding saw that his eyes were already big and dark, his smile beatific.

"I heard you all were having a little party tonight." Harding gave Murphy the beer and sat down on the sofa across from the door.

"Yeah," said Murphy. "There's a couple more guys coming out. They're both grunts. You remember anybody named Jones? A lance. Or Corporal Tate?"

"No. Are they in Force Troops?"

"Not your outfit. They were over the same time as us. You want a beer?"

"That's why I brought it. Where's Shelby?"

"Greetings." Shelby stood yawning in the doorway of his room. "I'm still catching up with myself after that little walk."

Murphy handed Shelby and Harding a beer and took the rest into the kitchenette. He and Morrison were drinking Coke with the grass. Morrison was smiling and shaking his head as he watched himself work.

"He's on his way." Murphy watched Morrison stick his tongue in the corner of his mouth as he rolled the joint. "We'll probably need some more Coke later."

Morrison handed up a joint to Murphy, who took a drag and offered it to Harding. Harding shook his head. "I'll do it on beer awhile."

"We got plenty. Our contact man in Fifth Marines is going to New York this weekend."

Murphy passed the joint along to Shelby, and Harding sipped his beer and watched Morrison twist the ends of one of his creations and strike a kitchen match that flared blue and white.

"Hey, I know what you'd like." Murphy went into the kitchenette and checked out several cupboards. He found what he was looking for and brought it back, with a glass.

"I got this in Jacksonville the other night when I was feeling hairy, but then I couldn't stand the taste of it." He handed the bottle to Harding.

"Tequila?"

"Not just tequila. That stuff is special." Murphy set the glass down and rummaged through a stack of magazines in a rack by the sofa. "Where is it?"

Harding opened the bottle and sniffed the contents. He had only drunk tequila once, in Tijuana while stationed at Pendleton, waiting to go over. He was not sure he liked it.

"Where the goddamn hell is the goddamn magazine?" Murphy sat down on the floor with a stack he had brought out from behind a chair and shuffled through them, discarding them like jokers from a deck of cards. "We just moved in the place, and already—"

"What is it you're looking for?" Harding poured a little into the glass and tasted it. It was not so bad. He poured a shot and drank it. "Am I supposed to have salt or lemon or something?"

Murphy was busy, and he licked the rim of the glass, licked the back of his hand experimentally. He drank another shot and chased it with beer.

"Shelby, you want some of this?"

Shelby, working on a joint, shook his head. "I don't think it would mix too well."

"It's gone." Murphy was sitting amid his discards.

"What is?"

Murphy accepted a joint from Morrison, who was grinning like the cat in *Alice,* and sucked hard. Tears came to his eyes, and he closed them and leaned back against the wall.

A record on the stereo pulsed a slow hard rhythm into the little room. Morrison smiled to himself, maneuvering joints with a flat pair of tweezers until he inhaled more hot ash and leavings than smoke, recycling these carefully into fresh cigarette papers, working his mouth for enough moisture to lick the glue.

Murphy got up after a while and changed the two lamps, putting a red bulb in one and an ultraviolet in the other, so the room seemed cozy, the posters on the walls leaping out at them through the smoke. Harding relaxed on the couch, letting the music carry him. He tried to conjure up an image of Madelaine.

He suddenly missed Green, became aware, in a way he seldom was, of Green's absence. Green would have been at home with this group, would have added a cool touch of humor and his peculiar easy friendship. But Green was gone, lost forever in the briny deeps.

A hard knock came on the door and everyone jumped.

"God." Morrison sat with the makings of still another joint scattered over his lap, the cigarette paper stuck to his lip, his eyes wide. His mustache seemed to have stiffened. It lay on his lip like a frightened caterpillar.

"Easy, man." Murphy put a hand on Morrison's knee. "Don't go paranoid, old buddy." He looked close to it himself.

Shelby opened his eyes and said calmly, "Must be Jones and Tate. Or else we're all done for. Everybody ready for a rumble with the Ps?"

"Oh, my God." Morrison started to get to his feet, but Murphy growled, "Damn it, Shelby, don't say things like that." He patted Morrison again. "You want us all climbing the walls?"

"Maybe," said Harding, "we ought to answer it."

They thought about it a long moment, and Shelby sighed and got up. He kept the door on the chain and opened it a crack. "Who the hell is it?"

"Criminal Investigation Division!"

"Everybody's a joker." Shelby slammed the door and unhooked the chain. "It's them."

"You all still alive in here?" Two young men edged into the room, which seemed to Harding to have assumed the dimensions of a cell. A breeze came in the open door, and he took a quick deep breath.

"We gave up on you." Shelby locked the door again.

"Glad you could make it," said Murphy. "When I said to come out later, I didn't mean you had to wait all night."

"We got in a poker game. I hope the girls ain't asleep and the grass all gone."

"It'd serve you right. When you banged on the door, old Morrison hit the ceiling."

Jones leaned over and peered at Morrison. "He looks like he's feelin okay." Jones laughed and shook hands. He was a short, beefy, red-faced Southerner, voluble and loud. *A grit,* thought Harding immediately. His clothing was surreal, par for the evening. He wore maroon-and-blue-striped bell bottoms and a blue knit pullover with, stitched across the chest and upper back, a loud mélange of intertwined orange, green, blue, yellow and silver threads in a wild flowery pattern, so that his upper torso seemed consumed in cold flames or wrapped around by some Oriental serpent, or perhaps a particularly gaudy form of man-eating plant.

Jones started to tell about the poker game and how he had cleaned up because of his inscrutable face. His voice had no trouble rising over the music and Harding thought irritably, *Just what we need. A loud-mouth inscrutable grit.*

The other kid, Tate, looked young and tough, dark and quiet, much like Murphy. His hair was a touch over regulation length and he wore a black mustache. Tate nodded at Harding, shook hands, accepted a beer and a joint from Murphy, and sat down on the floor.

Harding felt uncomfortable. He was having trouble breathing and his mouth was dried out by the tequila and smoke. The night air had struck him like the memory of a cool green dream. He wished they had left the door open.

"I unnerstand you're a grunt too."

He did not realize he was being addressed until Jones tapped him on the knee with his can of Coke, then paused to take a hit, closing his eyes tight and causing the joint to glow, his face bathed in the red light from the lamp.

"What?" said Harding, mishearing. "Oh, no, thanks."

He listened to Murphy and Jones and Tate, sipping the tequila, no longer tasting it. Murphy had wanted a party tonight. His new girl was working and this was the next best thing, a kind of housewarming with all his friends. Harding thought that if he had not come out here tonight, his other choices would have been few: go to a movie, drink beer somewhere, or stay in the barracks polishing his boots or trying to read. Not much to choose among.

He thought about getting out, the old dream. He had discovered that as time went by and the reality neared, the notion changed a little, became less idealized. He had thought often of going back to school, and in certain lights and in certain frames of mind it seemed an appealing idea. He could return on the graduate program, study without the draft hanging over him, use the GI Bill.

But he wondered if he would be content to do that. It was a nice idea that got him through days in the field or in the office—but would he be content to do that? he wondered.

He had told Donna that he wanted to travel, to see America. But that too was more a notion than a plan. He had just driven across America with Shelby, and perhaps Donna was right, perhaps it was all the same to him now. He felt that he had been in the military too long.

"I unnerstant," said Jones, tapping him on the knee again with his can of Coke, "I unnerstant you're a grunt too. Murphy said something about you bein a grunt."

"He's the biggest hill-humper in the Corps," said Murphy. "Aren't you, Harding? Him and Shelby walked all the way to Bragg this week."

"Is that right? Are you in that outfit? I heard you all did some movin out."

"Not all the way to Bragg. We walked part of the way."

"Where were you in Nam, Jones? Maybe me and Harding were in some of the same places."

"Well . . ." Jones took a hit, sipped his Coke and smiled nostalgically. "I spent most of my time around Chu Lai. The golden sands."

"We were there."

"I guess I had cactus in my ass and had my boots pulled off in that sand about as much as anybody who ever went over."

"We were mostly around Da Nang," said Murphy. "And at Phu Bai."

"Oh, you was up there on them jungle mountain trails. That's where Tate was. Right?" he said, but Tate was sitting with his eyes closed, listening to the music. He nodded.

"Tate's gettin ready to ship for four more. He's a goddamn hero. He got a Silver Star."

Murphy's eyes opened wide.

"I didn't know that," said Shelby.

"Hey, tell them." Jones reached over and shook Tate's foot. Tate opened his eyes. "Tell them how you piled up them fourteen bodies that night on the hill."

"Let me listen," said Tate, closing his eyes again.

Jones laughed and turned to Harding, who was watching Tate tap his hand on the floor with the beat.

"So how was it with you? Pretty rough up there?"

Harding made a shrug with his mouth.

"I need some more Coke," said Jones. "You all got some more Coke?"

Shelby got up and stretched. "All gone. I guess it's time we travel down to the store. What do you say?" he asked Harding. "You up to taking a ride with me?"

"I sure am." Harding got up. He felt strange. He needed some air.

2. He let the wind bathe him through the open window as they drove the ten miles to the grocery, feeling himself move through the great Carolina night, one lost car penciling headlights across the countryside. He imagined himself out and free, heading north toward Michigan.

"What do you think of Jones?" Shelby's voice cut through his reverie, reminding him that he was not alone, that you are never alone in the military.

"He seems like the real thing. Just what the Corps wants."

"Yeah. Murphy thought you might hit it off, since you've been in some of the same places."

"Shelby, most of the guys we live with have been in those places. And the others are going."

"Don't I know it."

"Christ, did you see that kid's eyes? Christ, he's a cold one."

"They interest me, though," Shelby said. "I listen to those stories and I think, *Yes; so that's how it is. That really happened to people.* And then wonder what it has done to them, or done for them. What kind of person is Tate after that night on the hill? Different? The same? What is Murphy like, having zapped your friend Webster in the back? Is *he* the same?"

Harding didn't answer.

"You never say much about it, do you? I wonder why you went, with your attitude. Why you let them do that to you. You could have done your time here or in an office at Pendleton. Or up at Quantico at CMC."

"Commandant Marine Corps wouldn't have wanted anybody who felt the way I did."

"Or come to think of it, you could have gone into the Army and really skated through. No, no. You went where you wanted to go."

"Just like you're going to do. So what's your problem?"

"That's my problem. I know why I'm going." Shelby turned to look at him in the pale light from the dash. "But I don't know why you went."

"For America," said Harding. "I did it for my mom and Richard Nixon. I wanted to make the world safe for democracy, again."

"You're bitter."

Harding laughed and looked at him. "What makes you think it's worth asking about?"

"That's for me to decide. All you have to decide is whether or not you want to tell me."

"I'll tell you something, all right, Shelby," he said. "You're about the weirdest character I've met since I came into the Marine Corps. Do you know that?"

A shrug. "I'm curious. Because of the way you act sometimes. Things you say. I suspect you of being a romantic."

"Beau Geste? Beau Geste Harding. No. Murphy is a romantic. I am a corporal."

"You aren't going to tell me, are you?"

Harding looked at him again. "Let me ask you something. How did you feel when you came into the Marine Corps? You were drafted."

Shelby nodded. "I was scared. I had expected them to put me in the Army. When they called off my name for the Corps, I got weak inside. I was never able to see myself as a leatherneck. Not like Murphy, or Jones or Tate. Not even like you."

"Well, but— Then look how it was for me. I got my notice and I thought, God, no graduate school. I thought, Christ, I'll have to go to jail or Canada."

"But instead you volunteered for the Marine Corps."

Harding turned away from Shelby and looked out at the blackness.

"I decided against jail or Canada. But I had to do something. I couldn't just let them run me through the mill. I decided that since I wasn't willing to go to prison, or to Canada, if I was going to go through with it then I deserved the full measure. I had to do it all. Later I wavered. But never enough." He watched the dark wood beyond the headlights. "If that is what you call a romantic . . ."

"Well, I can understand it," said Shelby. "Gestures were the order of the day. What never fails to impress me is how people can have such finely tuned consciences in a country where that has so little effect. I've never been able to afford it."

"Liar," said Harding. "Besides, who can afford it? In America you live beyond your means."

They saw lights rising out of the trees far ahead, becoming the service station at the entrance to the highway. A mile to their right was a small hamlet, sleeping now. A party store that catered to personnel from the base was open. They bought beer and Coca-Cola and headed back, away from the lighted settlement into the countryside flanking the swamp, the maw of night and forest.

"How do you like the tequila?" Shelby's voice through fog. Harding closed the window.

"I guess it can do a job on you. Do you know what Audie was going to tell me? Out of that magazine?"

"He was probably going to show you the John Wayne interview. He mentioned that brand."

"Oh?"

"Yes. He recommended it highly. Said it's about the greatest stuff he's ever drunk. Said he liked it better than any Scotch or bourbon he ever had. Murphy figured John Wayne's recommendation on booze ought to be good enough for any U.S. Marine. Murphy was a little tight when he bought it."

"It's a hell of a drink, I'll say that."

After a while Shelby said, "Well, you're about as short now as a man can be and still be in."

"I suppose," said Harding. "Sometimes I think what I really ought to do is stay in the Marine Corps."

"There's a thought. I can see you and Murphy and Tate humping out into the swamp for the next twenty years or so, good old buddies. You'll be a top sergeant by then. You can retire on your pension and sit around looking at your scrapbook."

"I could go to OCS. I'd be a captain in a couple of years."

"Sure, if you could get them to take you with your bum shoulder. Do you think you'd be happy?"

"No. It's just that I'm so well acquainted with the job." Something turned over in his stomach. His shoulder twitched and he moved in the seat. "Besides, what's wrong with being a professional marine? It's an honorable calling, isn't it?"

"There are worse," said Shelby.

"What do they give you to re-up? A couple of thousand? Choice of duty station? Promotion?"

"You've already blown that one."

"Yeah. Still . . . I should ask Tate."

"You should shut up. You're taking all the edge off my high."

Harding pictured himself humping out into the swamp for the rest of his life. He shuddered inside. Yet, he thought, wouldn't that be a simple and effective answer? Harding the lifer. Captain Harding. If nothing else, it would be such sweet irony. He had been taught to appreciate that.

3. When they got back it was like walking into a bad party at school. The only things missing were pretentious conversation and horny young women. Or, thought Harding, was it vice versa?

Murphy met them at the door. "What'd you do, die on the way?"

Harding got a beer and poured out a double shot of tequila. Shelby had been right; he was losing the edge of his own high. The combination of tequila, beer, smoke, fresh air, and now smoke and tequila and beer again made him feel unsteady. He sat down on one end of the sofa. Morrison was out of it, collapsed against the wall in a prenatal position, semiconscious.

"Hey, you guys. See if these bring back any memories." Jones had been showing snapshots to Murphy and Tate.

Shelby glanced at Harding and moved down beside them, and Jones flipped slowly through the pages of his album, adding pertinent data to the photos.

"This is staging at Pendleton. Here's Okie. That red arch thing—"

"The gateway to the Orient," said Murphy. "You're all supposed to go through it. I got the same pictures."

"These're my buddies."

Harding imagined himself packing up his car for the final trip, the long voyage home. It would be a brilliant sunny day—*Even if it rains,* he thought, *it will still be sunny for me*—and he would head out that long drive, through the main gate, and never look back. He would never look back and he would never come back. The long, winding two-lane road that meandered its way slow as some old Negro through scrub land and woods bordering the military reservation, to Rocky Mount and Interstate 95 north—then straight up through Virginia to D.C., across Maryland to the mountains of the Pennsylvania Turnpike, across rolling Ohio on another turnpike to Toledo—and north on I-75 to home.

He wondered how it would feel, what his mind would be like. Would it be all excited adrenaline, or would it seem anticlimactic?

"Here's a string of ears we took in that same ville."

He felt his head throb with the beat of the stereo, felt sharp twinges in his shoulder, felt his head fill slowly as if with some liquid substance. He sipped tequila, gulped beer and accepted a joint from Shelby, sucking in a long draught of obscuring smoke, holding his breath as long as he could and then repeating the process before handing it on. He watched Morrison snooze like an innocent babe, watched Murphy grow excited over some picture. Tate asked him if he had ever cut off ears. He ignored the question, sipped tequila, chased it with beer, smoked grass. His shoulder hurt. He felt bloated.

He pictured himself at school two years ago. He had bought a brown suede overcoat with a wool-fleece collar and lining. Corduroy trousers, button-down shirts, wide ties. Boots. He liked to sit in the coffee shop of the student union and watch the trees in the wind. They had turned that into a hip bookstore now, where you could buy decals and literature about the Revolution. He had liked to walk through the snow, the trees covered with ice and the wind blasting around him, talking to some girl about nothing.

He could go back to that, it was all still there, still more or less the same. But he could not picture himself there now. He could not picture himself anywhere now except heading up a column of marines behind the squad leader, directing his fire team through the bush, sitting out on bivouac in a field jacket and combat boots, eating from a can of C rations.

"I don't have a shot of the sergeant we fragged. He was a bastard, though. They had to pick pieces of him out of a tree fifty feet away. We used a satchel charge."

"That was kind of a lousy thing to do," said Shelby.

"He was asleep, man, he never knew. He would have got himself blown away sooner or later anyhow—and probably some of us. We all hated him. He was such a stupid mother."

Harding looked at Jones and Tate and Murphy and Shelby and considered his notion of staying in the Marine Corps. There were things to be said for it. But the problem—one of the problems—was that he would live every day of his life with people like Jones, and Tate, and Murphy. With people like Morrison and Shelby and Webster, and people like himself.

As he thought about it, Tate gave in to the urgings of Jones and began to tell about that night on the hill, when he had piled up fourteen bodies and won his medal. Murphy was fascinated. Even Shelby was caught up in the story.

Harding took a long hit, a sip of tequila, a swallow of beer. Something in his stomach went *flip*.

He stood up and stumbled over the coffee table, banging his shin so hard he cried out. He got to his feet and slammed the door open and it caught on the chain with a noise so loud even Morrison opened his eyes. He kept slamming the door against the chain and finally broke it off and went outside. He vomited once at the side of the trailer, then managed to get out into the darkness at the back of the lot, out from under the stars into the shadow of the trees. He vomited until his stomach was empty but still could not stop, and he fell to his knees, his body shuddering, sweat breaking out all over him.

When Murphy came around the trailer a few minutes later, Harding was lying on his back on the pine needles, shivering, looking up at where patches of starry sky showed through the tops of the trees.

Murphy could barely see him. "You all right, Harding?"

"I guess I won't die," Harding answered.

"Dry heaves?"

"It's over now, I think."

"Come on back in."

"No," said Harding, lying in darkness. "No, thanks. I'll stay here until I start to come back together."

"I know how you feel, man. I've had them. There's nothing worse. It was probably all the stuff you were drinking, and the grass."

"Well," said Harding. "I'll tell you one thing. I'm no John Wayne."

A night wind came through the pines and Harding shuddered. He was still sweating. He felt as if he were freezing to death. But it was too dark for Murphy to see.

"You coming back in?"

"Yes. You go on back. I'll come in when I feel like it."

Murphy hesitated and stepped away. Harding listened to his footsteps until they were swallowed in the wind and the noise from the trailer, pulsing with the music in the night. He lay there shivering, feeling a knife twist in his shoulder, watching the tops of the trees. Thinking of marines on bivouac in the swamps tonight, thinking of privates freezing on guard duty, lost on patrol, thinking of winter in Michigan, of summer near Da Nang, shivering, watching the trees.

1. "Take your boots off and put them over there. Unblouse your trousers. Turn your pockets out. Stand facing the wall. Spread your feet apart. Unbutton your sleeves. Take your belt off and put it around your neck. Unbutton the top two buttons of your shirt and turn your collar up. Pull your shirttails out. Hold your arms straight out from your sides. —Sergeant."

The sergeant stepped forward and placed his right foot between the prisoner's feet. Starting at the upturned collar and with little pinching motions, he searched the man, working down all the seams, out along the arms and shirt cuffs, and on down until the seams of the trouser cuffs had been checked.

Murphy sat on the scuffed red wooden bench and watched the prisoner's face as the sergeant moved his hands down along the body, arms, legs, ankles. He knew who the prisoner was, even with the shaved head. He was a medium-size man, very black, and his face and his attitude, the manner in which he seemed to pay no attention to any of them, yet followed instructions, was familiar.

The sergeant found nothing and stepped back. "Okay, get ready to go out." The prisoner was doing it, not quite ahead of the order.

The staff sergeant at the desk pulled his piece of paper from the typewriter and turned to Murphy. "All right, corporal. Sign this and he's yours. Don't you have any cuffs or a night stick?"

"No," said Murphy, getting up. "I'm in a cheap outfit."

The paper was a temporary-release form. It said that PFC Simms, Calvin Edward, was being released into the custody of Cpl. Murphy, Thomas D., to be delivered first to his defense counsel, Captain Taggart, G.S., at Base Legal; then to Building 15 (Infirmary) for a physical examination; then to be returned to the correctional facility. It was not officially referred to as the brig.

Murphy signed the paper. The staff sergeant handed him a carbon and Murphy studied it while Simms laced his boots. The paper stated that PFC Simms had been admitted to the correctional facility three weeks before and was awaiting trial by special court-martial.

Murphy remembered him. It was he who had escorted Simms to the brig three weeks ago. Simms was being court-martialed for having struck a staff sergeant and been in unauthorized absence for sixty-eight days.

Simms was blousing his trousers. The sergeant unlocked the door that led to the walk between the receiving office and the outer gate.

"You ready to go?"

Simms was moving.

Murphy followed him through the barred door, out to the gate in the high fence topped with barbed wire. The corporal at the gate checked the paper and Murphy's military ID and chaser's card again, as he had when Murphy came in. He handed them back and Murphy buttoned them into his left breast pocket. The corporal unlocked the gate and swung it open.

"Let's go."

They walked out and made a right turn, Simms in front, Murphy one pace behind and in step. Cuffs, he thought. He had never even seen a pair of handcuffs or a night stick in his company. The CO did not consider them necessary and proper.

"You know where Legal is?"

"Yeah," answered Simms. "I been there lots of times, last few weeks."

"How they treating you in there?"

"Okay, I guess. They ain't done nothing much to me."

Murphy hated being a brig chaser. This duty was doled out to personnel chosen at random, six or eight from each company. They would be hustled off one morning to the base theater for a "school" taught by a sergeant from the brig. He would show his captive audience how to use handcuffs and the night stick, tell them what they were allowed and not allowed to do, and recount funny stories about harassing prisoners. Prisoners in the Marine Corps had few rights, most of these existing only on paper and only since the recent scandals and congressional investigations.

Having learned this, the chosen few would be given a card from the correctional facility authorizing them to escort prisoners as needed for a period of six months. They would then return to their regular jobs until their services were required by the company legal office. The duty might then last for an afternoon or for several days, depending upon its nature.

Murphy hated this more than anything else in the Marine Corps —that ordinary marines should be forced to do what was properly a military policeman's job. It was a side of the profession which did not meet his ideals, and he kept his mind off it, did not talk to his prisoners, tried not to know any more about them than necessary. He was called out only once or twice a month. After Christmas, when his card came up for renewal, he intended to do some dealing with Morrison, who was now the legal NCO, and get himself dropped from the list.

"Can we stop off and let me make a head call?" Simms looked back over his shoulder.

"Sorry," said Murphy. "Order says go right to Legal."

"It just take a minute."

"You should've done that before."

"I didn't have no chance to." Simms stopped and half turned.

"Let's go," said Murphy. "Captain's waiting on you."

Simms put his hands in his pockets.

"Let's move it."

"Man, I gotta go."

They looked at each other. Murphy had never had a problem with one of his prisoners, but it was a possibility that irritated him. Worrying about it made him think about them, and he sometimes wished in spite of his dislike for handcuffs that the battalion would comply with regulations.

He considered giving in but was reluctant. He looked at Simms' face. It was long and hollow, the lips full and the jaw slack in a perpetually stupid look, reminding him of Webster. But Simms' eyes, unlike Webster's, were very quick and did not look stupid.

"You going to give me trouble?"

"Shit, man, I'm just askin a decent—"

"Take your hands out of your pockets." Murphy decided if it came to a fight, he would probably have to explain later why Simms was so messed up, as Simms would be if he forced Murphy into it. But he did not really want that to happen, and he thought, *Christ, what a job.*

"Well, if you ain't a motherfucker." Simms gave him an aggrieved look and took his hands out of his pockets.

"Move your ass." Murphy took a step forward, and Simms backed away and started moving again, Murphy one step behind.

"I'm gonna tell the captain you wouldn't let me make a goddamn head call."

"That's all right. I'm not authorized to make any stops. If you and the captain want to work something out, that's up to you and him."

He let his breath out, feeling an intense dislike toward Simms for making it hard. *Just like Webster,* he thought, wondering why there had to be so great a difference between such people and Green. He despised Simms even more because he had had to put Simms into the brig three weeks ago, shortly after Green died.

He hated going to the brig, hated even to pass by it. He did not think there should be any brigs. And he hated the prisoners, because if it were not for them he would not have to do this, play hard-ass and deny a man the right to make a head call. He hated them, not for going UA but for getting caught. Murphy had always sworn to himself that if he ever went UA he would make sure he was not caught. He would never give the brig guards a chance to play their games with him. He had been at Pendleton when the investigators came in, when the magazines published their true stories about the terror in that place, the torture. It was better now, they said, and this was Lejeune and not Pendleton—but it could never get that much better in a military "correctional facility."

The building had a red sign beside the walk, with yellow letters that said BASE LEGAL OFFICE. Murphy followed Simms up the steps and through the door into a hallway with a row of chairs. Little signs with officers' names on them stuck out into the hall from doors along each side.

"Wait a minute." Murphy pulled the paper out of his pocket. "You know where Captain Taggart's office is?" But Simms was already opening a door, sticking his head inside.

A young captain pulled it open. "Okay, Simms, come on in. Corporal, you can have a seat there; this won't take long. Let me have his papers."

Murphy took his cap off and sat down on one of the chairs in the hall. It made him feel tired to do this job, tired inside and outside. He could not get used to the idea of herding another man like a sheep or a steer.

He decided that he probably should have let Simms make the head call. He felt bad about that, although his orders had been clear. He wondered what Green would have done. Even Green had bent the rules on occasion, and Murphy had known him to break them outright when necessary. But what was necessary?

What he could not stand about this duty, what made him sweat and made his stomach churn, was having to be responsible for another person, a marine, having to treat him as something less than a man. He wished he did not care about that; had they not been fellow marines, he might not have cared about it—but they were. He did care.

2. The day three weeks ago when they had called him to the company office to escort Simms to the brig, he had felt so low he could hardly speak to anyone. All he could say to Morrison when he was handed the green duty belt was, "Why the hell did you ask for me?"

"They all say that." Morrison rolled a sheet of paper into his typewriter. "I didn't ask for you. We just call up the unit and tell them we need a chaser. Your top sergeant shuffles the names."

"I wish he'd shuffle my name right out of the deck." Morrison smiled sympathetically. "Where is he?" growled Murphy.

"In with Lieutenant Frost." Lieutenant Frost was the legal officer.

"What did he do?"

Morrison leaned back in his chair. "He's in a mess. He just shipped for two more years a little while back—shipped for promotion to *lance corporal.*"

"Wow."

"Yeah. So then his wife buys a color TV and a set of encyclopedias and a lot of other stuff. She runs him into debt. So he goes UA for two weeks to try and borrow some money. He straightens it out, comes back and gets busted to PFC again, with two years in and two more to go."

Murphy shook his head. "PFC."

"And so then the wife buys a car. He can't get leave, his platoon sergeant hassles him, so he slugs the guy and goes UA again for two months. They caught him working in a foundry."

"Son of a bitch. Will I have to put him in the brig?"

Morrison nodded. "He's waiting for a special court. You'll have to tuck him away."

"God damn it." Murphy sat down on the edge of the desk and glared at the people who came and went, and Morrison typed a page and scribbled on some papers.

He waited an hour and a half before the lieutenant was finished and Simms' gear had been brought in from the barracks.

"You got a chaser out there?" called the lieutenant over the wall separating the offices.

"Yes, sir," Morrison answered.

"Let me see him."

Morrison motioned him in. On the way he passed a black kid coming out.

Frost was a first lieutenant, an ex-infantryman from New York. He had an overly aggressive disposition. The only people he liked were the young civilian women who worked in the office next door, and they would have nothing to do with him.

When Murphy stepped into the office, Frost glanced up and began to play with some papers. "What's your name, chaser?"

"Corporal Murphy, sir." Noncommissioned officers were generally addressed by their ranks. It irritated Murphy that the lieutenant should ignore this courtesy.

"Okay, Murphy." Frost looked up again, shuffled papers. "What you passed coming in here was PFC Simms. I want you to get him over to the infirmary for a physical and put him in the brig. Don't take any crap from him and don't make any other stops. You got that?"

"Yes, sir."

"Okay. Move it."

Murphy felt momentarily like a private again. He turned and left the office thinking, *Fuck you, sir.*

Simms was sitting on his sea bag, watching Morrison type out his forms.

"This him?"

"Yeah." Morrison tapped the keys of his machine and Murphy looked at Simms, at his long dark slack face and his sharp, alert eyes that watched Morrison, and now slid around to return his stare.

"Where'd they catch you, man?" said Morrison.

"Indenaplis." Simms lowered his lids once and let them slide back up, *flap,* like dark window shades. "My wife turn me in," he added mildly.

"No shit—your *wife?*"

"She thought she was doin right, I guess. I about made up my mind not to come back at all."

"Your *wife* turned you in to the Ps?"

"She turn me in to the FBI. She thought . . ." Simms hesitated and looked at his hands. "She didn't know."

"Son of a bitch," said Murphy. "Tell your wife I said thanks, next time you write her. I might've got the afternoon off."

Simms did not look up. "Me too."

Murphy sat on the edge of Morrison's desk and watched the hands on the clock move through fifteen minutes while Morrison dawdled. "Come on, man. If we don't get going they might not take him today. I'll have to lock him in the linen room in the barracks and go through it all again tomorrow."

"Bout finished," said Morrison.

Lieutenant Frost came around the corner. Murphy stood up.

"For Pete's sake, are you still here? What do you say we get a move on."

"I'm waiting for his papers, sir."

Frost turned to Morrison. "Come on, lance corporal, hurry it up. I want him out of here."

"Just about done, sir." Morrison continued pecking away with his two index fingers.

Frost started to go back and noticed the sea bag Simms was sitting on. "What is *that* thing still here for?" He threw Murphy his best intimidating look. "Haven't you even got his gear over to Supply yet? What are you waiting for?"

"I didn't know I was supposed to, sir."

Morrison turned briefly from the typewriter. "That's my fault, lieutenant. I forgot to tell—"

"How long have you been a chaser?"

Murphy looked at the lieutenant. "Couple of months, sir."

"Don't you even know the job yet?"

"None of my other prisoners ever had their gear."

"I forgot to tell him, lieutenant," said Morrison, typing. "It's my fault."

"Do I have to do everything myself around this place?"

No one answered, and no one laughed. Morrison, rather languidly, kept typing. Murphy knew the lieutenant did little anyway, except harass the enlisted men—especially now, when the first sergeant was on leave.

"Get him and take his gear over and put it in Supply and make sure they give him a receipt. Do it while Morrison is playing with his toy there. I want that prisoner *out* of here. I want him out of my sight. You hear me?"

"Yessir." Murphy slurred it a little.

"You got all your stuff in there?" Frost said to Simms.

"I don't own much," answered Simms without looking up.

Frost came over to stand in front of him, hands on hips.

"What did you say?"

"Said I don't own much."

Frost's mouth became prim and hard; his back stiffened.

"Do you know how to speak to a lieutenant?"

Simms remained silent, looking at the toes of his tennis shoes.

"You say 'sir' when you speak to an officer. And you stand up when an officer addresses you. Do you hear me, marine?"

"I ain't no marine," Simms told him quietly.

"You may be piss poor, but you *are* a marine, and you'll act like one when an officer speaks to you. Or I'll make you wish you had."

"I ain't no marine," answered Simms.

The lieutenant grabbed the front of Simms' shirt with both hands and jerked him to his feet.

Morrison paused and looked curiously over his typewriter. Murphy, standing behind the lieutenant, saw Simms clench his right hand into a fist. Their eyes met and Murphy shook his head.

Frost let go of the shirt. "Now I asked you, PFC, if all your gear is in that sea bag." He still looked as if he wanted to hit him.

Simms glanced back and forth between the lieutenant and Murphy. Murphy shook his head again. It took a long second for Simms to decide.

"It all in there," he said. "Lieutenant."

Frost's lips became a straight line again, but he decided to go with this. He faced Murphy.

"Get this man out of here right now. When you get his receipt, come back and pick up his papers and go put him away. I don't want to see him again. You hear me?"

"Yes, lieutenant."

Frost gave Murphy a two-second glare that seemed to waver in an indecision precisely like Simms'. He turned to Morrison. "Get that damn thing done."

"Coming up, lieutenant," said Morrison, typing away.

Frost marched back into his office. There was no door for him to slam.

Morrison let his eyes drift up to Murphy's, raised his eyebrows and grinned.

Murphy made a face. "Thanks, friend."

"I'm sorry, man. I forgot all about his gear."

Murphy said, "Are you ready to go dump that?" and Simms silently hefted the sea bag. "Back in a minute. Have the papers ready, will you? Don't screw me again."

"Coming up," said Morrison behind his two fingers.

Outside, the wind was cold and there was no sun. Murphy walked behind Simms, who lurched along beneath the green bag, his sad face turned into the wind, like a parody of Santa Claus.

"You came pretty close to hanging it up."

"I guess," said Simms, "I try out the brig first a little while, before I do anything drastic."

It went thereafter without a hitch, at Supply, where Simms got his receipt; back in the company office, where Morrison had finally pulled out the last of his documents, clipped the papers together and leaned back in his chair with a Coke. At the infirmary Simms was stripped and prodded and punctured and weighed, asked if he was an addict. "No, man," he told the Navy doctor, a captain, and dressed again. And then the brig.

It stood inside its barbed-wire fence across the street from the central area theater, in about as public a place as could be without having been set up in the PX. It resembled a small prison: guards in towers, an exercise yard, an almost windowless main building. Murphy's barracks was nearby, one of many, themselves lined in rows like prison buildings. He could never go anywhere in the area without noticing the brig—it seized his attention, passing by. At night it was lighted like an exhibition, and in the daytime the voices of inmates playing basketball in the yard floated to his ears across all the fences.

He had been inside the brig four or five times, enough to loathe the place without even beginning to get used to it. He knew the sequence: having his chaser card and ID and the prisoner's papers scrutinized at the gate and again at the door to Receiving, and finally the receiving procedure itself—Simms stripped again, searched, his belongings inventoried, questions asked and answers recorded. Simms took his time about all this, never moving faster than he had to, as Murphy supposed he might do in the same situation, which itself was to him a horrifying thought.

"Okay, corporal."

The staff sergeant kept some of the papers, returned others to Murphy. "Take him up to Supply for his bedding, then to the third floor for In-Dock."

He followed Simms, directing him down a hall, up a stairway, Simms showing no apparent interest in his surroundings and Murphy hardly blaming him. He felt sorry for anyone who had to be here, felt sorry for himself for having to be here even briefly.

At Supply Simms scrawled his name, his tennis shoes were taken and he was given a mattress and blanket and pillow, no linen. Then up a stairway, through a door with an electrically controlled lock and a sign: IN-DOCK. Beyond this point Murphy had never been.

He had heard from some that this brig was not so bad, had heard from others that all brigs were nightmares. It hardly mattered to Murphy: the concept itself was a nightmare. After putting a man into the brig, Murphy was set for a night of drinking or smoking grass, or taking something that would send him much farther out among lights and pictures. At such times he came closest to wondering if the Marine Corps was everything he had believed it to be—and that night three weeks ago, without Green to tell him that it was, was all right, was a necessary and proper part of the smooth-working, efficient system, he cried.

3. He sat for half an hour, went down to the water fountain at the end of the hall for a drink, and was beginning to doze off when the door opened and Simms and Captain Taggart came out. Simms looked shaken and his eyes for the first time had lost their sharpness. Murphy stood up.

"Here are his papers, corporal. Take him on back. I'll be seeing you again, Simms."

Simms was silent, looking away. As the captain turned to go into his office, Simms said quietly, "What about my head call?"

The captain hesitated and looked at Murphy, who was putting on his cap. "Let him make a head call when you get to the infirmary, corporal."

"Yes, sir."

Simms went slouching outside ahead of Murphy. It had become a beautiful late autumn day, the sun out just warm enough to offset the chill in the air. Murphy took a deep breath and came awake, felt almost good for a change. Simms kept his mouth shut, head down, moving as if he were asleep, dragging himself toward the infirmary. He had such a hangdog look that for once Murphy was curious.

"Bad news?"

Simms looked over his shoulder at Murphy.

"Captain say maybe he can get me off with a BCD. That's what I want. But I probably got to do some brig time. Maybe even Portsmouth."

"Oh . . ." said Murphy. "Oh, great." A bad conduct discharge could be lived down, at least lived with. But the thought of Portsmouth Naval Prison made him feel cold. If you were tucked away, claustrophobic and tight, in the brig, how much more so were you lost to the world at Portsmouth? Portsmouth scared everyone. Like the Camp Pendleton brig, Portsmouth was the subject of stories that Murphy had thought, upon hearing them, could not be true. Yet they had been true at Pendleton.

"Jesus Christ, Simms!" he said suddenly, his horror breaking into hard anger that he should have to suffer vicarious anguish for this stupid black who had got his crazy ass caught. "What the hell did you have to trust your wife for?"

Simms looked around at him curiously, as if the question had awakened something in him, and his eyes looked almost sadly amused. He reminded Murphy, for just a moment, of Green.

"Now who the hell," he said slowly, "can a man trust if he can't trust his own wife."

"Sure," answered Murphy. "And she turned you in to the FBI."

"I know." Simms nodded and grinned. "I guess she thought she was savin me from myself."

"If my wife ever did anything like that to me, I'd get even if it took the rest of my life."

"Well," said Simms, "I thought about that. I got the rest of my life to think up ways."

They went in the back door of the infirmary and Murphy let Simms lead the way to the first-floor head. It was small, two urinals and a basin on the right, a single booth and commode straight across from the door.

Simms went into the booth, closed and snapped the door. Murphy leaned against the wall across from the sink. There was, he noticed over the top of the booth, a window inside the booth, the only one in the room. It occurred to him that Simms might make an attempt to escape—Murphy would have. The window was closed, but as he thought about it, Simms pulled away the Venetian blind and opened the window a few inches.

Murphy watched Simms' feet below the door of the booth. He began to consider the possibility. He thought he might be able to break open the door with a hard blow from his shoulder. Otherwise he envisioned himself, working it out in his mind in careful detail, leaping up to grab the top of the door, pulling himself up, swinging over, dropping on the other side. He could see it all happening with great clarity in his mind, as if it were a memory rather than a possibility, a déjà vu of something in the past or future, predestined by some quirk of the time element.

He would follow Simms through the window and chase him in the direction he was likely to go, toward the woods that stretched across, five miles deep, between the central area and the highway outside the main gate. If he got into the woods he would probably escape. He would have quite a head start, but of course there was considerable traffic between the infirmary and the woods. It would be a run of perhaps half a mile. Murphy was very fast, and in that sizable distance there would be many people he could call upon for help.

He thought about it, leaning against the wall. If Simms escaped, Murphy would be called on the carpet in front of Lieutenant Frost and probably the CO as well. Of course, he had had a direct order from a captain to allow Simms to make his head call. He was in the room and would pursue his man as required by regulations. He should be safely covered.

But Murphy knew that a man was never really covered in the military. He could always be done in if they were in the mood for it.

Simms flushed the toilet and stood up. Murphy heard him fasten his belt, zip his fly.

Simms, he thought, but could establish for himself nothing more coherent than that. *Simms . . .*

"Simms!" he said sharply, not certain of the note in his voice, not sure what response he desired or if he desired a response at all.

And then it was happening, so quickly and so slowly he felt as if it were an old-time movie, perhaps a silent comedy. He heard the blind snatched back and the window go up. He heard the sound of feet on a windowsill and threw himself against the door of the booth just as he had rehearsed it in his mind. The door held, as he had known it would, as he had *arranged* for it to hold, and he leaped and caught the top of the door and pulled himself up and over like a stunt man and dropped to his feet on the other side in time to see Simms leap. He followed Simms through the window, losing his cap, and jumped the six feet to the ground. He landed running.

Yes, he thought, *Simms*—and Simms cut to the right, around the end of the building, across the walk and the wide lawn toward the street, and beyond that Murphy could see the appointed stretch past the bowling alley and behind the PX to the woods.

Simms had a good lead. *I don't think,* Murphy decided, *I'll be able to catch him. Unless he runs out of wind in the half mile.* Simms was sprinting as if he were doing the hundred-yard dash. *Better ease up,* thought Murphy. *You can't keep it up, and I'm going to try hard to get you.*

He relaxed his own pace a little, and felt as if he were out for an autumn jog, the pressure off, the commitment made by each of them, the woods far away like a finish line, and he didn't have to feel anything now, no worry, no guilt, no sweat. Just run—and they crossed the street without being hit and passed the bowling alley with no one near, and Simms began to slow down.

Easy, thought Murphy, stepping up his pace. *Don't quit now. Don't throw it all away this time, Simms. No wife here to turn you back, no staff sergeant to hit,* just the gray-and-gold line of trees looming closer. Murphy opened up his pace a little more but decided not to spend himself, and thought, *I'm not going to catch you, Simms. You're on your own now if you can just hold a steady pace. No brig for you, no Portsmouth, and who knows, maybe they'll just mail the BCD to your parents if you can lie low for a while without your good wife finding out where you are. Or maybe Canada, Simms. Kick your wife's ass good for you and me both and head north. You were right—you're not a marine. It isn't for people like you.*

They crossed behind the PX twenty yards apart, both of them slowing. *When he gets into the trees,* thought Murphy, *I'll go back to the bowling alley and call the MPs. They'll never get him.*

A lieutenant in a winter uniform, slim and tall and with the green sunglasses that were *de rigueur* for young officers, was getting out of his car in the PX parking lot. He looked at Simms heading for the trees and turned to watch Murphy.

I'll have to call him, thought Murphy. *It's part of the game and there's no way not to. He's too close, he's right on the scene and he's an officer. I'll have to.*

"Halt," he cried, pointing at Simms, who was making a last sprint for the trees. "Stop that man!" And he thought, *Move it, Simms, move your ass.*

The lieutenant did not hesitate. It was as if he had been waiting for a signal. He went into motion like a released spring and he ran with the effortless, lovely, breath-taking ease and speed of a natural athlete. He ran right up to Simms at the edge of the woods, grabbed him around the throat with one hand and threw him down hard. A sound of anguish came out of Simms, and the lieutenant put a knee into his back, holding him until Murphy arrived. He looked at Simms squirming beneath the lieutenant's knee.

"This man a prisoner?"

"Yes, sir," gasped Murphy.

The lieutenant grinned. "Pretty close, huh?"

"Close," said Murphy, watching Simms, who had paused with an arm under him, heaving for air.

"I saw a military police truck around front when I came in. I'll hold this man while you get them."

"Yes, sir."

Simms was trying to get to his knees. The lieutenant put his weight into Simms' back and he collapsed again.

"Spread out your arms and legs and lie still. If you mess up my clean uniform I'll be mad at you."

The MPs, a sergeant and a corporal, rode Murphy back to where the lieutenant was standing now with a highly polished shoe in the middle of Simms' back. He returned their salutes.

"Here's one of your boys. He must not have cared for your hospitality."

"Much obliged, lieutenant." The sergeant got Simms up, cuffed him and put him in the back of the truck.

The lieutenant scratched at a grass stain on his trouser cuff. "Well, good luck, corporal."

"Thank you, sir." Murphy threw him a salute and watched the lieutenant walk back to his car. *Luck,* he thought. *A simple case of luck.*

The corporal got in behind the wheel of the truck and the sergeant held the door for Murphy.

"You want to go with us? You'll have to turn in his papers and make out a statement."

"I lost my hat back there. I'll get it and come on over."

He watched the truck pull away. He could see Simms' face through the wire grate, looking out at him. His eyes were not angry or afraid. They looked dull, dead, as if they had never had life at all.

Murphy thought about that as he walked back to the infirmary. It reminded him of Webster and of Green, at different times and for different reasons. He wished he had never given Simms the chance to run, wished he had made him keep the window closed, keep the door unlatched.

"He almost made it, though," he said aloud. "I let him almost make it." He shook his head and looked around at the autumn trees. It did not make sense. What he had done did not make sense. What was happening to Simms did not make sense.

1. Harding stood in the Friday-morning formation and watched the wind blow the branches of the trees across the street, dozing on his feet while the company gunnery sergeant read his notices, bitched about NCOs trading duty assignments without permission, bitched about broken cues in the poolroom.

"This shit," he said, "must cease."

The men shuffled away to work, and Harding crossed the street and went over to where Murphy's formation had just been dismissed. Murphy and Morrison waited for him.

"Morning."

"Hi. Is Shelby coming?"

"He took a guy's duty in the barracks," Harding told them. "For ten bucks."

"Smart," said Murphy.

"Where you working today?" Harding asked Murphy.

"I'm humping ammo at the dump."

"We have some guys out there too. Want to give me a ride?"

"Yeah, we got a truck."

"How you doing?" Harding said to Morrison. "Are you straight?"

"Straight enough to do my job. I gotta get to the office. Since our little almost-crisis the other day, Lieutenant Frost is putting on the screws. Thanks to your buddy here. See you all." Morrison cut away toward the company office and Harding looked at Murphy.

"Any repercussions about that?"

"Nah. He was pissed, he went through the whole act. The best thing was he said he didn't want me for a chaser anymore. Said he can't depend on me."

"I'll bet that broke your heart."

"Not so you'd notice it. What're you going to do this weekend?"

"I'm not sure," said Harding. "Get out of here for a while, is all I know. Go hide somewhere and pretend I'm discharged."

"You heard anything about that?"

"Not a word, son."

Murphy climbed up over the tailgate of the truck that would take them out to the ammunition dump. Harding had trouble.

"Give me your good hand." Murphy pulled him up.

"You wouldn't think they'd keep a cripple around to get in the way, would you?" Harding sat down on the wooden seat along the side of the truck and offered Murphy a cigarette. "Have some death."

"You ought to write your congressman."

"I did. I got a letter back that said he's checking on it."

"Oh." Murphy leaned forward and Harding gave him a light. "He's checking on it, huh?"

"Right. How's that for action?"

"Nothing slow about those boys in the Capitol."

The truck bumped out onto the street, swung around the circle and headed out the main boulevard past the power plant and the PX. Harding rubbed his shoulder and puffed the cigarette. "How are you and Cherry making out?"

"Good," said Murphy.

"I'll bet."

"No, I mean it, really." Murphy looked at the end of his cigarette.

Harding said carefully, "I hate to be crude or anything, buddy, but what about your wife?"

"No letter this week. She's too busy."

"You ought to go see her, Audie. You should have her here with you, in base housing. Then everything would work out."

"No, it wouldn't. I don't even like her anymore. Ever since I came in the Marine Corps she's been getting even."

"Maybe she just didn't have the service in mind when she married you."

"Oh, she knew I wanted to come in. She thought she could change my mind, get me into the University of Texas. We were going to move up to Austin and she'd work and I'd play football. Only they didn't come through fast enough with a scholarship. So she had other ideas. I could start an apprenticeship or something, or have a kid, for God's sake. Anything to screw up the draft board. Football was the one thing I might have thought about. But settle into some goddamn suburb and play house the rest of my life? No chance. I shouldn't ever have got married."

Harding watched the smoke disperse in the wind that came around the canvas flaps at the back of the cab. It was a cold day, cold enough for gloves.

"I feel sorry for you, fellow. That attitude—"

"Feel sorry for her. I'll make up for all of it. She leaves without even telling me until she's moved in with her aunt in Atlanta. Got a secretary job. What kind of a wife is that? And if she's doing what I think she's doing, I might just shoot her."

Harding looked at him. "Don't even say that. You're not serious. You have to work these things out."

Murphy didn't answer. He inhaled deeply and the cigarette burned down to his fingers. He put it out on the floor of the truck and stuck his hands into the pockets of his field jacket. He blew the smoke out in a thin stream and leaned back against the side of the truck.

"I'll work it out," he said.

Harding got off early, and fired his car out the gate, southwest on highway 17, past Jacksonville, through Verona, Dixon, Folkstone, Holly Ridge, Edgecomb, through the blasted countryside, past swamps, passing farmers and black folks in their rattletraps, around marines swooping south for the weekend. Through Hampstead and

Kirkland. At the outskirts of Wilmington, that fabled city on the Cape Fear River, last Confederate port to be closed by Union troops, he turned due south on highway 132, ran into 421 and drove into Carolina Beach at dusk.

It was a small summer town of motels, restaurants, arcades and beer taverns, with a boardwalk and a mile of decent beach. In the winter the town was mostly deserted, cold, turned off, a lonely place.

It was what Harding wanted. He checked into a motel with cheap winter rates, parked his car in the empty lot by an empty blue-painted pool that still sported a gaudy umbrella over a rusted table, and lugged his flight bag up to the room. He had had the pick of the place and had taken a corner room with a window that looked out on saw grass, the long weathered plank boardwalk and the Atlantic. The tide was in and the cold moonlight showed little of the beach itself.

He looked at the room. The walls were imitation knotty pine, with pictures of Civil War gunboats, a broken ship's-wheel barometer that had sprung itself at *Storm,* and some sort of fish on the wall over the bed.

Harding liked the effect. He was ensconced for the weekend. He jumped onto the bed, kicked off his shoes and watched a monster movie on the little TV set that only brought in one channel. After the movie there was an hour of country music with a guitar-picking warbler in a sequined cowboy suit, Billy or Jimmy somebody who appeared to be about forty-five and on the downhill side of a hard life. His presence on the tube made it *seem* like the South, although the man looked familiar and Harding supposed he had seen him before in Michigan or California, which these days were just about as South as the South.

His cohort was a bosomy piece named Sue-Ellen, packed into a flower-print full-skirted dress. She spoke with an accent Harding could have sliced into twelfths with a bayonet, and sang in her choked, crying country voice of lost loves and cheatin hearts, pressing herself into the microphone.

She turned Harding on, and he undressed and lay under the blankets, grabbing himself when Sue-Ellen breathed. She was finally replaced, to his chagrin, by a fat teen-age banjo player who knew how to frail but keep getting tangled in the strings when he tried to pick with three fingers. He grinned at the camera the whole time he was on, and Harding's passion ebbed.

Then Billy, the old cowboy, came back and sang about his big red motorcar, which seemed in poor taste to Harding, and then Sue-Ellen again, breathing and sighing and crying into the microphone. The whole gang got together for the finale and sang "Amazing Grace" in a way Harding had never heard it done, with guitars and fiddles and banjos.

When the program ended, Harding got up and turned the sound off, took the tube of skin lotion he had got in the hospital in California and lay thinking of Sue-Ellen's bosom. His image switched dreamily to the dancers in the Pussycat and then to the girl photographer. He shifted among all of them until it was over, and as he cleaned himself up he shook his head sadly.

"Another jackoff in the Old South. Onanism is death. This shit," he said, like the gunnery sergeant at the morning formation, "must cease."

He looked at himself naked in the mirror on the back of the bathroom door—and it was like a flashback in time to California, to Anaheim, that bad Friday night before he had met Donna. He raised his left arm as high as he could, working it around and watching the scarred flesh move as he felt it resisting on the inside.

"Caught a little somethin in the shoulder, there, boy," he said, moving the arm, and he looked and looked at it and thought, *Christ, Harding,* but he could not take his eyes away. *Why?* he thought. *Why did he do it?* and it was still like something that had never happened to him, was only a dream or something he had heard about. He said aloud to his image, "Why, Webster? Jesus Christ, why?" And he thought suddenly with cold fury, with hatred, *I'm glad Murphy wasted him. I'm glad the mother is dead. I wish to God I could have seen Audie blast him, pof-pof-pof, twenty hard ones right up his fucking yellow spine. I wish I'd done it. I wish I'd done it first.*

He broke his gaze from the ruined shoulder and looked at his face, and what he saw made him turn away from the mirror.

He sat down on the edge of the bed. "Harding, old buddy," he said, fingering the scars with his right hand, "I thought you were all over that by now." But apparently not. He was just the same; he had learned nothing. Or perhaps a little. Not enough, not nearly enough.

2. In the morning, while he waited for his breakfast, he looked out the window of the restaurant at the arcades and taverns and dime stores that sold bathing suits and beach supplies in the summer. Nothing much was open yet. He thought about what he might do to spend the day, and watched a girl walk by outside. It was the photographer from the Pussycat.

He found himself faced with the choice of denying his eyes—*Such things don't happen,* he thought, shocked—or taking advantage of what, impossible or not, seemed provided expressly for his benefit.

He jumped up. "I'll be right back!" he called to the waitress, and before she could turn he was out the door.

The girl was a dozen paces away, looking at the posters outside an adult theater. He started to call to her and felt a spasm of uncertainty. He had only seen her for an instant and now her back was to him. Gritting his teeth, he approached.

"Hey, there."

She turned, and it was indeed the girl with the camera. She had one with her now, a Nikon. She stared at him blankly for a moment and a look, not particularly pleased, crossed her face.

"Small world," he said. "How are you, Madelaine?"

"I don't know. I was all right a minute ago. Where did you come from?"

"I was in the restaurant and I saw you walk by. I wasn't sure it was you."

"I sometimes feel that way myself. Well," she said. She noticed he wore no jacket. "You'll catch cold, running out of restaurants like that every time a woman walks by."

It was true; he was freezing. He tried to think of something witty, but his head was numb. He had to make do with the truth. "It wasn't just a woman. It was you."

She seemed unconvinced.

"Have you had breakfast? Would you have breakfast with me?"

"I've already had." She seemed impatient. She looked up at the sky and around at the street. She shook her head and he was sure she was going to walk away and leave him there.

"Would you drink a cup of coffee with me then? They're working on my breakfast right now. You must have really gotten up early."

The impatience now appeared to be uncertainty. She turned her head and looked at the hot colors of the movie poster, two men struggling, one girl waiting. "The light is best early in the morning." She held up the camera.

He suddenly shivered so badly his teeth clicked. But she did not speak, just looked at him again with her lips pursed into a line against the chill or against him, and he could no longer stand the suspense.

"Look, Madelaine. Will you please come and have some coffee while I eat breakfast? I'm freezing to death."

"Okay," she said. "You can buy me some coffee."

"Thank God." He took her arm and hurried her back to the restaurant.

"I don't think your husband would mind your having a cup of coffee on a cold morning," he said, bringing two cups over himself. "What are you doing way down here?"

She had slipped out of her coat and was wearing a white turtleneck and gray wool slacks. Her thick dark hair was a little windblown and she wore no makeup. She was staring out the window.

"I don't know whether he would mind or not. Fortunately for you, he's in the Mediterranean."

"Literally?" He tried to sound hopeful.

"He's on a cruise," she said, turning to the coffee and to him.

"It's lucky I happened to see you walk by."

"I guess," she said, "we'll find out."

He ate his breakfast and she watched the sunlight slant across the façades outside and then watched him, sipping her coffee.

"You haven't told me why you're down here."

"I take my own pictures on my own time. All the winter beaches around here; they are very pictorial."

He finished eating and the waitress brought more coffee. "Tell me about your husband."

"Now why," she said carefully, "should I want to do that?"

"Because I'm asking you."

She leaned forward with her elbow on the table and looked at the ring. "Tell you . . . what?"

"Anything you want. What's his rating? His job? Anything. Say it now. I won't ask you after this."

She looked up at him and closed her fist, and he thought it was over.

But she said, "He's a captain. He's in warehousing with Second Marines, Second MarDiv. He did a tour in Viet Nam and a Caribbean cruise before this one. I met him in California and married him there. I'm from Long Beach. He's from San Diego. We've been married almost four years. We don't have any children. Is that enough?"

"It's enough for me if it's enough for you."

"It is." She picked up her cup. "It's time for me to start taking advantage of the light."

"Can I walk with you, Madelaine?"

She was looking at her hands, watching them leave the cup and move to the camera. "Just tell me one thing honestly, please. Did you have any idea I would be in Carolina Beach today?"

"Absolutely not," said Harding. "It is genuine fate."

She looked at him openly, her eyes a little wide, expressionless.

"Well, I'd like you to walk with me, yes. I'd like that very much."

The sun was a bit warmer and the breeze had died. Harding and Madelaine continued in the direction she had been going, away from his motel, on down the mall. Some of the taverns and arcades were open now and other restaurants gave out seafood and pizza smells. Madelaine stopped occasionally to shoot the front of a restaurant, or an empty arcade where bouncy roulette music came from loudspeakers. They reached the end of the street and turned left, up a ramp to a partly covered dock that stretched far out over the water at a right angle to the beach. It was another arcade, with colored lights and pinball machines, more happy music, but almost no people.

"You haven't told me why you're out here today." Madelaine opened the diaphragm of her Nikon and took slow exposures by the clear white light that came in the ends of the building. They went through and walked out on the open dock.

"I had to get off the base for a while," he said, and she clicked and wound, clicked and wound. "I guess I'm taking a vacation from my job too."

They walked back through the arcade and turned right along the boardwalk that paralleled the beach. She reloaded her camera and shot a few exposures: of the almost empty beach, a vacant lifeguard tower, the saw grass around a broken life buoy, a Guess-Your-Weight booth and a closed-up hot dog stand that faced the sea. When they came to where the boardwalk ended they stopped and sat down on the edge of the steep bank between the boardwalk and the beach.

"My husband and I had a cottage right on the beach."

"Really?"

"Yes. At West Onslow. A strange thing happened. After his cruise left, I was out there one day, moving some of the last things back to our house on the base. And a very strange thing happened." She told him about Murphy and the dolphins.

"It sounds like him," said Harding. "The man who was killed was named Green. Both of them, close friends of mine. But especially Murphy."

"Yes," she said. "It was funny seeing Murphy with you that night at the Pussycat. Do you know—I wanted him to make love to me that day. I was lonely and depressed. It's very strange."

"It isn't so strange. Murphy is young and good-looking. He's very successful with women."

"And he was so preoccupied with his friend's death, I don't think he even really saw me. He drank a cup of coffee and left."

"Well, he and Green were close. The fact that he didn't go for you is an indication. I can't think of anything else that would have kept him from it." He did not mention Murphy's wife. "So you were lonely and depressed, and made a pass at my buddy."

"Yes," she said.

"And how are you lately?"

She didn't answer. He drew her down in the dry grass, unbuttoning her coat and slipping a hand inside. She kissed him.

"I want you," he said.

"Oh, I know you do."

"Will you come with me?"

She nodded into his shoulder.

When they got to the room Madelaine sat down on the edge of the bed, looking uncertain in the drowsy light that came through the curtains. He stood her up and put his arms around her, and undressed her with a sureness she seemed to appreciate. He started to take off his clothes, and stopped.

"Listen," he said, feeling the sudden coldness in his stomach. "Madelaine..." He thought fiercely, *It's all right. Remember Donna?* "I was wounded."

"Oh?" Now that she was nude she seemed to have gained confidence, and she stretched out on the blanket, her pale skin smooth against the scratchy wool.

"It's a shoulder wound. It isn't very pretty."

"Take your clothes off, dear."

When he pulled off his undershirt she said, "Oh, that isn't so bad." In fact, it seemed to excite her, and later, resting, she kissed him and played her fingers where his smooth skin met the rough scar tissue.

"What happened to you?" she whispered.

"I was shot," he said, and began to move again.

When Madelaine awoke it was after noon. She sat up and watched Harding, feeling a peacefulness she had not had in a long time. She wondered why, and knew why without needing to admit it.

She reached out a finger and touched his lips, thinking how soft they were, how gentle he was, how considerate, touching again, very lightly so as not to wake him, the ruin of his shoulder, almost crying inside for him. She felt a sudden helplessness. She could see the future for an instant, a future, and she touched his hair, smoothing it until he opened his eyes.

"Good morning."

He smiled, and she traced his smile with her finger.

"I thought you might like to take me out for lunch. I have to go back soon."

He yawned and sat up, propping himself on a pillow. "You don't have to go back."

She nodded firmly. "Yes, I do. I have to work tonight."

"Why? Do you need the money?"

"Money isn't everything."

"It's the only thing." He smiled. "Suppose I asked you not to go?"

"I can come back tomorrow," she said, wondering then why she had to go back at all.

"But I want you to stay with me tonight. I love you."

"Oh, *don't,*" she cried, turning away. "Please don't say that when you know it isn't—when we've only just met and we don't really know each other. And you know I can't—" She put her face in her hands.

"I'm sorry. Madelaine . . ." He touched her and she wanted to run but turned back and he held her.

"Oh, I hate being alive," she said, knowing it was not what she meant; what she meant was that she hated her life as it was, no life at all, worse than death because she was aware of her pain every minute of the day.

"Stop it." He kissed her and she shook with an awareness of her vulnerability. *What is the matter with me?* she thought, clinging to him. He held her for a long time, apparently no end to his patience, and she felt afraid at the goodness of him, the gentleness that turned her weak with need.

"Would you like to get some lunch?"

She nodded against him.

Outside, the sun was warm and the wind blew in from the sea in sharp gusts that smelled clean, salty, pure. She held his hand as they walked back up the boardwalk, where, incredibly, a few hours before she had been so alone, where she had been in an agony of indecision that had been equally dangerous either way. Now she was calm, and she thought, as they walked along the mall, *Thanksgiving is coming. Next Thursday is Thanksgiving.* It was the first time she had thought of it.

PART 3
Causes

1

1. And now, driving away from the heart of it, heading south through springtime Virginia toward the Carolinas, on the downhill side of the trip as, at long last, the last downhill falling-off part of the military —leaning toward freedom such as it might be said he could ever have that—he sat in the car and took another glance, of the one continuing long look, at his country.

In another week he would be out, at long last out, released. Sitting behind the wheel in the car with Shelby and Morrison, Harding yawned in the Virginia afternoon and listened to the vibration of engine and tires and thought about the three of them. Morrison, Shelby, Harding—not these, but three others: remembering an evening in the rain when they had talked and shared their coffee and thought of getting out. . . .

Harding and Murphy and Green.

It was as if his mind had played a trick with time, as if a cog had been missed between autumn in California and spring in Carolina. How could it, he asked himself, be *March?* And had it happened at all: that night in the rain, the lieutenant and Webster—and later, Donna, Green's death, Murphy by the dock at Sneads Ferry, just before Christmas . . .

Too much had happened in that slipped cog of the clock in himself

—and he should have been gone long ago, in November instead of March.

"Fredericksburg." Shelby nodded at the sign.

Morrison leaned over from the back seat. "Wasn't there a battle around here?"

"Oh, yes." Shelby, fellow student of American history, smiled sadly. "There are battlefields all over this area. I do have a thing about Fredericksburg."

Harding looked in the mirror at Morrison. "You wouldn't, I suppose," he said to Shelby, "be interested in stopping?"

They had spent most of the previous day in the Smithsonian, gazing at Confederate and Union carbines and equipment, uniforms and flags.

The exhibits had struck Harding with a sense of immediacy that he found surprising: the old flags and uniforms seemed more sad, more honorable than his own, the Causes more relevant than his own dubious commitments.

"What's at Fredericksburg?"

"Just a cemetery and a view of the battlefield from Marye's Heights—"

"What's that?" asked Morrison.

"It's a hill on one side of the town. It's where the Confederates dug in and were assaulted by the Army of the Potomac. You can see very clearly how the battle went. If you were interested, I could tell you about the battle, and point out—"

"There's the turnoff." Harding slowed down. "What do you say?" But he was already edging over.

"I don't care," said Morrison. "Why not?"

Harding made the exit. As they curved off the ramp he watched the deceptively green trees and wondered where he would be when summer came. In Michigan—home—he thought, hoped, thought he hoped.

He wondered if he had a home. He pictured himself slumped stubble-cheeked in the doorway of a living room, uniformed, ill at ease, surrounded by his gear—useless in the real world—and someone saying, perhaps, "So that's where you've been! Too bad—you've missed your life." Too bad—and what to answer? "I'm sorry; I am very sorry. . . ."

He had seen a film on television, *The Best Years of Our Lives,* Fredric March and Dana Andrews and the wounded Harold Russell, who never made another movie, coming back from the Big War to Small Town U.S.A. to take up the threads of their lives again after making the world safe for democracy, again. A nice film, and who, Harding had thought, would not like to take up his life with the likes of Myrna Loy and Teresa Wright?

But he had not made the world safe for anything and, perhaps worse, had known he was wasting his time and the world's time and America's time, of which there seemed on occasion not so much left, playing America's Tommy Atkins in Uncle Sam's variation of the Song of India. . . . He felt like such a fool whenever he read a magazine and again was jolted with the cold-as-ice reality that simply because *he* had hung up his life for two years, that did not mean the rest of the world had joined him. All of the world that mattered most to him had gone spinning away; likely his world of the sixties had changed more in two years than Rip Van Winkle's in twenty.

Rip Van Harding.

Lying awake in the barracks nights when the drunken children were weaving in from town under the cold moon's eye, he felt that the worst was, he would not remember such life as he had lived these twenty-odd months (twenty odd months!) of the closing of a low, dishonest decade. Another low, another dishonest, another decade. He would repress it so fast he would be left with a twenty-month vacuum.

And Christ, did he *want* to remember? Someone would mention a mass killer by name and he would say *Who?*—or a violent confrontation on some campus, and his *Where?* would stop conversation. Men landing on the moon . . . All manner of foul or meaningless events he had not been privy to, lost in the confines of boot camp with no radio, no newspaper, lost at Pendleton learning to be a soldier, a *marine,* dear God, at this late date. Twenty-four years old, dropped-out graduate of the University of Michigan, where, as a sophomore, he had listened to Huntley and Brinkley report on Lyndon Johnson's decision to send major forces to Asia. The hand beginning to write on the wall even then. Would he hate Lyndon Johnson until he died? Playing tick-tack-toe with the draft board in Detroit all through college, a history student about to become Private Harding, 2575849 USMC. For America the Beautiful and President Thieu.

Or did Thieu come later?

The oddest thing, perhaps, he reflected during bouts with this sour malaise-of-the-soul, was how little he had mellowed with the experience, how, after twenty months of accustomedness and adaptation, he could still hate—not the Marine Corps, horrible backward ingrown disaster though it was—for it had always been there, *Semper Fidelis* whatever the job, however dirty, and perhaps—no doubt—rightly so. No, not that, but something far more fundamental. A notion, an attitude, almost a religion.

Was that what impressed him about those old flags, those stars and bars and grays and canteens stamped C.S.A.—full of shot holes and Minie balls—the fact that indeed there had been a time once, long ago, when it was possible to doubt the inevitability of the United States of America? When it had not been safe to be complacent? Looking at those crossed chest straps, that spent currency with J. Davis enshrined, a ghost, haunted and haunting in his own lifetime—was that what made him feel like crying?

Not that the one Cause had had any more validity than the other —to lose no more signified moral validity than to win—but that what had emerged from such a cataclysm could last another century and still be so . . . He did not know the word, was tempted to say: *fallible*. Or human. Whatever, how sad, how sad, thought Harding, must be the study of history. He had tried it.

They followed little signs on U.S. 1 that marked out the route to the National Military Park, maintained by the National Park Service, and all the way Harding was beside himself, not certain why. Perhaps because the great conflict of ideologies had, briefly, centered here once upon a time in the days of Lincoln and Lee. He tried to avoid what was for him the real question, the problem of how to readjust to a life whose birthright he had sacrificed. It was this that kept him awake nights after taps, when he would sit on his bunk and talk with Morrison or Shelby if one of them remained on base—or, failing that, with anyone in the barracks, anyone who, like Harding, would remember the Marine Corps best on midnight drunks as he pushed his way into late youth, into middle age; anyone who kept the silent, lifelong hurt the Marine Corps gave you, pride and shame in the same moment of remembering; anyone who hated, who loathed, with that separate, automatic loving, what had happened to him for a time in his nation's maddest military outfit in his nation's maddest moment.

The love-hate death match: what was it Murphy had said once, bitching in the mess hall about some detail to which he had been assigned? "Between us, I'll bet we've got enough hate to break a fucking egg. All we'd have to do is set it right here, and we could just look at it and break the damn thing."

But Murphy did not hate the Marine Corps. He had learned too much from it. "If I was a couple of years younger," he had said, "mean like I used to be, I wouldn't stand for this." He was twenty.

And he could never otherwise have been as mean as he learned to be in the Marine Corps, as creatively mean, as violently nonchalant. That was the specialty: the wedding of violence to innocence, the cultivation of natural aggression to produce the surest sort of killer. The institution had done it successfully for a hundred and seventy years, and never more successfully than during the 1960s.

Or so it seemed to Harding. Had it not, after all, done some sort of creditable job on himself?

2. Shelby had come around after work one evening a week ago with an offer. Harding was sitting on his bunk with a copy of Wallace Stevens' poems, lent to him by Shelby, who seemed to acquire personal libraries, whatever his living conditions, faster than anyone else Harding had ever met. Harding had found a poem that seemed to have been written for himself.

"Listen to this," he said, and with various rock sounds and the normal barracks pandemonium as a background, he read aloud:

"The wound kills that does not bleed.
It has no nurse nor kin to know
Nor kin to care.

And the man dies that does not fall.
He walks and dies. Nothing survives
Except what was. . . ."

Shelby made a noncommittal movement. "Sounds like one of his minor ones."

"You unfeeling son of a bitch. This is *me* he's writing about. Can't you see that?"

"Not really, no. I can't."

Harding slid the book under his pillow. "What the hell are you doing around here on a week night? Why aren't you out at Trailer Acres, or whatever you call that place."

"I have a proposition for you, old stalwart heart, old wound-that-does-not-bleed. Morrison wants to drive up to D.C. this weekend. Do you want to go?"

"Yes," said Harding. He needed to get off the base and away from Madelaine for a while, somewhere in the real world where he could again, as he did periodically, place himself in perspective with all that had happened, though nothing much had occurred since Christmas except that his discharge had been approved by everyone and—with nudging by his senator—was in the last stage of processing. In a couple of weeks it would all be over, and before that happened he needed to get away and fit himself mentally into the picture. There were things to consider, not the least of which was Madelaine. And, of course, again, perhaps always, Murphy.

As it turned out, Morrison's car broke down on Friday morning.

Harding was too much up for the trip by then to do anything except offer his own car, and Friday afternoon they got off early and made it out ahead of the weekend traffic, grinding north in the early spring weather. That evening they were in Washington.

Harding had been there before. Shelby had been there several times but Morrison never had, and the others took him in hand and did the monuments, the National Gallery, the Smithsonian.

Morrison was more impressed than he had expected to be, and Harding too felt in spite of himself the presence of the place, the historicity, the factualness of what had happened and was happening there. He was at the heart of the matter, the whole vast machine-and-amoeba, and his desire to place himself in context failed abysmally. He was in it, of it, and against it.

Yet he wanted to feel that, if nothing had been learned, if there was indeed no way to mitigate what he had participated in, then at least it was a forgivable error, a human failing, one that had perhaps been inevitably and repeatedly made, would doubtless be made as many times as there were opportunities for men to err so grotesquely. He had wanted to be exceptional; he longed now to be ordinary. In that, he felt, lay his peace of mind.

He believed this because, though for sure the war would end, though the controversy and the relevance would fade, yet for some few, and himself among them, the war would last on and on throughout their lives: they would measure out their lives in terms of values stated, accepted, lived up to, or falsified, betrayed, rationalized, compromised, at this particular brief stage of their youth. What held true at this time, or in his case, Harding felt, what might be salvaged, was the raw material of the future of some portion of America. Now was their Depression and their Second World War. America would stand or fall, not now, but twenty and thirty and forty years from now, on what was decided, accepted here and now, as the new decade pushed off from the corpse of disaster toward some vague hope.

They were all, he felt, comrades in arms against the darkness, the void, the black spaces between the stars. He and all the others would either wreak some small wisdom out of the chaos of these years, the ruined decade that had begun with so much promise—or they would not.

They drove along a sunken road behind a stone wall and Harding pulled off at a two-story brick house with a parking lot, the museum. There were a few tourists, and as Harding got out of the car he was aware of a vast silence.

"It's very peaceful," said Morrison, hesitating in the parking lot to look at the house, the stone fence by the sunken road, the hill to their right.

"Yes." Shelby looked around, renewing his acquaintance with it. "It's as if the place itself knew what happened here."

"What *did* happen here?" Morrison asked him.

They moved toward the museum and Harding thought, *How strange.* To come so far to be away from questions of great gravity —he was thinking, again, of Murphy—only to find oneself here, where questions hung eternally in the air.

3. Coming out of the museum later, Harding looked ahead to where the low stone wall paralleled the sunken road at the base of Marye's Heights. A hundred-odd years ago men had thrown themselves at that wall and died. He recalled the words written in the front of the guidebook he had bought. Captain Oliver Wendell Holmes, 20th Massachusetts Volunteers, later Chief Justice of the U.S. Supreme Court, had said (Harding looked it up again):

> In the midst of doubt, in the collapse of creeds, there is one thing I do not doubt and that is that the faith is true and adorable which leads a soldier to throw away his life in obedience to a blind accepted duty, in a cause which he little understands, in a plan of campaign of which he has no notion, under tactics of which he does not see the use.

Yes, thought Harding. *And Sail on, O Ship of State*— or was that someone else? *Ask me about it,* thought Harding. *Ask my friends. Ask a marine. True and adorable.*

The wall had been destroyed and later rebuilt. The sunken road was now a paved street, and just across it they climbed the steep side of the hill, terraced with rows of graves, and, coming over the top, were faced with the cemetery, row upon row of small square stones and larger monuments, back across the wooded hill as far as Harding could see. He stopped, his throat catching as Shelby moved ahead.

"Of course," Shelby was saying, "these were not all killed in the Fredericksburg battle. The dead from Chancellorsville, the Wilderness and Spotsylvania Court House are buried here too. In the four battles, there were over a hundred thousand casualties. This cemetery covers a large area."

"So I see," said Morrison.

And turning, Harding looked down the hill that fell sharply away, past the museum and across a plain now grown over with trees, running perhaps a half mile to the river, the Rappahannock.

"The trick was to move fast." Shelby walked along until he came to a cannon a few feet back from where the hill dropped away toward the invisible river. He folded his arms and leaned against the wooden wheel.

"December, 1862. Robert E. Lee had no intention of making a stand at Fredericksburg; he would have preferred to do it farther south. When the Union commander, General Burnside, got his army here to take the city on the way to Richmond, the Confederates had only a small force at the town. But Burnside was afraid to force a crossing. He was waiting for pontoon bridges to come down from Washington. They were late, and by the time they arrived General Longstreet was here, and Burnside was still too timid to cross. He had an army of a hundred and thirty thousand, against Longstreet's thirty-five thousand. But he waited too long. Lee and Jackson arrived and made this hill impregnable. Even the men in the ranks could see it. If Burnside had attacked as soon as he got here, he could have taken the city, kept Lee's forces divided and possibly moved to Richmond. Instead, he waited three weeks, and that made the difference."

Harding looked at the stone markers that seemed to go on forever, across the hill, through the gently rolling wooded land. He tried to imagine what it must have felt like. The Confederates would have been determined, confident; they had every reason to be. They were well fortified, covered by artillery, their infantry had a hill and three hundred cannon at their backs, a stone wall and a sunken road for cover, and a half mile of open plain between themselves and the enemy. Few armies ever went into battle with so much in their favor.

The Union troops, then, he thought. What must it have been like to know your commander to be an incompetent, to look across that open space, at that hill, that wall—and for what?

The faith is true and adorable.

What faith? he wondered. Faith in what?

He knew what he would have felt. He would have felt like escaping.

He thought he might have identified with them. Perhaps all of them, himself and Murphy and Green, for all their differences, could have understood any of those soldiers who, true and adorable faith be damned, must have known the great machine was about to grind them down. But too late; they must have looked across that empty plain and cursed the slogans that had brought them there. He would have, Harding knew.

And yet . . .

Part of the reason he had come into the Marine Corps was that he did not totally disbelieve in the institution. He had not wanted to come into the service at all, particularly during this war, this Cause which seemed even more ambiguous than that other Cause, which had laid these young men down. He at times pictured himself in the guise of other soldiers-in-the-ranks in other questionable conflicts, dark companions unsure of their moral ground. He was an Englishman in the American revolution, or in India or Africa. He was a Frenchman in Algeria—or, indeed, in his very own Indo-China, two decades back. Was he also, he wondered, a German in Poland or Belgium? A Russian in Hungary or Czechoslovakia?

He had suspected that military experience could prove valuable to a man—Shelby's song—particularly in retrospect, and that as such, as raw experience largely devoid of responsibility except on the most minimal level, it might be considered morally neutral at worst—or, as he now believed, at best. He had set out, after deciding against the few and radical alternatives, to make as worthwhile as he could what seemed at any rate inevitable, and he had acted on that premise as long as possible, and after it became impossible, he had not been sure exactly where he had gone wrong.

But he thought of Webster, of Murphy and Green and Lieutenant Whitcomb, and it was only too obvious in retrospect that he had gone wrong.

So much, he thought, for the value of hindsight.

Shelby and Morrison had walked forward to the edge, where the hill dropped sharply, and were looking toward the faraway river. Harding, drawn by the inevitability of the tragedy, came up as Shelby pointed.

"You can see where Sumner's division started from. They had the unenviable assignment of pushing through the city and taking the hill. Actually the battle began farther downstream. On the morning of December thirteenth, General Meade's Pennsylvania Division lead the attack on General Hill's division of Stonewall Jackson's corps, near Hamilton Crossing. Hill's men were dug in behind a railroad embankment. It was there, while the Federal troops were swinging into battle formations with their flags and bugles and drums, that Robert E. Lee, watching from a hill that was later named for him, made his famous remark."

" 'It is well that war is so terrible,' " said Harding. " 'We should grow too fond of it.' "

"Yes," answered Shelby. "And then Lee's artillery hit them, and I suppose it wasn't pretty anymore."

"Still," said Morrison. "They almost made it."

Shelby nodded. "The closest the Federals came to winning was at the outset. Meade hit a weak point in Hill's defenses and broke the Confederate line. But he couldn't hold; Jackson threw in reinforcements and the Federals were confused in the smoke. They fell back, and that was as close as they ever came."

"And here it was worse," said Harding.

"Here it was worse. Sumner's forces moved through the town and were hit by Lee's artillery as they formed for the attack. They moved off across that plain there, coming right at us. There was a drainage ditch that broke their alignment. Burnside refused to admit its existence. The artillery slaughtered them, and what was left when they came under the range of the guns had to face the infantry at the wall.

"So they kept falling back and regrouping under fire, attacking again. Burnside threw wave after wave into the field, division after division. One officer broke down and cried. 'Oh, God, see how our boys are falling.' There was a great deal of heroism. Many of the officers from the reserve volunteered to go out and help, but there wasn't any help—there never had been. Not a single man so much as reached the stone wall.

"It lasted all day. Some of the wounded froze to death that night. The next day Burnside wanted to try again. He would lead an attack himself. But his officers talked him out of it. Then again he didn't know what to do; he waited still another day and finally withdrew during a violent rainstorm, back across the river to the camp at Stafford Heights. They stayed there for weeks, and finally moved back through the rain and mud to Washington, humiliated, their morale gone. Burnside was relieved of command. The Army of the Potomac was finished for the winter."

"What were the losses that day?" said Morrison.

"Over twelve thousand for the Federals. About five thousand Confederates."

"For nothing," said Harding quietly. "Really—for nothing at all."

"For nothing," Shelby agreed.

Harding walked away, looking at the small stone markers that ran all the way up to the crest of the hill. Shelby followed. As they walked along, Harding felt tears come to his eyes. Disgusted with himself, he tried to rub them away without Shelby noticing.

"Fredericksburg," Shelby murmured. "Well, America has had its Fredericksburg now. She has gone where England had to go, where France had to go."

"All those guys," said Harding. "On both sides, all those good guys . . ." He shook his head, looking at the stones. "I don't like these places."

"Cemeteries?"

Harding shrugged. "Cemeteries, yes, especially places like this, monuments to insanity."

"The monuments aren't for the strategists. They're for the ordinary guys."

"But they were insane too," said Harding. "Or they wouldn't be here, dead."

"They'd just be somewhere else, dead."

Harding ignored this, and said, "They ought to have turned them back into the soil and tried to forget where it was. Or planted trees over it. I don't feel proud or uplifted at these places. I just feel sad."

"That's because you're still in the military. After you've been out awhile and had time to stop hating the Marine Corps, it won't be so much like that."

"I have nothing against the Marine Corps," said Harding, "except that it was so reluctant to let go of me."

"I think you hold more against it than that."

Harding sighed. "You're right. I do. What happened to Webster—and to Green and Murphy—to all of us. It was such a waste, such a waste."

"Webster should probably never have gotten in at all," said Shelby. "From what you've told me."

"And having gotten in, he should have been weeded out of boot camp, with that twenty percent who supposedly get dropped. That doesn't happen when you need a lot of bodies, when you're taking all volunteers and even using the draft. That's how you get people like Webster carrying an automatic rifle in the bush. The proud professional organization became just another military outfit."

"What is more frightening is what happened to Murphy and your friend Green. Ideal marines, four-year enlistees, plenty of motivation . . ."

Harding nodded. "I think it was the country's worst tragedy that people like Murphy fought this war. Wide-eyed, like kids playing cowboys. Murphy did it just the way he played football, hard and serious. Us against Them."

"And so cool about violence. No sense of—of outrage."

"Violence doesn't produce a sense of outrage in Americans anymore. Shelby, until you get over there, you won't be able to realize how casual we are about it, how unaffected these kids can be by their own acts against other human beings. It's pointless to talk about how violence is nurtured by everything kids grow up with now. But it's so. They get numb to it, deadened. The potential is there, and the Marine Corps simply taps it."

"Yes. Poor Audie." Shelby looked at the stones that surrounded them. "Do you think he went a little crazy?"

Harding began to think about all that had happened before Christmas, from the time he had met Madelaine in Carolina Beach until Murphy took his leave and headed south.

"Maybe at the last," he said. "But what does that mean? He was acting the way everyone acts, as he saw it. He was looking out for himself. And as for me—"

"You can't predict how people will act," said Shelby.

"No. You can't—but you should be able to help. God knows I did little enough of that."

1. "I don't know if I ever really loved him."

She could say it now, a measure of the growth of her self-awareness, a new knowledge of the practical and emotional need to face up to what had become, at best, a marginal situation, a marginal relationship.

"It was simply, I think, that I wanted to be married. It's the way I was raised, with that goal all prepackaged and hanging out there like the gold ring on a carrousel. I was getting nervous."

Harding, sitting on her bed in the little house on base, held up a black-and-white print of the weather-beaten lifeguard tower at Carolina Beach. It was shortly after Thanksgiving.

"How did you happen to pick him?" He glanced at the studio color photo in its silver frame on the night table by the bed. Young, heavyish, clear hard eyes, close-cropped hair, the garish dress blues like a part of his personality, all self-assurance, all assertion, looking out from the frame as if passing judgment on the photographer, who had not in this case been his wife.

She could almost hear Harding think: *A lifer all the way*—and so he was, hard-nosed and innocent, a killer, an American boy.

She moved a pile of photographs off the bed and put her arms around Harding, hugging him close from behind, looking over his shoulder at the tough boy in blue with the silver captain's bars.

"He was good in bed."

Harding compared two shots of the beach, empty except for a figure far away from the camera, looking out to sea in one shot and directly at the camera in the second, which needed cropping.

"You should do your own darkroom work."

"I used to, but there isn't room here. Does that bother you?" Madelaine pressed herself against his back. "That I thought he was good in bed?"

"He's your husband, isn't he?" Harding reached back and stroked her thigh. "I didn't find you in any convent, darling girl. I found you at the Pussycat."

"But doesn't that upset you? To think of him making love to me every night, and me liking it? Doesn't it make you rage inside?"

"Nope," said Harding, although it did.

She bit his ear, but he twisted her away and said, "Be good," and kept looking at the prints. He had said he wanted to see her real work, and he was scanning the prints as if he expected to find out all there was to know about her, as if they were a collage that would form, ultimately, a picture of Madelaine.

She lay back on the bed and watched him. He had a good face, strong and clear, but not like her husband's. Her husband's face—she glanced from Harding to the picture—was all-American in its blue-eyed openness. Harding's face seemed to her much older (he was actually, she knew, a year older) and already there were small lines at the corners of his eyes as if he had seen too much of something and his eyes had broken a little from the sight.

"You know what you should do?" He stacked the prints and put them in the box she used. "You ought to go over to Chapel Hill and get involved again in what you like. You should quit this crazy job and go meet some people with a taste for what you do in these." He indicated the box and set it on the table, moving aside the picture of her husband. "Actually, you ought to be out of this state. But at least this part of the state. Go someplace worthwhile."

"I tried it once," she said. "And you see, there is the husband."

"Get rid of him. You can't love him much. You're young, there's plenty of time for you, and plenty of options. Use them. Otherwise you'll end up a company grade officer's wife going to Happy Hours at the club. You won't be content with that life."

"You don't know what you're saying." She pulled him down beside her, breathless at his audacity in telling her what she knew, had known since she grew away from her husband. But it was one thing to know it and an entirely different thing to be told, especially to be told by him. It filled her with a sense of the possible. *Plenty of time, plenty of options...* She wondered if Harding was one of the options.

He had paced back and forth in the small living room, complimenting her ability to offset the green walls and furniture from the base warehouse with art prints and wall hangings. He had shuffled through her record collection and discovered that she had taste in music. He had looked out the windows in every part of the house, all of which gave onto identical green or white houses full of identical used furniture.

"We used to live on the beach. I gave up the place."

"You should have given up *this* place," he said, and took her to a movie at Midway Park.

So that lying with him now, when they had undressed and gone to bed, the room a filled container of blackness, the two of them gone to touch and smell and taste, herself falling with him and falling for him too, and knowing it, and afraid of it—he seemed like the voice of reason. He was telling her, told her every minute by his presence, of her life.

They made love and she gave up thinking and countered his strength with her giving, running her fingers lightly through his hair and through the sad rough hollow of his ruined shoulder. She was happy with the darkness and the warm strong feel of him.

When he had broken himself on her she held him and finally moved away, gliding naked to the kitchen, returning to the sound of his breathing with an orange and a package of cigarettes. She lit one and, taking it deeply, passed it to his lips.

"Have some death." It was his phrase, and she smoked only after having him and it had become a ritual of love and death, no mere habit.

"Hey," she said. "What I want to know is—"

"What you want to know is." He made the cigarette glow.

"What I want to know is, why did that boy shoot you?"

He made the cigarette glow. "Give me a slice of your orange."

She put it in his mouth. He finished it and made the cigarette glow and she took it away from him and inhaled deeply. She said. "Why did that boy shoot you, Robert?"

"I'm sure of one thing. He didn't like me much."

"But didn't you ever stop and really try to figure it out?"

"No," he said. "Oh, gee, no, I never thought to stop and really try to figure it out. Hey, maybe I ought to do that, huh?"

"All right," she said. "I'm sorry." She reached out and touched him inadvertently on the wound.

"You think you're sorry," said Harding, taking the cigarette, making it glow. "But you aren't sorry the way I'm sorry."

"Do you think it was an accident?" she said.

"Jesus Christ, darling. Don't you have anything interesting to talk about? Like the weather?"

"But just think though. If he really was trying to save your life. It would be so . . . really kind of sad, kind of ironic."

"Yes, kind of," said Harding. There was a silence, and he took a deep breath and let it out. "You're forgetting the lieutenant," he said, as if he could not help getting into it. "That kid you're trying to picture as a would-be lifesaver knew I suspected him of murdering an officer."

"But you don't know that he did it."

"No, I don't know it. I only know what he said to me. I only know he hated Lieutenant Whitcomb, and the lieutenant got a grenade in his tent, and he hated me and shot me in the back."

"And your friends killed him?"

Harding drew in the smoke, and the cigarette glowed and faded and he put it out, sighing the smoke out into the room.

"They never admitted it, but I'm pretty sure they did. Probably Murphy. Green was too much a professional to do something like that. Murphy hated Webster as much as I did. When Webster shot me, Murphy got even."

"What a strange thing," said Madelaine. "All of you wearing the same uniform, and shooting each other and blowing each other up. My husband said it happens more than a little, and I didn't believe him."

"It happens, all right."

Harding touched his fingers to her hair, and she moved over to kiss him. She wondered what was the point of all of it, the draft and the training and the propaganda, all these young men sent there to accomplish nothing but their own deaths, perhaps at the hands of their fellows. It did not seem very professional to her, nor very honorable.

2. Later she dressed for work. Harding watched her, feeling drained, ready to sleep or drink to excess, turn off his battered consciousness and his body. He had never been able to justify to himself taking another man's wife—not, as in the case of Donna, unknowingly but in full view of the possible consequences. He had told Donna that he did not go looking for wives, and it was the truth. Yet here he was, slipping deeper into a situation he already did not want to stop. He had, it sometimes seemed to him, an infinite capacity for rationalization, for adaptation. In the past two years it seemed as if everything had gone by the board; he was starting over from the ground up, building a new Robert Harding out of pieces he was not sure he liked.

He watched Madelaine as she dressed with quick efficiency, becoming again the self-assured scourge of the Strip, capable of separating some dozens of boys painlessly from their money, trading them a token of romance—and it was such a lie, he thought—for hard cash.

It struck him—he had not considered it since becoming her lover —that she was as much a purveyor of sex without feeling, the empty image of passion and love, as any of the dancers in the clubs, only a little less tarnished than the whores themselves, who did exactly the same thing with natural equipment. A dull distaste rose in him and he sat up against the headboard and lit a cigarette, watching her sure movements.

"I want to ask you something," he said in a voice that made her turn and look at him. "Do you think we should be doing what we're doing?"

"You mean—because of him?" She glanced at the picture on the night table.

Harding nodded.

"Well, I don't know," she said, pursing her lips. "Probably not. Do you want to stop?"

He shook his head.

"Neither do I. We'll have to think about it sometime, and probably make some decisions. But not yet. Not for a little while yet. Now"—she turned back to the mirror—"I have to get ready to go."

"Madelaine."

She turned to him again. He looked at his cigarette and said, knowing better, "Doesn't it ever bother you, using all those kids, taking their money? I mean—"

"Oh, come on," she said. "I don't exactly 'use' them, do I?" But he didn't look at her, and she said, "Hey . . ." and he still did not look at her, thinking, *You'd better say something*—and she cried, "Oh, *fuck you, Robert Harding!*"

They looked at each other and she turned and began to make up her face.

"Sorry," he said then, too late. "I just . . . Well, I mean I was thinking about it."

"I'm going to throw something at you if you say any more." She began to cry.

He got out of bed and went to her, feeling ridiculous in his skin, despising himself for his stupidity.

"Hey." He knelt beside her, but she would not look at him. "Hey, do you know I love you?"

"Shut up." She pulled Kleenex out of a box and dabbed at her eyes. She blew her nose.

"I'm an idiot," he said. "And I didn't even mean it. It was just something I said without thinking about it."

"I don't want to talk," she said. "I have to go to work."

"I'll drive you," he said, stroking her hair.

She shook his hand away and said, "I will drive my goddamn *self.*"

She dried her eyes and did her face, and he put his clothes on, thinking, *Congratulations, goat. Harding is the goat.*

When she was ready to go she got her coat and her camera. She would not let him help with the coat. She put a fresh magazine in the Polaroid, slung her photo case from her shoulder and turned out the lights. Outside, she walked directly to her car.

"If you should accidentally find yourself in the Pussycat, just pretend you don't know me."

"Hey, look," he said, but she slammed her door and started the car, sitting patiently with her eyes straight ahead until he moved his car out of her way. She spun gravel and was gone without a backward glance.

Harding sat for a while with his engine running. He slammed his hand down on the seat.

"God *damn* it!"

He put the car in gear and threw speed shifts like a frustrated teenager all the way out Lejeune Boulevard, past the used-car lots and hamburger stands on one side, the deep black woods of the base on the other. The drive-in theater was showing four motorcycle films. Cars stretched back a quarter mile in the right lane, full of eighteen- and twenty-year-old Peter Fondas with gasoline and motor oil in their rebellious young born-to-be-wild never-gonna-die American blood. Harding sneered and called "Fuck you all! You goddamn babies!" crashing by in his hot used Volkswagen at ten miles over the speed limit.

He came up behind a Jacksonville cop and stomped down to thirty-five, cruising sedately into Sin Town to lose himself in drink.

He went to the USO and made a quick tour, checking the TV rooms, the record rooms, the main lobby with its rock music that was so loud he could hardly hear himself swear, noticing there were a few crazies for whom the noise was never loud enough. They wore headphones to hear it better. *I hope you all go deaf,* he thought. Somebody was screaming a song called "Run Through the Jungle."

Harding checked the pool tables, the Ping-Pong tables, and found no one he knew. He paid a dollar and three cents for a chili dog and a Coke, and sat down at a table with one of the logbooks in which lonely marines scribbled their thoughts, such as they were. The local censor, who kept a close watch on the contents, had already been there. Harding began to leaf through the pages.

Oct. 7 [somebody had written in ball point ink]. *I hate this ▆▆▆ hole.*

Oct. 7 [someone had added]. *Me ▆▆▆ too.*

Harding smiled a little and ate his chili dog, turning the pages and wishing he had beaten the censor.

Oct. 9. Just arrived back from "The Nam." God bless Our American Soil and American Girls. Amen.

October 12. Hi Mom, Hi Dad, Hi Jim, Hi Stevie. I know you all can't see this, but in 24 days you will all be seeing Yours Truly In Person. 24 AND A WAKEUP!!

Oct. 15—I been in this ▆▆▆ town for six months. I come in the U.S.M.C. to fight for freedom, and all I can do is sit around Montford Point and Mainside learning to be a cook. I will never get to the Nam. I don't want to be a cook. I come in the Corpse to kill Charlies, not to cook and spend my time in the mess hall. I have got three years and six months left in the U.S.M.C. I DON'T WANT TO SPEND ALL MY TIME AS A COOK AT CAMP LEJEUNE! *I will never re-up at this rate.*

Signed——

But he had apparently thought better of it and left the signature off.

Oct. 21. I just want to say that I got my orders today. I go to Pendleton tomorrow morning for staging, and then WesPac. I was supposed to be a supply clerk but somebody ▆▆▆ me over good and I'm now an 0311 grunt. *I don't want to go over, especially not as a grunt. I hope all of you who read this will remember that I didn't want to go. But I guess it is my duty, and lots of other guys have done it before me. But I have a bad feeling about it.*

A group of Californians was singing, "I wish they all could be California girls . . ."

Harding finished his hot dog and skimmed through the pages, killing time. He focused on the past month.

Oct. 28. Good luck to all the guys of B.L.T. 11, leaving from Morehead City next Tuesday, bound for the Med. I wish I was going, guys. Wm. Hackett, L/Cpl.

Nov. 26—I am just drunk enough to know I made a bad mistake coming in the ▮▮▮▮ *Crotch. I would be in Kansas City right now if I hadn't of been such a dope. I been* ▮▮▮▮ *over already so much it's not funny, and I only been in eight months. I still got sixteen to go. I hope I can last.*

R. J. Thompson, PFC

Nov. 1. Last Wednesday one of my best friends died in a landing accident at Onslow Beach. I was with him. We were riding in on an amtrac and the driver lost it for a minute and we got swamped. My friend went over and nobody knew it till we were almost on the beach. I don't know whose fault it was or even if it was anybody's fault. I'm afraid he might have just jumped. Nobody will ever know. This is dedicated to the Memory of Eddie Green of Waco, Texas, CPL, A Co. 1st. Bn. 5th Marines, 2nd MarDiv. He was the best Marine I ever knew.

Signed, Murphy, T. D.
Cpl. USMC (A Co. 1/5, 2nd MarDiv.)

Harding read the entry over several times.
Somebody was singing, "No time left for you. . ."
He turned to the last entry:

Nov. 25: Tomorrow I head up to New Bern and take a good old Piedmont flight to D.C., then Delta to Defiance, Ohio. I want to wish everybody in the Marine Corps—especially the guys at Courthouse Bay—Happy Thanksgiving, Merry Christmas, and a Happy New Year. I hope all of you are as short as I am.

Signed: Ex-Cpl. John Ellison, USMCR
H&S Co. Supply Bn. 2nd FSR Force Troops

Harding closed the log, finished his Coke, watching marines come and go in the lounge. "Dream, dream, dream," sang the music, with the big red letters USO glowing in the window.

3. He walked into Shelby, Morrison and Murphy in the Hideaway.

"Harding!" they cried, well into their evening already—and, feeling sorry for himself, drinking beer to forget his sorrow, Harding surrendered to an old-fashioned bender.

The Hideaway had installed a new pinball machine, and Morrison, an expert, rabid pinball player, took on all of them and did not lose a game. Shelby finally sent him to the bar for pistachios so he could challenge Harding. Harding beat him and then beat Murphy, who tended to grow surly when the machine would not perform for him. Harding took on Morrison and lost again, and sat in the booth listening to Perry Como sing "It's Impossible" while Morrison kept the machine going on one quarter. Already three or four awed marines stood around him, watching to see how long he could make the machine award him extra games.

Harding wondered if it still was fun when you got to Morrison's level of competence. He seemed to be neither working nor playing. He looked like an IBM technician checking out a computer, with no stake in the performance, no real interest in the print-out. Only the audience cared.

Morrison finally shot off a ball while sipping his beer, removing his left hand from the paddle. The ball immediately scratched without making a point. Morrison yawned and sat down, not even checking his score.

"Gets to be a drag after a while. Standing up that long."

Harding started an argument with Shelby about who was the best leader of cavalry in the Civil War. He contended that Jeb Stuart was overrated—possibly true—and, further, that Phil Sheridan was a more effective cavalryman than Nathan Bedford Forrest. Harding knew this to be untrue, but it got Shelby off on a long and detailed comparison of Stuart, Sheridan, Forrest, John Hunt Morgan, Andrew Smith and Samuel D. Sturgis. He drew battle plans on a napkin while Morrison and Murphy—and Harding—watched, fascinated.

It reminded Harding of a night during staging when he and Green and Murphy had run into an old drunk in Los Angeles and bought him a beer. The man asked them where they had served and they said they were just going over. He had then claimed to be a retired sergeant major who had fought in the Pacific, and to their amazement proceeded to diagram the battle of Guadalcanal on a napkin with a ballpoint pen. Green and Murphy in particular sat dumbfounded as he told them of the Matanikau River fighting, and they had taken turns buying him Scotch.

In the beery comfort of Shelby's lecture, the warm atmosphere of the Hideaway with Morrison a celebrity and a friendly waitress, Harding cheered up. He forgot that Madelaine was angry with him, forgot that his shoulder ached, that he hated the service. He forgot that Green was dead and that he wanted to ask Murphy something. He let himself glide in the collective letting-go of a townful of lonesome children, most of them in training to head west, or to the Med or the Caribbean. When the town closed down at eleven-thirty and they stood outside in the cold pre-Christmas night, he even liked the garish lights of Jacksonville. They were like Christmas lights, wishing everyone well.

"Beautiful, isn't it?" he said to Murphy as they walked to Morrison's car to deliver Harding back to the USO parking lot.

"It's a fucking dump," said Murphy.

"Oh." Harding looked at him carefully. "You going to Cherry's tonight?"

"I don't know." Murphy hunched his shoulders, hands in pockets. "She doesn't like me when I'm drunk. I shouldn't of drunk so much. Do I act like I'm drunk? Do you think I'm drunk?"

"No," said Harding. "Of course not. You're not drunk."

"I wish I hadn't of drunk so much. She doesn't like me when I'm —and that slut bitch roommate of hers doesn't like me *any*time."

"Hey," said Harding.

"Goddamn bitch whore. Goddamn dyke."

"Hey, why don't you go see your wife this weekend?" Harding put an arm around Murphy's shoulders. "When was the last time you saw your wife, Audie?"

"Don't even mention *her*. I'm not in any mood to think about her."

"Yeah, but why don't you go see her, Audie? I mean she's your wife."

"Stop it, man. Stop it, God damn it. You'll mess up my whole evening."

"Audie, does Cherry know about your wife?" The subject suddenly seemed very important to Harding.

"No!" Murphy shook his head violently. "Just shut up about her. She wouldn't be any good this weekend anyway. She's sick or something."

"Sick?"

Murphy nodded. "That's what she *says*. She's got the flu or something. I did call her, I *called* her. And she said she—didn't want to see me this weekend." Murphy stopped and coughed, wiping his nose and face and eyes with his handkerchief. "I been calling her," he said.

"Hey. Man, maybe you ought to go anyway, maybe she just said that. I mean," Harding added, "to see if you'd come. Or maybe she is sick, and you ought to go anyway."

"Fuck it." Murphy almost ran into Morrison, who was unlocking the car. "She's lying, she's screwing somebody. I *know* it man. . . . Hey, Harding, are you going home for Christmas? Are you taking Christmas leave?"

"No." Harding pushed him into the front seat and got in and closed the door. "I'm too short. I'll take the money instead when I get out. If I ever do get out."

"I'm going to Atlanta," said Murphy. Morrison started the car and pulled out past the bus station and the long line of marines waiting in the cold for buses to take them back.

"I'm taking Christmas leave," said Murphy. "I'm going to Atlanta then."

"Good." Harding looked out the window. "Hey, it's snowing. Merry Christmas, marines!"

"I'm going to take Christmas leave and go see her and . . . see if we can't . . . you know, sort of . . . get back, like. I'm going to see just what the score with her is."

"Good," said Harding.

"Merry Christmas," said Shelby in the back seat. "Merry Christmas."

"But I don't know," said Murphy. "If it's what I think—if it's what I think it is . . ."

"Good," said Harding. "Merry Christmas, you-all."

"I'm going to kill her."

1. The next evening, Harding drove out the back gate to the trailer park, and he and Murphy went to Sneads Ferry for a seafood dinner.

It was Friday. Shelby was on duty—his own, this time—and Morrison had gone to Kinston with another friend. Secretly, Harding was glad. He had not been able to get away with Murphy in a while and now was the last chance before Christmas. He had felt the friendship slipping, despite Green's death, which should have pushed them together. Their lives had changed since the night they had sat in the rain near Da Nang, sharing their coffee. He sometimes felt out of place with Murphy now. He spent his weekends with Madelaine, and on nights he could not see her he stayed in the barracks or went to the base library.

Murphy was never comfortable without the radio, so they moved in a nimbus of black rock and crying country singers. The snow had not stuck, but the countryside was closing itself up until spring. In the headlight beams a rabbit darted out of the road, and once they saw deer grazing brown grass near the trees. It was cold: the heater was on, purring drowsily.

"Heard anything from your congressman?" Murphy turned the radio down as the lights of Sneads Ferry approached out of the wilderness and Harding watched for the turn to the restaurant they had chosen.

It is always the same, he thought, slowing down, watching. The same questions, the same conversation now. Not like before. *How's your wife? How's the shoulder? How's Madelaine? How's Cherry? How's the trailer? How's the barracks? Have you heard from your—*

"Not a word."

"Jesus. Hey, do you really think this guy's going to get you out at all? I mean with a medical? It looks like they're just going to fuck you over until your time is up."

"I don't know, Audie." He made the turn, accelerated around a curve. "There's not a hell of a lot left I can do except request mast all the way up. By the time I got past the colonel I'd be out anyway."

"The colonel might give you the discharge, though."

"Well, they know I've put in for it. They know about the letter to my senator. The CO tells me he's waiting for word from CMC. Actually it's kind of funny to see how long they take. It doesn't even seem to matter so much anymore."

They rounded another curve, and the restaurant loomed at the edge of the New River Inlet, bright-lighted on wood pilings, with boat docks and bait shops, a store, a service station. When they parked and got out, crossing the street, blown with sand though the air was still, a stray dog barked at them. There was a faint smell of fish in the air, as if something from the sea had been left out on the beach too long. Harding kicked up sand and felt his shoes sink into it. He started toward the steps and noticed something in the beam from one of the spotlights toward the rear of the restaurant, where the boats were.

"Hey, look."

Murphy followed him around the side of the restaurant. They found a dead shark, perhaps three feet long.

"Wow. What's it doing in the inlet?"

"They might have got it farther out." Harding nudged the shark with his foot. The smell was fairly sharp but not totally unpleasant in the cold air.

"Those mothers I can do without."

"Yeah," said Harding. "I guess so."

They went back around and up the wooden steps with whitewash peeling off the rail, six steps up and a glimpse of the inlet running straight out to sea.

There were a number of people in the restaurant, local families taking advantage of the Friday-night seafood special, and the place was so plain, so small and local and informal, that Harding felt he was in the real world, or one part of it, and quickly reneged on what he had told Murphy: it did matter, and *God,* he thought, sitting down and listening to the sounds of the place, *I've got to get free.*

They ordered and drank a quick beer while their dinners cooked, Murphy eyeing the place and seeming to catch a little of Harding's mood.

"We ought to bring the girls out here sometime."

"That's not a bad idea."

"How are you and Madelaine doing?"

"Okay," said Harding. "I called her up and we made peace. On the whole, we're probably getting along too well."

"I know. So are Cherry and me." Murphy drew a wet ring on the table with his finger. "The marriage bit is a drag, isn't it?"

Harding, not sure what he meant by that, nodded.

"Are you serious about her?" said Murphy.

"Oh, I don't think so. I don't know. I doubt it." He was not sure he felt like talking about it at all. He did not know how he felt about Madelaine, only that it was different from the way he was trying to sound.

"You're lucky, then." Murphy drew another, concentric ring. "It's an awful lot easier that way."

Harding saw their dinners coming. He finished his beer and they ordered another as the platters of shrimp and perch and clams and scallops and crabmeat steamed in front of them.

"The thing is," said Murphy, "Cherry doesn't even know about my wife. I mean it might matter to her."

"It might matter to both of them."

"But I don't care. I'm crazy about her. I really am." He said it almost sullenly, to his fish, not looking at Harding. "Did you ever feel like you were really"—he looked up at Harding, and it was the old look—"really in some kind of a bind? Did you ever feel like you were screwed no matter what you did?"

Why, no, thought Harding. *Gee, I never did.*

He nodded. "Yeah. Yeah." He thought, *God damn it, Audie,* and he said, "So you went and got hung on her, did you?"

Murphy shrugged. "Oh, I know. How can anybody get hung on a dumb Jacksonville dancer? How can it ever get beyond a turn-on? But it's more than that." Murphy looked at him as if trying to communicate with the look instead of having to articulate what he meant. "It just is. We're good together."

"Well, then," said Harding, and he thought, *All right, then, say it.* "So what about your wife?"

Murphy made a face, shook his head and finished his meal while Harding sipped beer and listened to the jukebox.

"I've been fucked over by women all my whole life," Murphy said at last. "If there had never been any women in my life, I'd probably be happy."

"Sure, you would."

"Okay. That's okay for you, you can say that. You've been hanging loose, going to school and not getting hung on anybody. You're a goddamn survivor type. I got fucking *married* is what *I* did. When you've been hassled like I been hassled, then you'll know what I'm talking about."

"I don't think you know yourself what you're talking about. It seems to me you and the ladies have come out just about even up to now."

"Oh, yeah? What about my wife?"

Harding sighed. "Audie, they have arrangements in the service for people like you. It's called married housing. You don't have to be at Camp Lejeune and have your wife living in Atlanta. Christ, you've got two and a half years to go yet! What are you going to do, send her cards on the holidays?"

"She won't do it," said Murphy. "She doesn't want to live on a military base."

"Then put her up in town. Live off base."

"It sounds so simple to you, doesn't it? If she wanted to be here with me, she'd be here. I'm not going to go crawling back there and ask her to come up here and be part of my life again. She's got her own life going. Her and me—she and I—we're two different people now than we were when we got married. I've been trying to hold on to her, but I don't know if it can work anymore. She won't write to me. She doesn't *want* to see me. I wanted to go see her this weekend; she tells me not to come, she's sick, she's got the flu—"

"She probably does have the flu. I'll bet she hasn't got anyone else. I'll bet she really loves you and you're selling her short."

Murphy looked at him for a moment. "I suppose Madelaine's husband is selling her short too."

"As a matter of fact," said Harding, "as a matter of fact, he is, yes, he damn well is."

"And she's playing games with you while he's in the Med."

Harding shook his head. "It's not the same thing at all, and besides, what I'm saying is it's *his* fault."

"I know what you're saying, all right."

"Well, then . . ."

"My wife hates the military. Because of her brother. He was in an Army outfit near Saigon that got hit by our own planes. It was an accident. I don't know why she married me, because I told her I wanted to join the Marine Corps. And when the time came, she tried to stop me, said it might be the end of us. She wanted me to live by *her* rules—and I don't do that, friend, I've never done that, let some jade tell me how it was going to be. The reason she hassles me is because I didn't stay home and spend one hundred percent of my time making her feel good. She thought she was marrying a football player, and what she got was a marine. And she just wouldn't take that serious. It's hard, to not be taken serious by somebody—"

"Okay," said Harding, but Murphy wasn't finished.

"Cherry is a lot like her, a lot like the way she was at first. Cherry wants to make *me* feel good. She doesn't worry about the Marine Corps or try to run my life for me. And that's how I like it. Anything could happen.... It's her fault," finished Murphy helplessly. "It's her fault, man. Her fault."

"Okay."

"Let's drop it. I don't even want to talk about it anymore."

"*Okay.*" Harding finished his beer and started looking for the waitress. "There's something else I've been wanting to ask you about anyway. I was over in the USO last night and I was reading through the logbook—"

"Why?"

"Why? What do you mean, 'why'? Because I didn't have anything better to do, and Madelaine was mad at me and I didn't know you were partying at the Hideaway. All right?"

"Yeah," said Murphy. "I just wondered."

"So I came across that entry you made."

"About Green."

"Right."

"Well, I had to do something. Didn't I? Hell, I walked all over the damn beach trying to find him."

"Yes, Madelaine told me about seeing you."

"So I couldn't find him, he was gone, gone. Like, I didn't have a buddy anymore, you know? Old Green ... and I had to do *something*, you know?"

Harding nodded. "Yes. So I want to ask you."

Murphy was looking at his beer.

"What makes you think Green killed himself?"

Murphy's head came up and they looked at each other as somebody sang about his motorcar. Harding recognized the singer and the song he had heard in Carolina Beach, the night before he had found Madelaine.

Murphy said in a quiet, almost pleading voice, "You don't think he did, do you, Harding? Green wouldn't do anything like that. Would he?"

"Wait a minute." Harding leaned forward, searching Murphy's

face, and Murphy looked down at his hands. "You're the one who said it, not me. I would never have thought he'd do anything like that, no."

Murphy looked up hopefully. "That's what I mean. He wouldn't ever do that. He wasn't that kind of a guy."

"But you wrote that you thought maybe—that you were afraid he did."

"Oh, I don't know. I was pretty messed up."

"Yes, but Audie—" Harding reached across and put a hand on Murphy's arm. "What I want to know is why you thought he might have."

"Oh, the hell with it. He *didn't,* so let's just—" Murphy shook his head once as if to clear it. "Hey, let's get out of here, Harding." He grabbed hs jacket.

"Don't you want to have another beer?"

"No. Hey, get the check, okay?" Murphy tossed a five-dollar bill on the table and got up, shrugging into his jacket as he went out the door.

Harding left a tip and took the checks to the cashier. She asked him if everything had been all right.

"Great," he said. He smiled at her and went outside. A breeze had picked up and was blowing sand across the road.

2. Murphy was not at the car, and the same dog that had barked at them before nosed at Harding's heels as he walked back toward the restaurant. He went around the side and walked out toward the boats lined up in the shadows by the dock. He could no longer smell the shark because of the wind.

Murphy was standing on the dock, looking over the side where a wooden piling drove down out of the shadows into the shallow water lighted by a spotlight from the restaurant. Harding followed his footprints through the blowing sand and walked out a few feet on the dock to stand beside him.

"What's happening, Audie?"

Murphy leaned against the rail in the deeper darkness at the edge of the spotlight beam.

"I don't know what's happening. A little while ago I was playing football in Galveston. Now I don't know what the hell is coming off. I thought I wanted to be a marine, a professional. A lifer."

"Well, there are worse lives." He remembered Shelby saying that to him. The wind died a little and picked up again in quick small gusts.

"But you don't really know. Nobody does, now. All you guys, drafted. Only Green and me—we were the only real ones. Like you talk about being a lifer sometimes when you're down. But you don't know anything about it."

"I know there's nothing wrong with it, Audie. You can get thrown into some lost causes—some bad causes, too, or no cause at all. But that can happen anyway. About the killing, I'm not so sure. For me it was a bad thing, evil. But not necessarily for you—or Green."

"I never wanted to kill anybody at all," said Murphy. "Now I don't know. I've killed so many VC, women and kids too. It doesn't upset me like it did at the very first. Toward the end it was almost sort of fun. Is that crazy?"

"I wouldn't be able to say. I do think it's sad. I think a professional should do what he has to, but not necessarily like it." Harding thought for a moment. "Do you think Green ever got to where he enjoyed killing?"

"No. I know he didn't. He wasn't afraid to do it, but he didn't like it sometimes. . . . Oh, Christ," he said quietly. "He didn't jump off that amtrac, did he, Harding? He didn't, did he? I mean if he did —what's the point? How much of a professional can you be? I mean, damn it, you can't go by every goddamn rule in the book. Sometimes you have got to *do* what has to be done. But after Webster, I don't think he ever felt clean anymore. He thought he was a bad marine."

"You mean," said Harding suddenly, "Green was the one who murdered Webster?"

Murphy looked at him quickly. "Murdered?"

"I'm sorry," said Harding. "But that's the word. That's what they call it."

"Yeah. That's what they call it." Murphy knocked his fist against the piling and looked down at the water. "Who did you think gave it to Webster?"

"Hell, Audie—I thought it was you."

"Me?" Murphy smiled and Harding looked where he was looking. A school of minnows darted back and forth around one of the pilings in the light, shining like bits of metal. "Why would I have done that?"

"Well—" Harding stopped, confused. "I always thought you did it to make up for him shooting me. Jesus Christ!" he said. "*Green* did it. Are you kidding me? You wouldn't put me on about something like that? *Green* killed Webster? But Webster *liked* Green!"

Murphy nodded. "I know it. Green knew it too. Green was the only one Webster ever tried to be friends with. Green blasted him, shot him in the back—I mean, he had it coming. I'd have done it if he hadn't. I *should* have done it; I wouldn't have lost any sleep over it. But Green did. Do you know, Harding, the day he died he was on—drugs—I think because of that. He was shooting."

"*Green?*"

"Yeah. Green. The day he went off the amtrac he was high. That's why I wonder."

"I never even saw him smoke a joint!"

"No, he always stayed away from all that stuff. He didn't want any part of it. But this was afterward, see. He said you don't do that to another marine. Fuck, Webster was no marine. Webster was a turd. But he wore the uniform and that was enough for Green. So he shoots up and swims off an amtrac. . . ."

"But why did he do it?"

Murphy looked at him. "I just told you. That's what I'm trying to—"

"No, no." Harding felt suddenly cold inside, out of balance as if some liquid at his center had leaked away like the alcohol in a cracked compass. "Why did Green kill Webster? *Why?*" He shook his head as Murphy watched him. "Not because of me? Green and I were friends, but we weren't that close, not to make him do something like that. Audie, why did he?"

Murphy sighed. "Oh, Christ, man, don't ask. Look, he was pissed at Webster for zapping you. Everybody was."

"No, though. That wouldn't have been enough. For you it would have been, but not for Green."

"Well, I would have done it. But Green did it."

"Wait. I know." Harding took a deep breath. The wind had stopped and the smell of the shark came to him. "Was it because Webster killed Lieutenant Whitcomb? He might have done it for that. He would have had a good reason to do it for that."

"Yeah," said Murphy, standing against the rail. Then he said, "No."

"What do you mean?"

"Oh, hell," said Murphy. "Oh, Christ, Harding."

Harding looked at him but could not quite make out his face.

"Look," said Murphy tiredly. "Man—Webster didn't kill the lieutenant. I killed the lieutenant."

It seemed to Harding that he had not heard it, as if it had been a sound the wind makes around boats and pilings, approximating speech.

"Oh, Audie. No, man. Hey, come on. . . ."

"I fragged the lieutenant," said Murphy. He struck the piling hard with his fist and walked away past Harding, off the dock, away from the odor of the shark and out of the lighted area of the restaurant, walking in the sand above the line of the tide.

Harding followed him and when Murphy stopped Harding came up and said again, "Hey . . ."

"He was a crazy-ass. He would have got all the rest of us killed like he did the first platoon. He caused twelve of those guys to die for nothing. Just because he was such a crazy hard-ass mother. He was no good, man. He had no goddamn business leading troops in the bush."

Harding sat down in the sand, cold but not noticing it, numb with that and the rest.

"I always thought Webster did it. He practically said so."

"No. It was me. Webster was shooting off his mouth, just like always. Green knew about it; he hated the lieutenant too. But he wouldn't have anything to do with it. He tried to stop me. It offended his sense of honor."

The wind rose again. Harding listened to the waves slap against the dock and the sides of the boats. A family came out of the restaurant, their voices and laughter blowing with the sand—and Harding could think of nothing to say, could not make himself grasp what Murphy had told him, what Murphy had done. He remembered the corpsmen laboring over the lieutenant when he was already gone, remembered too the twelve members of the first platoon, cut down when Whitcomb sent them into an ambush.

"Well, so there it is." Murphy stood looking down at Harding, who sat there with the sand blowing over his shoes.

"I don't know," said Harding. "I don't know, maybe I should have figured it. I knew you well enough. Maybe I just wanted to blame it on Webster."

"I blasted the lieutenant," Murphy said again. "Somehow or other Webster knew it was me. He was into the hard drugs and Green was trying to make him quit. Green was going to square him away, or else turn him in and get him out of our outfit—at least he said he would. I think he really believed he could make something out of that bastard."

"Not even Green could have done that."

"No, but you know how he was. For a while I even thought he might. So he kept the stuff away from him, and Webster said he'd shoot his mouth off about me. That pissed Green pretty bad, and it didn't make me love him either. I would have zapped him anyhow after that. He was as good as dead. Then when he shot you, I scratched some crosses on a whole magazine full of rounds. But Green got him first," Murphy said as if he too was amazed by the fact. "Green got him."

"God." Harding remembered what Madelaine had said to him:

What a strange thing. All of you wearing the same uniform, shooting each other and blowing each other up.

"So then," said Murphy, "he acted funny after that, even after we got back to Pendleton, and here. And one night I caught him. I caught him—doing that."

"Maybe I see why," said Harding.

"Well, *why?* He knew better than to do that. He never would have done that before, he was too smart for that, he was too— He was too *good.*"

"Not as good as he wanted to be, though."

"Listen," said Murphy. "You don't think he jumped off that amtrac, do you? You knew him. He wouldn't have done that, would he? Do you think he would have done that?"

Harding looked up and smiled. "I had everything wrong, Audie. I'd be the last one to ask what he would or wouldn't have done."

"No, but you knew him too." Murphy knelt down and took Harding's arm tightly. "He wouldn't have done that, would he? *Would* he?"

"No." Harding looked at Murphy, their faces six inches apart, both of them blinking at the sand that was blowing like dust. "No, Audie, I don't think he would ever have done that. He probably slipped when the wave hit you."

Murphy looked at him a moment longer and nodded. "That's what I think too. Right. Right. He must have—his hand must have slipped or something. And he was high. That's what must have happened." He kept nodding.

Harding felt the cold then and, forcing Murphy to let go, he stood up. "Let's get going back, Audie."

They walked, a few feet apart, back toward the restaurant and across the street to the car.

3. All the way back they were silent, only the wind outside and the low faraway gaiety of the radio inside, the noise of the heater, the soothing lights on the dash.

When they got to the trailer, Murphy sat for a minute and said, "You want to come in? Have a beer?"

"No, I think I'd better go back and crash, Audie."

Murphy nodded. "Well. It was good, in a way. I needed to ask you about—you know. I hope—I hope you're not too put out about the lieutenant."

Harding looked at him. "Put out . . ."

"I mean that it was me. I hope you're not mad at me. You're my friend, Harding. You know that, don't you?"

Harding sighed and could think of no response. He finally said, "The strangest part of all, to me, is still . . . why he shot me. Why he shot *me.*"

"Yeah. You know, we never did figure that out. Me and Green talked about it a couple of times. Then he didn't want to talk about it anymore."

"I thought maybe," Harding said with lost hope, "he might have told Green, or something."

"No." Murphy shook his head. "Green said more than once he couldn't figure it. It would have made more sense for him to shoot me. *Or* Green." He considered for a moment. "I think," he said, "Webster just looked at you and for some reason saw the enemy."

Harding almost jumped.

"He was so high he probably thought you were the VC. Or maybe he got you mixed up with one of us. Maybe," said Murphy.

"I guess."

"Well." Murphy opened the door. "If you want to come in awhile. . . ."

"No. No, thanks, Audie."

"Okay. See you then. See you, man."

Murphy closed the door and stood looking in the window at Harding. Then he turned and went into the trailer.

Harding drove around to the back gate, let the sentry wave him through and watched for deer on the way back to the central area. He did not think, did not know what to think. It all seemed too old now to matter anymore. He did not even let himself ask *Why?* But he could not help hearing Murphy's words, over and over:

Webster just looked at you—and for some reason, saw the enemy.

4

1. The following Saturday, Harding and Madelaine drove to Chapel Hill to see the University of North Carolina. As they headed west on U.S. 70 in the bright morning sunshine, Harding cheered up for the first time in a week, and he winked at Madelaine. The car ticked along like a clock, through Kinston and Goldsboro, on toward Raleigh and Durham. The land began to roll as they moved away from the coast, the pine trees giving way to more domesticated sorts, and the countryside became prettier.

He had had time enough now to know her, and to wonder what would happen when his discharge came. But he had decided nothing, for himself or for her. He was spending out his days in a spilling of time, a distraction uninvolved in day-counting or planning or making decisions.

What he had feared might happen was happening. Long before he faced Murphy on the cold beach at Sneads Ferry and learned the truth about him and Green, and something of the truth, perhaps all he would ever know of the truth, about Webster and himself—even before that he had begun to adapt once more to being where he was. As the time drained away, as encouraging words came from the doctors and from the company office, the import he had placed on being free, becoming again a civilian, was fading into the days of working, nights in Madelaine's arms, when that seemed enough to think of and marvel at.

Sometimes it still jabbed him sharply, the need to be out. But she said to him that night in Chapel Hill in the motel after walking the wide lovely campus, lunching at the student union, watching Frisbee players—she said, lying in darkness, warm against his side, "I want you to tell me something."

"You want me to tell you something. Tell you what? The population of Vancouver, British Columbia? About half a million."

"How do you know that?"

"I had occasion to check on it once."

"I thought you'd considered Montreal."

"Among other places. The city of Quebec. Sault Ste. Marie, across from northern Michigan. Moose Jaw, Saskatchewan."

She snorted. "I don't believe you. What's the population of Moose Jaw?"

"Something over thirty thousand, by my old gazetteer."

"How would I know if you were lying?"

"You should only ask questions," he said, "whose answers you are sure of."

"Maybe you're right. But tell me something . . ."

"Tell you something. Tell you what."

"Tell me—what's going to happen."

"Fire and flood," he answered. "Famine. Pestilence. Earthquakes, tidal waves. Only the pure will be saved."

"I'm serious."

"Oh," he said. "And those aren't?"

"Your discharge is going to be coming through any time now. My husband's cruise won't be back until spring."

"Yes," said Harding. "Yes to both of those."

"I just want to know. I'm not trying to make you say anything at all. I just want to know what you think."

"Yes," he said. "Yes again. Give me a cigarette."

She reached over, moving away from him as her hand searched the floor beside the bed. His side felt strange where her warmth had been.

She lit a cigarette, inhaled, and passed it over.

"Have some death."

That day, after their late lunch at the union, with the sun bright and unseasonably warm, they had heard the odd displaced wail of Scottish bagpipes, rising and falling in a reel at once pleasant and disconcerting, and they followed the strained crying notes to the campus clock tower, where, at its base, safe inside a maze of hedges too high to see over, they found a music student practicing his first love to an audience of six. And watching him, and looking up at the hands of the clock in the slender tower, listening to those highland wails in the American South, standing with another man's wife from California, he seemed so incredibly far from his own place and life, from all that he had ever had and been, and he knew more strongly than he had often known, more strongly than he had known for months at least, how far and into what bizarre, *eldritch* twists and alleys of reality a life could be drawn, and how easily; and he was aware then, in the most immanent of ways, of being alive.

Later, in a good bookstore, he looked at copies of Thomas Wolfe, saw from a poster that he had missed a reading of W. H. Auden by just two days and felt, again, a sense of displacement: as if he were, as perhaps he should have been, at home, in Michigan, on his own campus, where his life had had meaning and he had never felt the incredible tastes of violence, regimentation, where his friends had not been murderers and he had never taken another man's wife as *his due,* as something supplied him, like his meals and his identity, by the Marine Corps.

Walking across the night campus later, a remarkably large and beautiful campus and much less crowded than the one he had been used to, crossing several wide courts and leaf-strewn malls and walkways under bare trees and soft round yellow globes, he felt that perhaps he could return to it and make the other not be, fade to a memory of something only read about—and he touched the shoulder, the ruined part of him, and gave up, and was a marine pretending to another life, and he drew the girl close.

And now drawing her close again, not answering, not knowing what or how to answer and saying finally, "I don't know, Madelaine," and sighing as if that was a defeat. He wanted to know and felt he ought to know and soon had better know.

"I'm sorry I asked. I had no real right—"

"It isn't a question of rights. If it were, of course you'd have the right. You can ask anything. Except I don't know. I could say that I love you—"

"You don't have to do that."

"—and it would be true, I think. I think it would."

"Hey," she said. "Stop. You don't need to say any more."

"But I do need to. I think of taking you away—"

"Oh, Robert—"

"—of getting you out of here with me when I go, away from this place and away from him. I mean I *think* about it; I'm not suggesting it, at least not yet. I'm not sure I want to do that, and you probably don't know if you'd go."

She moved up and sat cross-legged, the ashtray in front of her, and they passed the cigarette.

"I feel as if my life has run off its bearings," she said. "And I'm sidetracked, a long way off and in very different circumstances from what I ever imagined."

"That's right," said Harding. "That's how I feel, too."

"When I was in high school I got restless. Long Beach is an okay place, it's a lot better than most places, as far as that goes. But you know how it is with places you were born."

"Sure. In my part of the country, all the kids want to leave and go to southern California."

She laughed. "See, but I couldn't do that. I was *there*. So I moved into my own apartment and I was lucky and got a few modeling jobs, very small stuff, not even a beginning. I was unhappy. I signed up for some night courses at UCLA. Photography. I was living alone and hating it, and I met my husband. It all seemed to make very good, very quick sense. He was the answer, the way out."

"But you didn't know," said Harding, "he had a warrior's heart. Did you?"

"No," she said. "I didn't know. But along came the war. We were married too late for him to get a deferment. His father and uncle had been marines; the uncle was killed in the Pacific. And there, as marines say, it is."

"He decided to stay in?"

"Oh, yes. They gave him a promotion and a new car to ship over when his first three were up. Made him a captain. Much money, *beaucoup jing*. Well, not as much as he'd have made as a civilian. But there was the responsibility, you see, and the chance to play war."

"You remind me of someone," Harding told her. "A girl in Anaheim, a WesPac widow. Funny, though; she was from Memphis."

"I guess anything's funny if your sense of humor is warped enough."

"No, I mean the two of you—she was in almost exactly the same position you're in."

"How nice for you."

"Come on. It's funny that I should meet her in California and you here."

"Anything's funny if your sense—"

"Okay." He shut up, but it was, he thought, strange.

Later she said, "What I want to know is—"

"What you want to know is—"

"Are you going back to school when you get out?"

"Maybe," he said. "I doubt it. I'll probably never go back to school. School wouldn't feel right now. Do you understand?"

"Of course not."

"Good," he said. "Understanding women are a drag on the market."

"A drug on the market?"

"What I said."

"Well, what will you do, then? If you aren't going back to school."

"Go fishing, maybe. Operate a string of lobster pots. Become a crabber. Steal a yacht and go to the Virgin Islands."

"Like your friend wants to do with Cherry."

"Yes," he said. "Like my friend wants to do. My friend Murphy."

"Can I go with you?"

"I don't know," he said. "I don't know, and you don't know too. Either."

"How do you know I don't?"

"I know you don't. Because I don't, and that applies to you too."

"Oh."

"My friend Murphy is married," said Harding.

"I know. You finally told me. Cherry doesn't know it, though."

"Cherry will find out," said Harding. "Murphy's wife is married to a marine and she doesn't want to stay with him."

"Oh," she said. "And so there it is. Well, I don't think my husband is like Murphy. Not at all like Murphy."

"And you aren't anything like Murphy's wife. And I'm not anything like what I think I am."

"No," she said sharply. "No; we aren't any of us like that. And I think you're just letting your conscience run away with you. I think Murphy is a completely different kind of person."

"You think," said Harding. "You think so."

"He is a murderer. I don't care if he is your friend—he is a murderer."

"Yes, he is. He is that, all right."

"And I don't think his wife had anything to do with that. She didn't have anything to do with that."

"No," said Harding. "But she left him and you want to leave your husband."

"So *what?*" she cried.

"So what," he said.

"Let's just drop it," said Madelaine. "I don't even want to talk about it anymore now. I don't like you to compare us to—them. To any of them. We're *us*."

"Are we?"

"I don't even want to talk about it."

2. Harding was sitting on his bunk after lunch a few days later, reading *Billy Budd,* when Murphy came in.

"Hi."

"Hi yourself."

"What's happening?"

Harding had avoided Murphy for over a week, since the evening at Sneads Ferry. He did not know what to do, did not know how he felt about his friend now. What was different was the new knowledge. All the aspects of their lives that had drawn Harding and Murphy together were now changed because of it, and Harding, although he wanted the friendship to remain intact, found himself otherwise preoccupied.

"What's ever happening?" he said.

Murphy sat down on a footlocker, crisp in starched utilities, his boots polished, a bright black eagle, globe and anchor and the letters USMC ironed onto the left breast pocket of his field jacket. He had got a haircut and looked as if he might be a candidate for drill instructor school.

"Listen, I want you to do me a favor."

"All right. What is it?"

"They called me at work. Western Union. There's a telegram over there for me. I want you to walk over there with me."

"Do you know who it's from?"

"No," said Murphy. "I don't know who it's from. I want to go over and get it before I go back to work. I want you to walk over there with me."

"All right." Harding closed the book and put it under his pillow. "All right, let's go."

He put on his field jacket and gloves and they went outside. It was a bitter, windy December day, gray and sunless, threatening rain, or worse. They walked the two blocks to the Western Union office across from the bus station, in the little building that also housed the airline ticket office. Murphy went over to the grille and leaned his elbows on the counter.

"You have a telegram for me," he told the girl behind the grille. "Thomas Murphy."

She found the telegram and Murphy signed for it. He walked over and sat down beside Harding on the bench across from the counter. He tore it open and looked at the typed signature.

"It's from my mom."

"What does it say?"

Murphy read the telegram. "It just says, 'Call home.' " He blinked, looking at the thin yellow paper. "It must be some kind of emergency, like I figured. Something must have happened."

"Maybe they only want to hear from you," said Harding. He hated telegrams for just this reason.

"No. Something's happened." Murphy kept looking at the paper. He folded it neatly and buttoned it into his shirt pocket. He zipped his jacket back up and looked at Harding. "Let's go."

"You can call from the bus station," Harding told him.

"No. I've got to get back to work. I'll call them after work." He got up and Harding followed him out.

"You shouldn't wait that long," Harding said when they were out on the sidewalk. "If your mother sent you a telegram, she must want to hear from you pretty badly."

"Yeah." Murphy hesitated, his hands in the pockets of his field jacket. "Yeah, you're right, I guess."

"You ought to call home right now." Harding was thinking of Murphy's wife, who had said she was ill.

"Yeah," said Murphy. "I guess I ought to."

"Come on." Harding put a hand on his shoulder. Murphy was looking at the bus station. "Come on, let's go over there and do it."

"I guess," said Murphy, taking a reluctant step forward, led along by Harding's hand. "I guess I will."

Harding moved him across the parking lot to the telephone booths at the bus station. Murphy halted outside a booth.

"I haven't got enough change."

"You can call collect. Do you have a dime?"

"Yes." Murphy reached into his pocket. "I've got a dime." He stood there looking at the coin in his hand.

"Go on," said Harding. "Or we'll both be late getting back to work."

"Something bad has happened." Murphy looked at him and Harding felt the tautness in his gut change to a queasy apprehension.

"Go on," he said nervously, pushing Murphy into the booth. "Do it."

Murphy looked at him accusingly and turned and dropped his dime into the telephone. He hesitated and turned back.

"I don't know if I want to do this. I don't know if I want to find out what it is."

"God damn it." Harding felt like hitting him, suddenly conscious of a strong desire to be elsewhere. "You've got to do it sooner or later. It may be an emergency. Now go on and *do* it."

Murphy dialed the operator and put through his call. When he said, "Mom? It's me. What's happened, Mom?" Harding stepped away and sat down on a bench by the door. He took out a cigarette and wondered at his feeling of estrangement. A bus came grinding in, sat with its engine running, and a mob of marines got off and scattered, and another mob came out of the station and lined up impatiently to climb onto the heated bus and ride out to the industrial area for work. Harding felt like climbing aboard and hiding at the back.

He did not want to be here, and he hoped—not so much for Murphy's sake but for his own—that nothing was wrong. He felt himself withdrawn from his friend, felt ashamed too, but that did not change it. His affection was still there, but no responsibility remained to complement it. His friendship felt at this moment like another bit of nostalgia, something that had once been necessary and agreeable, but limited in duration. He hoped nothing had happened because he did not want to have to console Murphy, did not feel capable of that now. He was back at a more preliminary position, where nothing might be demanded of him, where nothing was offered and he had no desire to offer it—had, in fact, quite an opposite need. He had not even known until this minute that he had withdrawn so far.

Murphy hung up and stood in the booth for a minute, and Harding watched him out of the corner of his eye, tapped his foot and smoked the cigarette fiercely without knowing he had it. The bus closed its doors with a *whumph* of air and whined around the corner and out onto the street.

Jesus Christ, he thought. *It's something bad, all right. Oh, Jesus Christ.* He wanted to run before Murphy came out of the booth.

But he sat there, and Murphy turned and came out and Harding watched him walk over and sit down.

"You got another cigarette?"

Harding took the cigarettes out of the pocket of his field jacket and gave Murphy one, lighting it for him with his Marine Corps lighter, which flickered in the wind sweeping across the parking lot. He put the pack and the lighter away.

Murphy's face was tight but unemotional. He dragged on the cigarette and did not look at Harding.

"Well, I was right, all right."

Harding sighed out the smoke. "What happened?" He tried to hold down his desire not to know.

"My wife. My goddamn wife."

Harding nodded. "I guess I sort of expected it was that."

"Yeah. Me too. Well, she died." Harding felt a jolt, and barely heard him say, "She saved me the trouble of doing the job."

"Oh, Christ, Audie, I'm sorry. I'm sorry, man."

Murphy looked at him and one side of his mouth curled up in an unnatural grin. "Yeah. Aren't we both."

Harding looked away, blinking, feeling dizzy, and said, "What was it? Was it pneumonia?"

"Pneumonia?" Murphy shook his head and kept grinning his half smile. Harding looked back at him, but Murphy was gazing straight ahead. "Not hardly. Not fucking hardly. My mom talked to her on the phone the other day. She was feeling great. Not even a cold. I didn't believe that anyway. I figured she was lying. Oh, that *bitch.*"

He slapped his hand down on his knee and stood up. "Come on, let's go back. We'll be late for work."

"But what happened?" Harding followed him away from the bus station, his reluctance overcome by curiosity.

"She was with some guy in a camper, heading down Interstate 16 toward Savannah. They were sideswiped by a truck. Rolled over. Both of them got it. She broke her neck."

"Oh, man. Oh, Jesus . . ."

"Yeah," said Murphy. "When I think of all the times I wanted to break her neck for her. So she went out and did it on her own. What a dope."

They walked back toward the barracks and Harding watched the naked trees shake in the wind. He could think of nothing to say that would be any good, so he said nothing. He wanted to get back to the office and shuffle papers. He wanted some dull routine to help him cast off the need to care, or even think about Murphy and Murphy's dead wife. He was tired of caring about people.

"At least now I can count on getting that Christmas leave. Maybe I ought to ask for an extra week. I'll just tell them I have to bury my wife who accidentally broke her neck while going camping in Savannah with a friend."

"It looks like you were right all along," said Harding, although that hardly mattered now, meant less than nothing.

"Should've shot her," said Murphy mildly. "Instead of talking about it, letting her play her games with me. Should've shot them both. People don't matter that much, Harding. I've learned that since I got out of school. Doing the two of them would have been as easy as any VC I ever zapped. Easier than the lieutenant. See, that's what happens when you go around trusting people. Everybody I ever cared about has screwed me one way or another. Even old Green, going off that amtrac."

"He fell off," said Harding.

"Yeah, but he was already screwed. Just because of Webster. Such a big deal out of wasting a loser like that."

"I imagine he made a pretty big deal out of what happened to Lieutenant Whitcomb too," said Harding without thinking.

Murphy stopped and looked at him.

"He did. Sure he did. But at least he didn't stop being my friend." Harding blinked and felt a deep resentment forming.

"I can't *see* it," said Murphy, walking again. "Those people all got what they deserved. What's the difference who did it? It's like VC: you kill off a few and there's always more. My bitch of a wife breaks her neck and there's a thousand more fucking up somebody's life. It doesn't mean a thing. The world is full of losers, Harding. They're as plentiful as collards."

Harding did not feel like arguing, but he said, "That's a hell of an attitude. People matter. If people don't matter to you, Audie, then what does?"

"Nothing, I guess," said Murphy. "Not anymore."

"What about the Marine Corps?"

"Not even that."

"What about Cherry? At least you're free now to do what you want with her."

"A waste of time," said Murphy. "Anyway, it's too risky. Trusting people."

Harding wished later he had said more, made a whole speech about opting for life. He believed that Murphy was wrong, did not think Murphy believed his own words.

But he was cold and depressed, irritable, ashamed; he wanted to go away and be let alone. He did not want to have to talk optimism to anyone. He was not in a condition where he felt much like opting for anything like life himself, much less preach it to someone in Murphy's position. Murphy was suspicious of him anyway, and, Harding thought, rightly so.

But he wished he had spoken. Another albatross to carry, he thought later; he had let the moment pass. He went back to work, and that night he made love to Madelaine and wondered if Murphy wasn't partly right. Losers seemed as plentiful as collards growing in a Carolina field. As, Harding felt, he himself had good reason to know.

1. She had never had very good luck in her life, had never considered herself a lucky person. But she had known people who were worse off, and she came of tough, hardy stock. She never expected much, and when nothing came she could live with her disappointment. She considered nothing her due. She had learned that.

Murphy called her as she was getting ready for work.

"I've got to see you."

"Well, I have to work, Audie, you know that."

"Call in sick. It's pretty important." He sounded tense, his voice hard, but that was the way he often sounded.

"Audie, I can't. I have a job."

"Listen," he said. "It's pretty important."

"Well, what is it?"

"I don't want to talk about it on the goddamn telephone. I want to come over and see you. I want you to spend the evening with me."

"Well—" She hesitated. Jill was waiting for her. "Audie—look, baby—"

"All right," he said. "That just figures."

"I *want* to see you. But I can't just take off work any time I feel like it. Look, can't you come over after work?"

"I don't want to come over after work. I want to come *now*. After work that goddamn bitch roommate of yours will be there. And I don't want to wait that long."

"Well . . ."

"Fuck it," he said. "Just never mind."

"Look—you're not being very reasonable. Look, maybe I can—"

"The hell with it."

"Audie . . ."

"Just forget it. Go on over there and take off your clothes and give those horny bastards what they want. I'll see you when I see you."

"*Audie—*"

He hung up.

Jill said, "Are you coming?"

All evening she tried to fog out her mind and work hard and not remember how he had talked to her. He had never spoken to her that way before, had never been so impatient or foul-mouthed or abusive. She thought several times of trying to get away early, and during a break she called the trailer and got no answer, and called the barracks and sent the duty NCO to look for him, but he was not there. She felt a premonition of something bad approaching, and she believed in such feelings. But she did not know what to do, and in the end she surrendered and tried to be fatalistic, gave up her mind to the mindless music and her body to the beat. She twisted her way through the crazy zodiac posters, the planets that whirled on the ceiling amid the galaxy of colored lights, and, late in the evening, she was able to know as always that, if need be, she could survive this way for some measure of time before an end came.

When she went outside after the lights were turned on and then off for the night, and all the marines had gone across the street to line up behind the bus station like wayward children, she pulled her coat close around her and ducked her head into the collar to keep warm, following Jill and her boss to his car for the ride home. She was so tired she could hardly walk, and she fell asleep in the car and did not know for a moment where she was when Jill woke her.

"Come on, baby doll. Home sweet home."

"Wait a minute." Her boss pulled a foot-long flashlight out of the glove compartment and beamed it on a young man sitting on the steps of their house. The boy raised his bottle and drank from it before he called out.

"If you don't get that light out of my face in about two seconds, I'm going to break your fucking neck."

Cherry sat up. "Audie. It's Audie." She forced herself awake and scrambled out of the car.

"It's okay," Jill said. "It's Cherry's . . . friend."

"Audie." She leaned down where he was sitting and put her arms around him as he raised the bottle again, and he carefully maneuvered his hand out from between them and took another drink. "I've been so *worried* about you. How long have you been sitting out here?"

"Don't know."

"You must be frozen. Come on." She turned as the car pulled away and Jill came up the walk. "Help me get him inside."

"What's the matter with him?" Jill stopped with both hands on her hips, looking at Murphy as he took another drink.

"Hello, Mom," he said to Jill. "Want a little touch of my bourbon, Mom?"

"Help me," said Cherry.

"Hell, let him freeze."

"Jill!"

"He's drunk, baby, can't you see? How long are you going to go around coddling drunk marines?"

"Jill, *help* me."

"I'm tired," said Jill, and as Cherry turned on her Murphy pulled himself to his feet.

"Fooled you. I don't want your grandma to lay a hand on me. She might lose it if she tries."

"Too bad we can't lose *you.*" Jill went past him up the steps and unlocked the door. She glanced back as Murphy and Cherry came up behind her, and disappeared inside.

"Bitch." Murphy put an arm around Cherry's waist as she opened the door. He followed her in and closed it behind him while Cherry turned on lights. Jill had gone into her room and shut the door.

Cherry came over and kissed him. "Come on, take off your jacket and sit down. I'll make some coffee. All right?"

"Coffee." Murphy grinned and took off the field jacket he was wearing. He set the bottle down on the TV. "I don't need any coffee. I don't need anything."

"Yes, you do." She moved him over to the sofa—he grabbed the bottle before she could get it—and sat him down.

"Please take it easy with that. I'm going to put some coffee on. Then we can talk."

She began to shake when she went into the kitchen, and she leaned against the refrigerator. Something was wrong, something bad. He had never been quite like this before. He knew she did not like it when he drank too much. She felt guilty for making him wait all evening out there in the cold and she bit her lip and tensed herself until the shaking stopped, then took a deep breath and let it out. She got the coffeepot and put it on to heat.

He was drinking from the bottle again when she came back into the living room. She sat down by him on the sofa and clasped her hands.

"The coffee is heating."

"Did you do a good job tonight?" he said without looking at her.

"I—I always work hard over there."

"Yeah. It's hard work. You know, I wonder how many guys at Lejeune have been to bed with you—in their minds, I mean." He looked at her now and smiled. "Let's see. You're the best-looking of the dancers, and the Pussycat is the most popular place in town—"

"Stop it, Audie."

"How many customers would you estimate the Pussycat has in a week? And then, I wonder what percentage of them go to bed with you when they get back to the base. Pretty high, I'd say."

"Please, Audie, don't." She reached out to touch his arm.

He looked at her for several seconds, then jumped up and began to pace unsteadily, looking at her and at the floor and at the room as if he did not know where he was.

"You tell me," he said. "You tell me why everything is so wrong.

Why can't you ever depend on anybody, why can't people ever be the way they ought to be, the way you think they are?"

She was looking up at him. "I'm sorry, Audie. I should have stayed home from work. I knew I should have when I went. Please sit down and tell me what's the matter."

He stopped pacing and came over, but when she reached out to him he grabbed the bottle instead and took a long drink from it, standing in front of her as she watched him. He stepped away, holding the nearly empty bottle, and began walking around the room again, looking at the pictures and posters on the walls, the paperback books in the little recessed bookcase, the movie and confession magazines on the coffee table.

"It's all fucked up," he said, looking at a cover story called *The Things He Made Me Do*. "Cherry, it's all a goddamn mess. A mess!"

"Don't yell," she said. Jill came out of her room and crossed to the bathroom, slamming the door.

"No," said Murphy. "Let's not have any hollering about how fucked up the world is. Let's just clench our teeth and do our duty like good marines." He laughed. " 'Clench our teeth.' I always did think that was funny."

"Audie, what's wrong with you? What's happened?"

"Happened?" he said. "Happened? Has something happened?" He grinned and shrugged. "Beats me."

She did not know what to do. She had seen him drunk and knew he could be incredibly childish and self-pitying. He could cry real tears about what he had believed his life in the Marine Corps would be like, and how it was not, how all his best friends had misled him and either died or changed on him. But he had always been more or less explicit about why he was crying or sulking or ranting—and this was different. She had the feeling, almost a certainty, that this was at least partly directed against her, and she had no idea why.

So she watched him and waited for him to get around to whatever it was. He finished the bottle and stood holding it and looked at her again. She remembered the coffee.

"I'll tell you something," he said.

"All right. Just let me get the coffee before it boils away."

She went into the kitchen and when she was pouring the second cup she heard a crash. She ran into the living room and he was standing where he had been. He had thrown the empty bottle across the room and there was a mark on the wall where it had struck. Jagged pieces of brown glass lay on the carpet.

She stopped in the doorway and looked from him to the broken glass and back to him, her breathing and heartbeat fast. She felt a little wave of irritation break through her patience.

"Well, that was a nice thing to do." She crossed the room and looked at the dark scratch in the plaster, carefully stepping around the broken glass. She could hear the shower running in the bathroom, and decided with relief that maybe Jill had not heard the noise. Murphy stood without speaking. "Don't you think so?" she said. "Isn't that about enough of this kind of behavior?"

"You don't even want to hear what I have to say," he said sullenly. "You don't care."

"Yes, I do. But I think maybe you're overdoing it a little bit. Don't you?" He didn't answer and she started toward the kitchen. "I'll get a broom and you can help me clean up that glass. It's a good thing Jill didn't hear it."

"You're just like everybody else," said Murphy. "You're just like all of them. Like her."

She stopped. "Like who?" she said, turning. He looked at her and she felt a tremor in her stomach. "Like who?" she said again. He still did not answer. He clenched one hand into a fist and held it against his forehead—it was like a gesture she had seen in high school plays. "Who am I like?" Maybe, she thought, maybe he meant Jill.

But he dropped his fist and looked at her.

"My wife. You're just like my wife."

She blinked and said faintly, "What?" or perhaps only thought it, and now she felt weak all over. He did not say it again.

She turned and stumbled into the kitchen, swallowing at a knot in her throat, trying to breathe. She took a sip of coffee that scorched her tongue, and she picked up the two cups and saucers and one of them slipped out of her hand and broke in the sink, reduced, like Murphy's bottle, to jagged shards. The other cup shook so that she had to set it down, and she leaned against the sink looking at the broken fragments, swallowing repeatedly, noticing with absurd clarity the delicate blue border on the stained white pieces of china, the gleam of the chrome faucet handles, her hands, gripping the edge of the sink, slender and lovely with long nails polished pink. It was as if she were high, and her standing there seemed to take no time at all. She was so tired. She felt as if she were slipping out of herself, disappearing into the familiar kitchen objects, the table and chairs and the stool in the corner, the chrome strip that ran along the counters, and the light-green refrigerator and the brass knobs on the cupboard doors . . . the tile floor she seemed to be floating just above, or falling away into, and the poinsettias in a white porcelain vase on the table, and a picture on the wall of children sledding, framed with bric-a-brac and a calendar that said December.

Merry Christmas, she thought.

2. When she came back in with the one cup of coffee, he was sitting on a hard chair in a corner by the stereo, patting his hands on his knees. He looked up and she handed him the coffee and sat down on the end of the sofa, folding her hands in her lap.

"I should have guessed something like this."

He sipped the coffee and put it on top of the stereo. "Wasn't any point in telling you. Wouldn't have done anybody any good. I didn't have the balls anyway."

She could think of nothing to say. She kept looking at his face.

"I came to say good-bye," said Murphy. "I'm going home, on leave. Christmas leave." She did not answer and he took the cup and drank from it and said, "It never would have worked with you and me. You remind me of her, a lot. I'd have ended up hurting you. Except you're better than she ever was. God, women . . . Maybe I had it figured in high school. If I hadn't ever got married I'd probably still be happy. I should have just got out of school and come in the Marine Corps, and I wouldn't ever have had to sweat it out with her. It was okay until I came in. But she never got it through her goddamn stupid head about me. She never did understand me. She didn't even try."

While he drank the coffee and talked, she felt herself crumbling, tired of herself and him and everything. She realized that she was not even hurting. It was such a normal thing to be happening to her that it almost did not matter—would not matter soon, when she had a chance to heal a little. Hard work was the answer, had always been her answer, and she had great faith in that. Later, perhaps, she would go see her sister in Kentucky. But now she wanted to go to bed and sleep.

He was still talking, more or less to himself, when Jill came out of the bathroom in a robe, her hair done up in a towel. She started to cross the hall and her eyes caught the broken bottle. She halted and came into the room, walking over to look down at the glass as Cherry had done. Murphy stopped talking and looked at her, curling his lip.

"Well, now, what is *this?*" Jill turned on him, hands on hips. "Sonny boy, you've carried your little tricks just about as far as they'll go."

"Shut up," said Murphy. "Get your ass out of here and let us alone."

"*You're* the one who's going to get your ass out of here. Right now."

"Jill . . ." Cherry was too tired to get up, to intercede.

"Don't you start. We've put up with Mister Tough Guy long enough. I live here too, and I don't have to have his damn bottles broken all over the floor to know when he and I both have had enough." She jerked a thumb toward the door. "Beat it, kid. Your time is up."

"Not quite," said Murphy. "Not quite yet." He put the coffee down and stood up. "I've got one more little trick you ought to be interested in." He unbuckled his belt and walked slowly toward her.

"Audie!" Cherry sat, unable to move, as Jill's face went white and she began to back up toward her room.

"I think maybe you'll appreciate this," said Murphy, and he pulled out his belt and looped it around his right hand, letting the heavy buckle hang. Jill's eyes caught the dangling piece of metal and she froze, staring as he lifted his hand and swung the buckle in front of her face.

"This is something you need," said Murphy. "This is something all of you need once in a while when you decide to start pushing too far. Little old Marine Corps trick. I learned it in boot camp, a long time ago. Watch."

He swung his arm and Jill broke her gaze and ducked as he brought the buckle down toward her face. It missed her and made a clean whistling sound, and Jill gagged something, her eyes wide, and ran for the bedroom. He started after her and Cherry screamed his name and then was holding him from behind. She did not know what was happening. She had not really seen what she had seen, and she closed her eyes tight and held on until he broke her grip and threw her to the floor. It was all so normal, so natural, so typical, and she kept her eyes closed and felt herself slipping away, and she heard the whistling noise and waited for the blow.

But it did not come. She heard the clank of the buckle as he threw the belt against the door, and then the door opened and slammed and she thought of the beach in early winter. She thought of Sneads Ferry, where everyone was together and happy and where things were always right—thought of that and the old lighthouse, and waves that crashed on the sand forever.

Murphy got his flight bag from beneath the porch steps and looked inside it, checking in the cold moonlight to see that nothing was missing. He put on his belt and field jacket and walked away from the house without looking back. He had almost made a mistake, he thought, turning up the collar of the jacket. He had almost got the wrong one.

Now his Christmas leave had begun. An unofficial leave, a necessary leave to set things straight that should have been set straight long ago. They would not look for him until morning formation, and they would not come after him for a long time, time enough for him to take care of things. Unless the bitch turned him in, he thought, remembering poor old Simms, who did not belong in the Marine Corps.

He would have to be careful. He put his gloves on and hiked out to highway 17, watching for the patrol cars of sheriff's deputies and military police. It would be a cold night if he did not get a ride, but everything would be better in the morning.

1. The girl with glass in her eyes sat in the back of the police car while they waited for the ambulance. The ambulance was slow in coming. She was trying not to cry but could not help crying because of the pain and because of the dead boy who was pinned in the Chevrolet in the ditch. Her crying consisted of dry unfeminine sobs that sounded as if they came from her chest, and the sobs and the blood on her face behind the policeman's handkerchief and her hands reminded the marine of a gook woman he had seen near Phu Bai during a fight with snipers. She had come running out of a hut with a little boy across his right front, and he had shot at her head with his M-16 and almost missed but blew her nose and checkbone away and killed the boy with his second shot. She fell down but, amazingly, got to her knees and covered her face with her hands in just this way, looking toward him and crying but of course silently with the firing.

The girl had gone through the windshield and was all right except for her face. The marine bent forward a little to smile at her through the window. She could not see him, and a policeman took him by the shoulder.

"What do you think you're doing?"

"I wanted to see her," said the marine.

"Do you know this girl?"

He shook his head. "I was just looking at her. She reminds me of somebody."

"Did you witness the accident?"

The marine nodded. "Wow, yeah." He looked over at the blue Ford where the other boy and girl were sitting waiting for him. They were looking at him. "We saw the accident. I was the first one to get to her. Her dress was up over her face. I guess she didn't know what she was doing. Her legs are beautiful. There was blood all over." He looked at the car in the ditch. "He's dead, huh. I could tell that right off."

"Yeah," said the policeman. "Did you talk to the other officer?"

"We gave him our names and addresses and all. He said we could go ahead and go." He looked again at the boy and girl, watching him from the car. "They're going home for Christmas."

"So were they."

Both of them looked at the girl, who seemed so helpless, so completely at the mercy of whoever took her blindness and pain in their charge, that the two of them stood listening to her sobs, looking at the red-stained blond hair and the arch of her throat and all the rest of her without her even knowing they were watching.

The marine smiled at the policeman, and the policeman took his arm and pulled him away toward the highway, where the other officer was directing traffic.

"If you've talked to him already, what are you still hanging around here for?"

"I wanted to look at her," he said.

The policeman said tightly, "I think you better move it out of here right now."

"Yeah," he agreed. "Yeah, I got a ways to go yet."

The policeman watched him cross the highway to where the Ford was parked.

The boy was facing straight ahead now over the wheel and had the engine running, but the girl was still looking at him. She was blond too, and tall, quite pretty.

"He's dead, all right." The marine nodded at the car in the ditch. "She's okay, though, except her face is hurt, her eyes—"

"Let's go," said the boy without turning. "Are you going with us or not? Or are you going to stay here the rest of the day?"

The marine looked at him. The boy's hair curled around his ears and he wore a moustache and a short beard and rimless eyeglasses. In the back window of the car was a sticker that said UNIVERSITY OF VIRGINIA.

"Yeah, if I can," said the marine. "Go with you. I mean I want to."

"Let's go then, God damn it."

The girl put a hand on his arm and he looked at her as the marine went around the car. He was about twenty, and so was the girl. The same age as the marine.

"We shouldn't even have waited for him. Sitting here like a couple of necrophiles . . ."

"Stop," she said. "Get in," she said to the marine.

"Yeah. Thanks."

He had decided to get off the freeway near Charlotte because no one would pick him up there. His last ride had taken him past the city and let him off more than an hour before, and nobody else would stop, and it was raining, a cold miserable pre-Christmas southern rain, fine and penetrating, soaking through the field jacket he had put over his head. He was drenched, and angry at all the cars that passed him by, people who would not pick up a serviceman in the rain. He tried it one last time.

The car did not actually stop for him. The boy had started slowing down too late and missed the exit. He pulled over to the side to let several cars pass before backing up to the turnoff.

But the marine had run over yelling, "Thanks!" and the girl said something to the boy. They engaged in a brief exchange while the marine stood there in the rain, trying to see the girl through the window. Finally she opened the door.

"Come on. Get in." She slid over and he got in beside her, placing his flight bag between his feet.

"Wow." He shook his head, wiping the rain off his face and hair.

"Wet out there. Thanks again." He arranged the field jacket over his knees like a blanket.

The boy slammed the car into reverse and backed up to the turnoff, shifted and accelerated off the expressway.

The marine turned to the pretty blond girl, who was looking straight ahead.

"Where you from?"

"We go to school in Virginia," she said, and her eyes came around to his. "We live in Columbia."

"South Carolina?"

The boy muttered testily, "How many Columbias are there in this part of the country?"

The girl lowered her eyes a moment. "Where are you going?"

"Atlanta."

"Oh, great." The boy leaned forward to look at him around the girl. "What the hell did you get in with us for? Eighty-five goes straight through to Atlanta. We're going down to *Columbia.*"

"Yeah. Well, when you stopped I thought you were going straight on. But to tell you the truth, it's not much difference. I wasn't getting anywhere. Maybe I can get a ride out of Columbia down twenty to Augusta and over."

"You should have stayed on the freeway."

The girl agreed quietly. "You really should have stayed on the freeway."

"Well, I was getting wet on the freeway. I'm not in much of a hurry. I'm on leave. You going home for Christmas?"

The girl started to answer, but the boy spoke first. "Isn't *everybody* going home for Chirstmas? Aren't *you?*" The rain was pelting the windshield and he wove back and forth a little on the road.

"Not really, no. My old lady died on me and I'm going home to bury her."

They looked at him, the girl with shocked sympathy and the boy with disbelief. He had said it so matter-of-factly, it even sounded untrue to himself.

"Oh, I'm sorry." She shifted toward him and almost put a hand on his arm, but checked herself and said, "That can be hard. I lost my mother when I was—"

"Not my *mother*," he said, looking at her quickly and noticing the hand. "My *wife*, for God's sake." He chuckled. "My mother. Jesus."

"Oh, *no*." The girl and the marine looked at each other, and the boy said shortly, "What happened to her?"

"Oh, it was pneumonia or something. It's not such a loss, though. I think she was going out on me while I was in Nam. My original intention was to come back and shoot her, you know? So now I don't need to. She got pneumonia or something. She died of pneumonia or something. All I have to do is go back and bury her. That's fair. I guess I can do that."

"How sad," the girl said.

The marine shrugged. He thought of something. He reached over and dug into the flight bag and came out with two pictures.

"Here." He handed one of them to the girl, a picture of the marine with a lovely blond girl on his lap. They were smiling at the camera and the girl was dressed in a sequined costume, her long slender legs in net stockings, one leg bent at the knee, the other straight out in a pose.

"That's her. She was a dancer." He looked at the other picture. "And these are some of my friends. They were all killed in Viet Nam."

A Chevrolet came up behind them, swung out to pass and too late the driver saw an oncoming car. The boy slowed down to let him in, but the passing car was slowing too and they stayed even.

"Christ," said the boy, weaving back and forth on the road. The Chevrolet skidded off the road to the left as the oncoming car went by, and as they braked they could see the Chevrolet careen off the guard posts, jump them and roll over and over into the ditch.

The marine was almost on top of the girl, trying to see out the back window. "Stop! Did you see that? Did you? Oh, wow!"

They pulled off the road and the marine jumped out first. He ran to the girl who had been thrown out of the car. He stood looking down at her as she groped blindly with her hands, blood staining her face, sobbing quietly and trying to get to her knees. She finally lay over on her back and pulled her dress over her face like a thin veil that crimsoned and fluttered in the breeze and the slow thin rain. Her legs were so beautiful and she looked so helpless, and he almost wished this were another place and time, his head filled with all sorts of quick déjà vus, and he placed his field jacket carefully over her face.

2. "I'm curious about why you joined the Marine Corps. Of all the branches of the military, if you had to go in, why did you pick the worst?"

The marine felt the girl look at him as the boy waited, felt her thigh resting against his but kept his eyes on the road. The boy's hands were locked on the wheel and because of the accident he drove more slowly. It was still raining, but not so hard, and to their upper right as they headed south-southwest the clouds were trying to break up so that now it was lighter, but still with no sun.

"I didn't have to go in," answered the marine. He had been thinking about his wife as she was when he met her: seventeen, with long hair he would not let her cut, and seemingly so innocent, so pure in appearance that he had been shocked at the things she knew, the things she was eager to do. He wondered if she would ever have gone out on him if by some chance he had not entered the service. He thought not, and then, remembering her better, changed his mind.

"Well?"

"Huh?"

"Then why did you?" The boy almost thrashed with hostility. "I've always wondered what kind of person goes into the Marine Corps, particularly during a war like this. And now I have my chance to ask. So why did you?"

"Stop it," said the girl.

"I wanted to," said the marine. "I always liked the idea. The way I see it, after high school you either go to college or go in the service. You learn some things in one place and some in the other."

"Is that right."

"Yeah."

"And did they just send you over, or did you want to go?"

"Of course I wanted to go. Why be in the Marine Corps and not be where the war is?"

"I see." The boy was nodding. "I suppose the kind of person who would join the Marine Corps would want to be in the war, no matter which war it was. Is that right?"

"Right. That's it."

The boy mulled that for a while and said, "I refused to be drafted into the Army. I've got a trial coming up and I may go to prison. What do you think about that?"

"Let's drop this," said the girl, but the marine answered anyway.

"I don't think anything about it. You got your problems and I got mine. They don't have to have anything in common."

The boy considered this, sliding his hands back and forth on the steering wheel, ignoring the warning glances tossed at him by the girl.

The marine was thinking about his wedding day two years ago, when his girl had stood there in the little church in Galveston and he had not seen any of the other people at all, none of all the relatives and friends who were there. The women kissed him and the men shook his hand and slapped him on the back and told him to hold out for the best football school. He could remember looking at her and feeling dizzy that she was his *wife,* not completely sure he ought to have done it.

He was eighteen then and had graduated, was already in the waiting period, fluctuating between college and enlistment. He had received a few scholarship offers, none of the ones he really wanted, but of several acceptable alternatives, one would have been to take a scholarship, marry the girl and go to college. Or to have not married her and enlisted.

Moving too fast, heady and nervous at his freedom to choose, he had done a little of both: married and then enlisted. She had not believed he would do that, turn down the University of Texas to go to boot camp.

But the University of Texas had waited too long, and he made his choice. He was tired of school, he wanted to be involved in bigger events, life-and-death events, great causes. That and the marriage had been the beginning of all his troubles.

They stopped at a drive-in restaurant and the marine sat across the table from the boy and girl, watching the girl's long blond hair. He thought of running his hands through it and twisting it around all over his face.

"What're you looking at?" The girl gave a kind of chortle.

He dropped his eyes, and could feel the dislike from the boy, but the girl seemed interested in him. "I was thinking about something," he said.

Her face became serious and she said quietly, "It must be terrible to be over there almost a year."

"No, not really," he said as the waitress brought their food. "It makes as much sense as being here. You get so used to the kind of life over there that sometimes it almost seems like you could stay and it would be normal—"

"Killing every day?" said the boy.

He shrugged. "You get used to that too. After a while it doesn't seem so bad. You do it and don't even think about it."

"I understand sometimes you even kill each other," said the boy. "Your own men."

He and the marine looked at each other and the marine said, "Well, things happen sometimes. Things just . . . happen." He was answering the boy but he looked to the girl for sympathy or understanding, and he thought he saw it in her eyes.

3. "My wife," he said later, "never understood me."

He put the picture away in the flight bag again and leaned his shoulder against the door, letting his left knee touch the girl's stockinged leg. The rhythmic vibration of the car, the heater pushing out warm air, made him sleepy, and he caught a quick memory of the girl in the accident with her dress thrown over her face, her white legs exposed all bare up to her black underwear, her thighs.

"She was popular and sexy. That's why I liked her at the start. She was the best there was in the whole school, and that was what I wanted. I think the reason I started loving her, though, was because she seemed to really love *me* and care about me. Maybe she thought I was the best she could get too," he said thoughtfully. "And the reason I wanted to kill her is because she didn't stay the way she seemed. She changed on me after I enlisted, because I enlisted. But that shouldn't have made any difference."

When he had told her—and he had told her many times—that he was going to enlist, she had always looked at him as if he were kidding; she had treated it as a childish whim and not something he would ever do. Her brother had done it and died, but *he* would never do that. She knew he would go to Austin, and their next few years would be much like the last few—that was *her* whim. She could not understand why, could not believe that he wanted to test himself in a more reckless game than football, to prove himself to himself—and to her—in a harder fire. The war had been so intrusive, so—convenient almost, so *timely*—but of course it could never have seemed that way to her, could never have represented for her what it represented for him in terms of opportunity.

She deserved to die, he felt, deserved actually and simply to die by his own young wronged hand. He could allow for her not seeing what it meant for him, but he could never forgive her inability—her refusal —to stand by him. She did not want to be married to a marine who was in Asia. She wanted to be married to the first string quarterback at Texas.

But a man, he thought, feeling the girl beside him and talking to her in his mind as he had tried to talk to his wife in his letters, a man could be things in the military he could not be in real life—outside, that is. It was like a religion, which allowed him—required him—to do what he had done to the lieutenant and would have done to Webster, to the VC, who were, like Webster and the lieutenant, a threat to what was good and right, to what he had with Green and Harding. And without something like that, so solid and frightening, so fraught with the responsibility and opportunity to deal in life and death—without it, how could you ever say you had been alive?

He was watching the girl's legs, there in front of her and him like an offering. He imagined her dress up over her face. Her presence aroused him, and although her face was interested and silent, he decided to answer the boy.

"You were asking me about how sometimes our own guys get zapped. It doesn't happen very often, especially nowadays. But it almost always is either an accident or because the guy deserves it. Like he's high at the wrong time and he could maybe get you all killed. I've known people who would shoot him for that. But it doesn't happen much."

"God," said the boy. "If it happened *once,* that would be too damn much."

"It's like an occupational hazard. You try to stay friendly with everybody. Combat does weird things to people."

"Obviously," said the boy. "You can say that again."

"I did; it does. I said it does."

The boy moved his hands back and forth on the steering wheel. He kept looking at the marine, turning his head so that the girl said, "Watch where you're going!"

"It's so depressing," he said.

"Oh, let it alone."

"There's no way of stopping this kind of thing, ever. I mean," he said, gesturing toward the marine, "*him.* The country is full of people like him. He's so typical, he's so goddamn—"

"Stop it," she said, and put a hand on his knee. "You expect too much."

"I shouldn't expect anything at all," the boy said grimly. "America does what it wants. It deserves what it gets."

The marine looked out at the day, bleak Christmas clouds hunching where the sun tried to break through. The rain had stopped.

It had been a day like this when he left his wife to go to boot camp. They had made love all night and got up in total darkness, with heavy clouds in the sky and rain threatening. Spring, that had been. But like today. She had driven him uptown to the bus station and they had made long and tearful good-byes while it got lighter out, grappling each other and promising all sorts of things neither of them meant. But he believed her at the time, as he believed himself. Later, when he took whores and bar girls and raped gook women, he refused to think of her doing more or less the same at home. He did not want to think of it now, or of how she had left and changed her life without him.

"They love it," said the boy. "That's why I can't help hating them. They really—"

"Oh, stop," said the girl. "Don't you see you should feel *sorry* for them?"

The marine looked at her. She twisted a little in the seat and her hip came against his, and he got a crazy idea.

He leaned over and unzipped the flight bag at his feet and reached in and took out the pistol. It was a .45 caliber automatic, an official United States military sidearm that he had bought at a pawnshop in Jacksonville.

The girl looked at him—at it. "Oh, my God."

The marine smiled at her.

The boy jumped. "Christ, I didn't know you had *that* thing."

"I got it in Nam," said the marine. "They're issued to officers and staff NCOs and a few other people—machine gunners and tank crewmen. It's a little harder for a grunt like me to get one, especially to get it back here, when they x-ray all your gear. But I got it. It's what I was going to use on them."

He had bought the pistol the evening before. He had not fired one in over a year. The handle was warm and it smelled of gun oil.

"The old United States Pistol, .45 Caliber Automatic, 1911-A1. Yes, sir."

"I hope it's not loaded, for Christ's sake."

"As a matter of fact," said the marine, and he slipped the magazine out into his left hand. The girl and boy could see the blunt rounds in the magazine. "No good to anybody empty."

"Please put that way," said the girl. "I hate guns. I hate them."

"No, but look...." The marine smiled shyly, playing with the pistol and the magazine. "I fired expert with this thing, did you know that?

Not many pistol experts around. I was just thinking—what I'd like to do is turn off at one of these side roads and sort of fire off a couple of rounds or something. See if I still got the old eye. That may sound kind of dumb to you—"

"It sounds goddamn *insane* to me," cried the boy, trying to drive and look at the pistol at the same time. His eyes slid around, his head turned almost imperceptibly, the way some men will eye others in a lavatory, just to check the size. The marine began to feel good, began to feel all Christmasy for some reason.

"Let's just turn off at one of these roads here," he said, looking out and leaning a little forward. "We got plenty of time."

The boy took a deep breath. "I'm not stopping this car or turning off at any road until we get to Columbia. Unless you want to get out. And if you don't put that gun away you can get out right now."

"Not gun—pistol," said the marine. "No, listen." He slipped the magazine back into the grip and they all heard the little click as it locked. "Just turn off at one of these side roads. Okay? I just want to take some practice shots so when the time comes—"

"The time?" said the girl. "You're not talking about your *wife?*"

He sighed and nodded. "I know how it sounds. But something like that is sometimes justified. It can be necessary and it can be right. I told her—"

"But she's dead." The girl looked into his eyes. "Didn't you say she died of pneumonia?"

"Oh . . ." He had almost forgotten. "Yeah, she did. It was pneumonia or something. That's right." He thought about it and it hurt as much as before. It was as if the girl had told him for the first time, and he looked at the pistol and felt a helplessness, an awareness of some great lack of justice in the world.

"Well, I could still take some practice shots."

The boy shook his head. "Jesus Christ, what is it with you? What's this thing you've got about shooting?"

"Oh, I've been thinking about this for a long time. It's why I bought the pistol. What good does it do to have her just die like that? Maybe if I can just— Maybe just shooting, emptying the magazine into the woods might help. Do you know what it's like to have everything taken away from you? Everything that ought to have been good, ought to have worked, and just got all fucked up somewhere, so nothing is the way it's supposed to be?"

The girl looked at him with sympathy. "Maybe I sort of know how you feel. But—"

"I'm glad," he said. "I'm glad you understand. She never did, or even . . . anybody." He said to the boy, "If you'll just turn off at one of these roads. At that one coming up."

"I told you—"

"Please turn off." He reached his left hand over and, with thumb and forefinger, snapped back the slide and released it, cocking the hammer and chambering a round.

The girl kept looking into his eyes and said quietly, "Please."

He put his left hand on her shoulder, feeling excited. "I just want to get it over with," he said to her. He pointed the pistol at the boy. "I don't want to hurt anybody. Please turn here."

The boy looked down the barrel and stepped on the brake and made the turn.

The girl was watching him with big eyes and he touched her hair with his fingers, stroking it down from her head to her shoulder. He let the hammer down on the pistol.

He laughed. "Boy, you'd think you people weren't going home for Christmas at all, you're in such a hurry. You'd think you were going off to spend a vacation together somewhere, or something."

"No," said the girl.

"Hey—"

"You'd think so."

They drove in silence for about a mile, and the marine said, "This is fine, right here. You can stop here."

The boy stopped the car and they all sat looking at each other with the engine running. The boy sat in silence, watching the pistol. The girl looked into the marine's eyes and said, "What are we going to do?"

"Let's take a walk," said the marine. "The sun's coming out. Let's all take a walk in the woods."

4. The woods were wet and glistening with the stray sunlight that broke into them and then faded to winter gray. Their shoes got wet and it was like a heavy dew that had fallen and it was not cold now; and a low smoky mist covered the ground in places and in other places did not show at all. When the sunlight struck it the mist seemed to change to a faint golden color and then fade to nothing, and when the sun went in again the mist was white.

The marine took aim at trees and acorns and squirrels, but did not fire at anything. He enjoyed the feeling of being in the woods. It reminded him of a time on patrol once when he had been point man for the platoon and had got too far out in front and they had lost him. He had thought at first that he could not find them again, and then that Charlie would find him first. He had started being afraid, one of the few times he could remember ever being afraid over there. But Harding and Green had found him.

When he turned to them the boy was whispering something to the girl, and she shook her head quickly.

"What are you really doing?" the marine asked them, smiling. "Are you escaping for the holidays? Are you married to someone?" he asked the girl.

"It's not anything like that," said the girl. They stood hand in hand watching him as he looked around at the wood.

"I'll bet it is." He looked at the girl again. "And what is your husband doing while you have your little holiday?"

She looked at him with her big eyes and did not answer, and he thought of the girl in the ditch, blind, her dress fluttering over her face and her white legs.

The girl said, "I think you've got this in your head because of your wife. But we're going home for Christmas."

"Yeah, my wife . . . You know, over there it's a very easy thing to do, it's the easiest thing in the world, and no one really minds. You kill somebody and there's just one less out of too many. She's like that. She'll be one less out of way too many."

"We're going home for *Christmas,*" said the girl, holding tight to the boy's hand as he tried to break away.

He looked at the girl in a haze of pain and desire, thinking of the girl in the ditch and knowing she could not see him. "Oh," he said quietly. "Oh—"

The boy took a step away to the side, forcing the girl to break her grip. He started forward and the marine reached over with his left hand and cocked the hammer and both of them froze as he lowered the pistol at them. He had seen that look before, and marveled at how exactly the same it was no matter what kind of face wore it. And she could not even see him.

He held the pistol in his right hand and braced it in the palm of his left just the way he had qualified long ago, the way he was taught to hold it because you really could not hit anything any other way, and shot the boy in the chest. The boy was flung back against a tree and sat down, his eyelids fluttering sleepily. The girl screamed and covered her ears as the shot went off, and immediately turned her face away, and her knees began to shake so violently it was almost funny. He let the hammer down with his thumb and shoved the pistol into his belt and she stood dumbly looking down as he had seen them do, and she let him help her over a few yards from the boy, let him pull her gently down on the wet ground and put her dress over her face, and she never made a sound as he took her, then when it was over just looking away until he shot her.

He stood up and looked around at the wood and did not know where he was. He could not hear a sound from the road, or birds in the trees, his ears muffled by gunfire and his nose smarting at the odor of cordite. It did not look or sound much like any place he knew, and he called to his friends and put his hand over his mouth, and then much of it was the same, with the sun going down, and the rays that came streaming through the clouds into the wood reminded him of just such an evening, though it was so long ago and far away he could remember very little of it.

1. At Fredericksburg, Harding walked a few steps farther and started back toward where the cannon stood on the new green grass. He had thought about death and honor for so long, in the many forms in which each routinely came to men in the service, that now he felt at peace with both. The stone markers surrounded him and Shelby, and he came aware again that it was spring and he was almost free.

"So his wife probably tripped him." Shelby moved along behind with his hands in his pockets.

"I don't know why he did it," said Harding. "Any more than I know why Green died—or why Webster shot me. You want answers, Shelby?"

"You blame it on the military, don't you?"

"Well, it was really more than just his wife. The military, the war, the country . . . The opportunity to do what he did, the *way* he responded to his wife's death, was fostered by the country and the war and the Marine Corps. He learned the uses of violence—not only the technique, but the attitude."

"It's a common thing, I suppose."

"A common thing. Two years ago Murphy was running a high school team to a state championship. He should be playing quarterback now at Texas. And where is he?"

They had found Murphy's body in a marsh, less than a hundred yards from the main highway. He had seen the cars passing and had waded out as if it were a rice paddy, and had attempted to swim the last stretch to firm ground.

Harding could understand it. He was a superb athlete, a strong swimmer, and he was already wet from the rain and the woods. He was lost and alone. He had misjudged the distance and the cold; he had tired; he had drowned. The weather had turned colder that night. They found him nosing a clump of frozen reeds that snapped like icicles.

Harding imagined him calling out to him and Green in those final cold minutes. He did not know why he imagined Murphy doing that as he died, but sometimes he lay awake at night, thinking about it.

They came on another monument. The inscription said:

IN MEMORY
OF
COL. JOSEPH A. MOESCH
KILLED AT
THE WILDERNESS
MAY 6, 1864

ERECTED BY
SURVIVING COMRADES

" 'Surviving comrades,' " said Harding. "Do you think any of those guys survived having the world turn upside down? Can anybody really survive something like that?"

"Yes," said Shelby. "Are you thinking about us?"

"I'm thinking about Causes," said Harding. "All the damn Causes that come along just in time to ruin people's lives. Do you think any of those 'surviving comrades' ever believed in anything again?"

"Yes. Maybe they were a little more discriminating. Maybe not even that. That will happen to you too. To all of us."

Harding smiled at him. "Always the optimist."

"Or, as an optimist would say, a realist. And you're feeling pessimistic."

"Or as a pessimist would say . . ."

Shelby laughed. "I don't think you're really that. You're just tired."

"I'm tired, all right. I'm tired of everything."

2. Corporal Harding, R. L., USMCR, lay on the mattress of his stripped bunk with his right hand behind his head, watching people come and go in the barracks. It was late afternoon of a rainy Friday. Marines were coming back from the mess hall and getting ready to go to Jacksonville or Kinston or, if they were luckier, Richmond or D.C. In a pile by Harding's bunk were his packed sea bag, a small zippered flight bag with an eagle, globe and anchor and the letters USMC stenciled gaudily on one side in gold fuzz, a pair of green canvas-and-steel jungle boots tied together by the laces, a tennis racket he had bought at the PX hoping it might, with diligent use, help restore some semblance of ability to his left arm, and a manila envelope with his name and service number printed on it in heavy black ink.

The envelope contained his separation and medical papers, his printed or photocopied discharge certificate, a superfluous Notice of Obligated Service (NAVMC 10228), superfluous because he would not be considered in service at all even in the reserve (although some clerk had given him a reserve ID card, by way, Harding supposed, of making sure there would be something to have to straighten out later), a certification of his serviceman's group life insurance so he could convert to a private policy, several papers from the base disbursing office concerning the status of his U.S. Savings Bonds they had forced everyone to sign up for in boot camp that he had never bothered to cancel although he would now, his separation and unused leave pay, etc., with a travel voucher to his home town allowing him six cents per mile, and a cardboard Certificate of Appreciation For Service in the Armed Forces of the United States. The certificate said:

Corporal (E-4) Robert Lawrence Harding 2575849/3042

I extend to you my personal thanks and the sincere appreciation of a grateful nation for your contribution of honorable service to our country. You have helped maintain the security of the nation during a critical time in its history with a devotion to duty and a spirit of sacrifice in keeping with the proud tradition of the military service. I trust that in the coming years you will maintain an active interest in the Armed Forces and the purpose for which you served.

My best wishes to you for happiness and success in the future.

The facsimile signature said, "Richard Nixon, Commander in Chief," and there was a pretty color reproduction of the seal of the President of the United States. In the bottom left-hand corner of the certificate it said, "DD Form 1 Jan 70 1725."

Harding's shoulder hurt. He was waiting for Shelby to get off work so they could eat a final meal together. Somebody was on the telephone at the duty desk, talking to his mother in Arkansas. "Yes, Mama!" he kept saying, as if he were trying to force his voice through the wire. *"Yes, Mama!* I said YES, God *damn!* —I'm sorry, Mama. I said—"

Shelby came in and sat down on Harding's bunk. He grinned and said, "So it's over."

Harding nodded.

"You know, I've been thinking. When I get out, maybe I really will go back to school. See how the university compares with the Marine Corps in terms of motivation. After I've been in Nam a few months I'll apply for an early out for the fall term at Columbia. Go on the GI Bill and pick up my degree."

"Sounds sensible."

"Of course, I have a few months yet to work it out."

"I've got my degree." Harding pursed his lips as he thought about it. "The idea of going back to graduate school still clogs up the back of my throat. Maybe I'm too old inside. I don't care enough anymore. So I guess I won't be getting any of that money."

"Too bad they don't pay retroactively."

"Yep. Too bad, too bad."

"Well, there are other benefits. Maybe the VA can find you a job." They both had to laugh at that.

"Hell, I guess I'll just stay in."

"I guess you just won't."

Harding was not in a particularly good mood for someone about to leave—someone, in fact, officially out of—the Marine Corps. His shoulder ached and the steady rain falling outside the window made him feel gloomy. He took his hand from behind his head and sat up against the end of the rack, rubbing his shoulder. He could raise his arm a little better than shoulder height now, but he had no strength in it. Sometimes in the shower he would still look down at it, a mangled reddish mass of scar tissue and pale skin grafts off his butt, and several square inches of nothing much where there should have been bone and muscle. Funny, he thought, what a single small 5.56-millimeter round entering from the rear could do to a man's shoulder.

The three of them, Harding and the battalion commander and especially the senator, had finally got the Marine Corps to commit itself, to acknowledge in the only acceptable way that somehow Corporal Harding had indeed been rather messed up. He was not very grateful except to the senator, because it had not been easy and without the senator might not have come about at all. They had made him serve almost his full two years. And he never had got the Purple Heart.

"Let's go eat." Shelby buttoned his raincoat and put on his cap. Harding got his raincoat out of the top of his sea bag and put it on over his civilian clothes, half hoping somebody would jump him for breaking uniform regulations. *I am a civilian,* he thought, saying it over again in his head as he had been doing, as he would keep doing for a while until it became unnecessary as he got used to it again.

They stepped outside and waited under the eave until the rain eased up. A line of trucks with their headlights on rumbled along the street between the barracks and the mess hall, and Harding remembered his last day at Pendleton so far back, another rainy day on the other side of the year, when he and Shelby had smoked a cigarette under an eave and watched the column pass. A déjà vu, and he said now, as then, "Never ride one of those again."

Shelby lit a cigarette and blew smoke out on the wet air.

"What are you going to do about Madelaine?"

"I don't know. Nothing, for a while. I've told her that. I'm going to go home, and her husband is going to come back, and we'll have to see. It's possible we may forget about each other."

"So it's over between you?"

"No," said Harding. "It's over with Murphy and Cherry. That's what 'over' means."

"Well, then."

"I'm pretty sure I need her. It's hard to say it: I need something from this past two years that will be real, something from this time that will last beyond the Marine Corps, the way it didn't last with Murphy and Green. I need some part of this time that won't be lost and wasted, the way all the rest of it has been lost and wasted."

"Well," said Shelby. "You have my friendship, for what that's worth."

Harding looked at him, and Shelby puffed the cigarette and watched the rain.

"It's worth something," said Harding. He took a breath and sighed. "I'll tell you what I think is going to happen. I think I'm going to go home and come as close to dying of displacement as it's possible to come. And I think Madelaine's husband will get back here and love her up awhile and then get bored again. And after that . . ." He shrugged. "That's what we'll both be waiting to see."

The rain faded to a drizzle and they ran for the mess hall. They waited inside while the duty NCO got people to show their meal passes and sign the number in the book. Somebody ahead of Shelby wrote down a low card number.

"Is that your IQ or the number of days you've been in the Marine Corps?"

"It's the size of my penis," said the PFC.

"What, in millimeters?"

When he saw Harding, the sergeant grinned. "I'm not authorized to allow civilians on the premises, even if they are wearing regulation raincoats over their civilian clothes."

"I don't see the mess sergeant around."

"Neither do I. Have a steak on the Marine Corps. Sign in the number you used to have, way back when."

"Yeah. This morning."

3. The rain had stopped when they came out, and they walked around puddles on the sidewalk, under the dripping trees.

"How far you going tonight?" Shelby asked him.

"I'll probably stop in D.C. Or Richmond, if I feel like it. I'll just do what I want to do when I decide to do it. There's a heady thought."

"I wonder how you feel," said Shelby, as they crossed the street and watched another line of half-tons approach. "You're in a place I won't be able to imagine for months. Next week I head over, and then all that is behind you will come to me."

"Not all of it, I sure as hell hope."

"But the essentials. The essentials. I won't have as long a tour."

"The Corps will be out of there before you even get over."

"No, it won't." Shelby grinned.

"Maybe they'll hold you at Okinawa."

"Maybe. I don't think they'll do that."

They stopped at the door of the barracks. Shelby spoke again.

"But for you—wow. You're going back out *there*—where the world is. You're like someone from Dante who's seen the Inferno and come back. You're like Melville."

"Call me Ishmael."

Shelby helped him carry his gear outside and load it into the car.

"So what happens now?" Shelby asked as if he needed a prediction, a sign.

"Well, for you," said Harding, "all kinds of things I can't begin to describe. And I hope you'll miss a few things I wouldn't want to predict."

"Well." Shelby grinned up at the rain, which had begun again. He was, Harding could see, more than ever looking forward to it. Harding tried but was unable to remember himself ever having felt that way.

Shelby said, "We'll see. But what about you? Civilian."

The word made Harding smile, hitting with that soft shock that was at once pleasurable and strange, when directed at himself, as it was twice only in a man's military experience: at the beginning, and now.

"Oh," he said. "All kinds of things too."

"And some you wouldn't want to predict."

"It won't be like the military, though. The military is something to be endured, something to be gotten through. Nothing that happens in the military is real, nothing means anything. The best that can happen is that you survive it. But nobody comes out clean."

"Still," said Shelby, "you did survive it."

"Yes." Harding nodded. "I guess I should be grateful. Not everybody does. Green and Murphy didn't. Webster didn't. Lieutenant Whitcomb. I'm probably very lucky. I'm probably very fortunate."

"I think," said Shelby, "it should mean something to you. It is one of the central experiences any American could have had in this decade. It doesn't have to be a total waste."

"No, it could have been valuable," admitted Harding ruefully. "It would be nice to have come through without this—" He indicated the ruin of his shoulder. "Or to not have killed anyone. Or to not have been involved in that whole thing I was involved in with my friends. But how do you propose to avoid such things, Shelby? How are you going to get your valuable experience and come out of it as clean as sand?"

"I don't know," said Shelby. "Maybe it's impossible. But I think it will be interesting. I want to do it."

"Why?" said Harding suddenly, impatiently. "Why can't you learn? Why do you insist on repeating the same mistakes everyone else has made?"

"Because I think," said Shelby, "there is something to be learned in going there, in doing whatever is done and falling prey to whatever happens. I've always thought that, since the day I was drafted. But I was afraid until very late. It will be a primary experience for me, as it's been for the country. Do you understand? Not just an experience, but a *primary* experience, one that can be used to make me and our generation and America better for having done it, wrongly or not."

"But the country made a grave error," said Harding. "I made a grave error. Why do you insist on making it?"

"Because I'll learn something from it that I need to know—just as America has. I feel that. Something that will stay with me—and you—and the country—for the rest of our lives. Something we'll always be able to apply."

"I don't think there is anything to apply," said Harding, "or anybody capable of applying it. I think it was a disaster for all concerned, and will always be that. I feel older and dirtier, and that's all. That's what will happen to you."

"I hope to be wiser from it," said Shelby. "That's what you'll realize someday has happened to *you.*"

Harding got into the car and took a quick superfluous look around at the dark rain-drenched barracks with lights just coming on, at the trees and grass, the scattered buildings and trucks and marines running to their cars in the rain. He decided again it was pretty for a military base. He shook hands with Shelby.

"I hope it proves out for you," he said. "I hope it will be more valuable for you than it's been for me and everyone else. When you've been there a couple of months, write and tell me what it's really all about, and how we'll all be better for it."

"You're kidding," said Shelby. "But I'll do that. Chances are you'll already know by then. If not, I'll spell it out for you. Some night on duty. It'll give me something worthwhile to do."

"Good," said Harding. "I'll look forward to seeing your letter."

"Give me three months," said Shelby.

But three months later he was dead.